p 60: Cordelia Nightwing

Kissed by Smoke

[Trichnosis] Disease
from
BACON.

Also in Shéa MacLeod's Sunwalker Saga

Kissed by Darkness
Kissed by Fire

Kissed by Smoke

THE SUNWALKER SAGA, BOOK THREE

Shéa MacLeod

Montlake
Romance

Text copyright © 2011 Shéa MacLeod
Montlake edition © 2012

Published by Montlake Romance
P.O. Box 400818
Las Vegas, NV 89140

ISBN-13: 9781612185644
ISBN-10: 1612185649

For the real Kabita

Chapter One

The spray of warm blood hit me full in the face.

Gross. Seriously gross. I swiped at it, clearing away the arterial spray. Probably leaving an almighty mess behind.

The vampire I was currently trying to kill had obviously just fed; otherwise, the blood would have been cold. Not sure which was worse, to be honest, warm and sticky or cold and coagulated.

At least this particular vamp wouldn't be sucking anyone's blood anymore. I watched as his hands clutched his throat. Red liquid spilled through his fingers, pouring down the front of his white shirt and turning it black in the moonlight.

Eyes wide, he staggered back, stumbling over the uneven ground in his attempt to get away. Not that it would do him any good. I hopped down from the low retaining wall circling the park, which had given me just the right amount of height to slit the vamp's throat. Slowly, I stalked him deeper into the park. I was feeling particularly nasty tonight. Or maybe it was the darkness in me. Sort of PMS on crack.

"No point running." The voice was my own, but the taunt came from somewhere deep inside me where the darkness lived. I shut it down, quick. This was an ordinary hunt. I didn't need the darkness, despite what it might think.

It snarled back. I ignored it. It was a little game we played these days, the darkness and me. It was somewhat debatable which of us was actually in control.

"You know you won't survive the blood loss. Let me end it for you," I coaxed.

The only answer was a gurgle. The vamp swayed on his feet, barely keeping upright, as his stolen life force leaked out onto the ground. One more step backward and he collapsed under a tree at the edge of the playground. The shadows were deep there, and I couldn't see him clearly, even with my superior night vision—just one of the many perks of the vampire attack I'd survived three years ago.

I was pretty sure he was down for the count, but still, I approached cautiously. I've been a hunter long enough to know better than to go rushing into somewhere I can't see. It is a good way to get dead.

I was right. The vamp was down. He didn't even have the strength to keep his hand clamped to his throat any longer. Not that it mattered. The gush of blood had slowed to a trickle, which meant he'd nearly finished bleeding out. If he were still human, he'd have been dead by now. As it was, he'd meet the end soon enough.

Unless some idiot came wandering through the park and happened to trip and fall on the vamp's fangs, there was no way he was going to survive. Still, it wouldn't do to leave the trash lying around.

I knelt down beside him. Glassy eyes stared up at me, begging me. For what? Not to kill him?

His lips formed a word: *please*. I frowned. Something moved behind his eyes. Something more human than the monster he was now. He formed the word again.

Maybe he wanted me to kill him, after all. Stranger things in heaven and earth. Though I would definitely rather be dead than turned vampire, most vamps don't agree with that line of logic.

I didn't pull out a wooden stake. I have a better way of doing things these days. Besides, I needed practice.

I placed my left palm flat against his chest where there should have been a heartbeat. Looking into his eyes, I whispered something I never dreamed I'd say to a vampire. "Go with the gods."

The look on his face was strangely peaceful. At odds with the pool of blood surrounding us, the blade still clutched in my right hand.

I cast a quick glance around to make sure we weren't being watched. The night was dark and cold, and it was well past midnight. In this residential area, everyone appeared to be tucked up safe in his or her bed for the night.

Then I closed my eyes and let the fire loose. It burned through me, turning my blood to rivers of molten lava. The relief of letting it free was nearly orgasmic. I threw my head back as flame burst from my skin to encompass the vampire and turn him to ash in seconds. He didn't even have time to feel the pain.

But I did.

The fire didn't hurt me. It was heat and light, but it didn't burn. I was its vessel. But for the first time, I felt *his* pain. The pain of the soul that had been trapped inside the vampire. A soul I'd just set free.

I'd never felt that before. After all, the vamps no longer have souls. Or at least, they aren't supposed to.

For a long time, I sat there, tears running down my face. I sat there until the wind came and gently blew the ash away.

The sun had barely kissed the horizon when I arrived back at the office. Still, Kabita was already at her desk, ink-black hair scraped back in a long braid, papers spread across her enormous mahogany desk, nose to the proverbial grindstone.

"What the hell?" I stood just inside the doorway and stared in bafflement. Kabita's office was wall-to-wall plastic, with drop cloths everywhere. Even the side of her desk was draped in the stuff. "Are you redecorating or something?"

"I'm trying to prevent you from destroying my carpet again." She leaned back in her chair, arms crossed, and gave me an arch look.

I glanced down at my perfectly clean clothing. "I showered before I came to the office this time."

"So I see."

Me, I was highly amused. I'd ruined her carpet at least twice in the last year alone. Bloodstains are nearly impossible to get out of cream carpet. Especially when they are vampire bloodstains. Those are particularly nasty.

I flopped into one of the visitor chairs, the plastic making a crinkling sound underneath me. I ignored it and flung one leg over the arm of the chair, letting my steel-toed hunting boot dangle over the side.

"Honestly, Morgan, you are just about the most unladylike person I know."

I shrugged and popped a stick of gum in my mouth. Spearmint. My favorite. "I hunt vampires for a living. Ladylike isn't in the job description." Thank the gods for small miracles. Not that I couldn't fake it when necessary, but why bother? Ladylike is overrated in my opinion.

She rolled her eyes. "Anyway, I've got something for you. Hand delivered. Very mysterious." She held out a small cream-colored envelope.

Everything is mysterious in our business. The sign on the door tells the world that these offices are a private investigation firm, but that is just a front. In reality, we are government subcontractors for a branch of the government's Environmental Protection Agency called the Supernatural Regulatory Agency. We are paranormal mercenaries, if you will. We deal with all kinds of supernatural incidents: demons, vampires, and most recently, the murder of an MI8 agent over in London. It is all very hush-hush. A hand-delivered letter isn't especially mysterious, though it is unusual.

I reached over and took the envelope from Kabita. My name, Morgan Bailey, was scrawled across the front in bold black lettering. I didn't recognize the handwriting, but that didn't mean much. Between texting, e-mailing, and instant messaging, I hardly recognize my own handwriting these days.

The envelope contained a single sheet of lined paper, which didn't match the snazzy envelope. Probably not a woman, then. I frowned at the message, then laughed. "It's from Trevor. His version of a birthday card. Listen to this: *Sorry I didn't have time to buy a card, but I wanted to wish you a Happy Birthday. You're the best little sister a guy could ask for.* Isn't that sweet?"

"Very sweet. Why didn't he just send you an e-card like a normal person?"

"Nothing beats a handwritten note." Dear gods, I sounded like my mother. Before I could say anything else, my cell phone vibrated, letting me know I had a text: *Meet me tomorrow. 1 pm. Warm Springs Café. Keep this on the down low. Lives may depend on it. Bring the darkness.*

"Huh. Talk about coincidence. Trevor wants to meet me at the café in Warm Springs tomorrow. Business." I figured that "down low" did not refer to Kabita, since she was technically my boss and therefore more or less responsible for my hunter activities.

Warm Springs is nearly an hour and a half away, on the other side of the mountain, on reservation land. Not exactly a hot spot for a business meeting and well out of SRA jurisdiction, though granted that is a little fluid. Still, the tribal elders have their own ways of dealing with the paranormal, and they don't involve hunters like me.

"Does he say why?" Kabita glanced up from the report she was reading.

I shook my head. "Nope. Just that 'lives may depend on it.'"

"That's a bit weird. Even for our friendly government liaison," Kabita said with a slight frown.

"No kidding." Trevor is not only my half brother, but our contact at the SRA. If the government needs our services, Trevor usually calls or shows up on our doorstep. He does not send cryptic texts.

I tried to send him a reply, but it bounced back unsent. That worried me. I tried ringing instead, but it went straight to voice mail. A shiver of foreboding snaked its way up my spine. Something hinky was definitely going on.

"Are you going?" Kabita asked.

I sighed. I so did not look forward to the drive, but there was no other choice as far as I was concerned. "Of course I am. It could be important." Not to mention the comment at the end of the note. It wasn't like I could leave the darkness at home, but it was obviously Trevor's way of telling me things might be dangerous and to watch my back. Fabulous.

I'd finally told Kabita about my abilities to channel darkness and fire. After everything that had gone down in London and what had happened with her cousin—and my lover—Inigo getting kidnapped by a psycho dragon hunter, I knew I couldn't keep it from her any longer. Besides, with what she'd been hiding from me, she didn't have a right to get mad at me keeping things from her. A fact I'd quickly pointed out to her, just in time to keep her from going ballistic.

Kabita was not one to forgive and forget, generally, but with the little matter of Inigo's parentage, not to mention her own family history, to wave over her head, I convinced her. Well, with that and a plate of homemade chocolate chip cookies. What can I say? I like to bake. And I find most people extremely bribable when baked goods are involved.

Kabita frowned. "Warm Springs Café? It's not exactly next door. And why the reservation? Seems like an odd place for a meeting. Are you sure the text is from Trevor?"

"Yes, it's from him," I confirmed. Well, unless somebody stole his cell phone and was sending me cryptic messages for fun. But that was unlikely. "As for Warm Springs, it's quiet. Out of the way." And not under US jurisdiction.

"Good place for an ambush," she pointed out. "Maybe somebody kidnapped him and is making him send you mysterious texts to lure you out there." She sounded almost hopeful over the kidnapping part. Another option I hadn't considered.

I gave her a look. "Seriously? Are you mental?" The very idea was ludicrous. Still, I couldn't shake the feeling that, despite the unusual message, this was important. "I know someone who might offer some invaluable insight."

Kabita's brow went up. "Cordy?"

I nodded. "Cordy. Since Trevor isn't answering his damn phone, maybe she can use her otherworldly connections to tell me a little more about the message. And what I will find out there in Warm Springs." Cordelia Nightwing's psychic abilities are often more hazy than helpful, but it was worth a try. Besides, I hadn't seen her in a while, and it was high time I paid her a visit. "I'll pop over for a quick chat."

"It's a little early for that, don't you think?"

I shrugged. Cordy kept odd hours. No doubt her unearthly contacts had already told her I was on the way. "I'll text you when I'm done, and we can have breakfast at Lola's." I was craving pancakes in a big way.

"Sounds good to me." Kabita rustled about in her desk drawer before pulling out a small ziplock baggie. "Here. You'll need this."

I caught the baggie midair. Inside was some kind of dried greenish herb. Not that I was an expert, but it looked suspiciously like pot. I gave her a look. "Don't tell me this is…"

She just raised an eyebrow.

"You've got to be kidding."

"Bastet will be your best friend."

I rolled my eyes. "Just what I've always dreamed of."

She smirked.

Bloody woman.

Chapter Two

Cordelia Nightwing still lived in her cramped one-bedroom apartment at the edge of the Park Blocks area in downtown Portland. This time of year, the trees in the park were bare of leaves and the grass was more brown than green. Still, it kept that aura of peacefulness that seemed to cling to it year-round.

Cordy flung open the door to her apartment the minute I knocked. It was just as jammed with stuff as the last time I'd been there. Possibly more so. I was pretty sure the Ming-inspired vase perched precariously on top of the bookshelf was a new addition.

"Morgan! I haven't seen you in ages!" There was the usual round of hugs, exclamation marks, swirling silk, and clouds of perfume. Today's robe was of the sapphire-blue variety, which matched her eyes. A golden dragon was embroidered across the back, and there were tiny gold dragons on the red chopsticks stabbed through the bun atop her head. Interesting, knowing what I do about her sister's connection to the dragon race. Underneath the robe, she wore her usual ordinary jeans and sweater.

"Love the robe, Cordelia. Where'd you get it?" Strangely, in all the years we've known each other, she has never mentioned her sister, the dragon child. I wondered if she'd do it now. If she even realized I'd met her sister, Sandra.

Cordelia completely ignored the question as she hurried down the hall to the living room. "Bastet has been talking about you nonstop for the past week. She'll be thrilled to see you."

"I bet." Especially once she found the catnip in my pocket. Yeah, that's right. Bastet is a cat. Apparently she talks to Cordelia.

I'm not sure if Cordy is just plain nuts, or if the damn cat actually talks. Honestly? I wouldn't put it past her. The cat, I mean. Like I said, stranger things.

Bastet was on her usual perch: sprawled over the mountain of decorative pillows on the couch. She gave me a baleful look through slit eyes. Also as per usual. I don't care what Cordy claims, I have no doubt that cat hates me.

Cordelia dropped gracefully into the only available chair, sending a perilously balanced deck of goddess tarot cards flying. They littered the floor in a colorful array of Cups and Swords and images of Isis. "Oh dear." She leaned over the chair arm and peered down at the cards. "Never mind. I'll get them later. Tea?"

Cordy is always fully armed with tea. I accepted a cup of the stuff to be polite. Honestly, I prefer a nice strong coffee any day. Tea tastes like dirty dishwater.

"I've got a present for Bastet."

"Oh, she'll be so pleased!" Cordy clapped her hands together. "What is it?"

I pulled the plastic baggie out of my pocket.

"Pot?" She frowned.

Glad I wasn't the only one. "Uh. No. Catnip."

She brightened. "How fun. She'll love it!"

I glanced at Bastet, who was still glaring at me. I had my doubts about that.

I peeled open the bag and edged it closer to the cat. She gave it a slight sniff, shot me a dirty look, then turned her back on me. Ungrateful wretch.

"Yep, she definitely hates me."

Cordelia laughed. "She does not. She's very pleased with your offering."

Offering. Like the damn cat is the goddess she was named after. Granted, it wouldn't surprise me in the least if she were.

"So, tell me everything. Eddie said you were in London?" Cordy leaned back in her chair and sipped her tea. Her blue eyes twinkled. For all her Mad Hatter persona, Cordelia Nightwing is one of the most intelligent and perceptive people I know.

I gave her a quick rundown of my most recent adventure in London with the dragons. Up to and including the end of my romantic relationship with Jack and the beginning of one with Inigo. I left out the part about Inigo being a half dragon. That was not my story to tell. Then I casually finished with, "Oh, and I met your sister, Sandra."

Cordelia gave me an enigmatic smile. "Ah, yes. Sandra. How is she?" For all the world like we were speaking of some vague acquaintance from the good old days. I didn't buy it for a minute.

"She's fine. Great, in fact. She shut up her shop in Soho and left London to go hang out with one of the dragon clans in the Scottish Highlands. She's absolutely loving it." Sandra's status as dragon child is proving beneficial in her position as liaison between the clans and the British government. Again, something that wasn't mine to tell.

Cordy's expression didn't change. "That's nice." She sipped elegantly at her tea.

I just stared at her. Cordelia has to be one of the most baffling people I've ever met. Then again, who am I to judge familial relationships? My own mother isn't exactly a picnic, and I only discovered I have a brother all of a couple of months ago.

"Now, sweetness," Cordy changed the subject, "tell me why you've really come. You have a question?"

Damn. I swear the woman can read my mind. I hesitated, debating whether or not to tell her. Trevor had asked me to keep things quiet, but Cordy had worked with us on many sensitive cases before. I knew she could be trusted, and with my brother MIA, I needed answers. "Yes. I got a text from Trevor this morning. It's a little unusual." I pulled out my cell and handed it to her.

She read the text, frowned, then read it again before handing the phone back. She stared thoughtfully into her tea for what seemed like ages. Finally, she thrust out her hand.

I knew immediately what she wanted. I gulped the rest of my tea and then handed her the china cup, hand painted with delicate pink flowers.

She upended my cup onto its saucer, then turned it right side up again and peered at the dregs. I've never understood how anyone can possibly make any sense of tea leaves. They just look like slimy brown gunk to me, but it seems to work for her.

"Well, obviously you should meet him." Her voice was matter-of-fact and held no hint of the airy-fairy persona she often puts on. "This truly is a matter of life and death." She frowned. "Mostly death, I'm afraid."

"Shit. What does that mean?" I so did not like the sound of it.

She shook her head. "I'm sorry, Morgan. It's not very clear to me. I only know that it is crucial you meet with Trevor tomorrow. The future depends on it."

Three cheers for the enigmatic.

Before I left, I decided to ask her something that had been weighing on my mind since I'd dusted the vampire in the park early that morning. Something so bizarre I could hardly bring myself to say it. "Cordy, do vampires have souls?"

"Of course not, dear. Everyone knows that."

Her assurances should have eased my mind, but instead, I felt more confused than ever. Not because of what she'd said, but because before she said it, she'd paused just a little too long.

I stared out at the gloom beyond the window of the Roxy. I am not a fan of winter. I don't mind rain. I'm from Oregon, after all. It kind of comes with the territory. But I dislike cold and I hate the snow. And yet, I was born on a cold winter morning in February. Go figure.

I sank back in the booth, taking in the giant wooden crucifix hanging side by side with autographed photos of famous drag queens and half-naked male models. The irony of the decor was half the fun of dining at the Roxy.

My mind was still in a whirl over the text from Trevor. It had sounded important, and yet the whole thing was just so out of character. I didn't quite know what to make of it. Part of me wanted to brush it off as a joke or an exaggeration on his part. But another part of me was worried it was something much more serious. Especially since repeated attempts to call him had gone straight to voice mail. Unfortunately, Cordelia was of the same opinion. And Cordelia has a habit of being right.

"Happy birthday." Kabita handed me a neatly wrapped package, then dropped into the seat opposite me.

The waiter sauntered over to pour her a cup of coffee and then left to get us our blueberry pancakes. I'd gone for the Britney Spears, a nice little two-stack. Kabita had gone all out and gotten the three-stack Anna Nicole Smith. Who says pancakes can't have a sense of humor?

Besides, blueberry pancakes are a necessity of life. Especially on one's birthday.

"Thanks." I turned the shoebox-size package over in my hands, the shiny purple paper sparkling in the café lights. Heavy. And it gave off a slight *thunk* as I turned it. "Can I open it now?"

"Not until after the ceremony."

"C'mon. Just a peek?"

She shook her head. "No way. Try to peek, and I'll take it back."

"Fine," I huffed. "When's the ceremony?"

Kabita is a natural-born witch and enjoys forcing me to participate in random rituals and rites just because she knows they drive me nuts. It isn't that I don't believe in them or that I have a problem with them, I just think they are incredibly boring. Plus, despite my strange supernatural abilities, I have zero affinity for anything magical, so I feel pretty stupid standing around chanting. This ritual, though, was all about me.

"Tonight. Your house."

"Why my house?"

She rolled her eyes. "You can't do a proper purification ritual without purifying your personal space too."

"Don't know why I need a purification ritual," I muttered around a mouthful of blueberry pancake.

One eyebrow went up. "Seriously? After what you've been through over the past few months, you don't think you need a purification ritual?"

She had a point. Between channeling the powers of fire and darkness, nearly getting killed more than once, confronting my murderer, ditching a Templar Knight for a dragon (or half dragon, actually), and discovering I have a brother I never knew about—crazy doesn't even begin to cover my life. Maybe I did need some purification.

"OK, fine. I suppose I should get a couple bottles of wine or something. Maybe bake some brownies." Brownies are another necessity of life.

She laughed. "Don't worry. I'm bringing cupcakes."

"I like cupcakes."

"Who doesn't?"

Good point.

"What did those poor pancakes ever do to you?" Kabita's tone had turned serious, and I glanced up from poking at my pancakes.

"What do you mean?"

She nodded to the shreds of cake and smashed blueberries left on my plate. "You've been picking at them for the last ten minutes. Now what's wrong?"

I sighed. "Trevor. I can't get a hold of him, and I'm worried sick."

"You know there's nothing you can do about it until the meeting."

"I know." I gave the pancake another vicious poke. "Doesn't stop me worrying though. Can't seem to get my mind off it." What I needed was a distraction.

Kabita's grin turned downright wicked. "You want to get your mind off things? I can help with that."

Curses. I'd fallen into that trap hook, line, and sinker.

She pulled out bills to pay the check. "I've got a very special hunt for you. Just because I love you."

"I'm going to hate this, aren't I?"

"Oh, most definitely."

§

I remember the first time I saw a demon. Who would forget that, right? It's actually easier to forget than you might think.

I had been crouching behind a Dumpster outside of the office where I worked, watching the demon laugh like a maniac while the place burned to the ground. It was pretty much exactly as one might imagine a demon to look: spiky horns, leathery skin, smoke billowing out of its nostrils.

My hands turned sweaty; my heart pounded against my chest. I felt like I was going to throw up. Or pass out. Or something.

My boss at the time, the Dragon Lady (not her real name, of course, but protecting the not-so-innocent and all that—granted, it's an insult to dragons, but I digress), didn't see it. Too busy cussing out the firefighters, who also didn't see it.

I could never understand why I was the only one who'd seen... well, what I'd seen. He'd been standing right there in front of everyone, and yet it was as though the creature had been invisible to everyone but me. For a long time, I'd thought that meant I was nuts. Or maybe had an overactive imagination. Which was highly likely.

Of course, that was all before I was attacked by a vampire, died, then came back to life with superpowers, so I sort of blew the whole thing off. Hello? Would you want to admit, even to yourself, that you'd just watched a seven-foot-tall demon who looked something like a giant fire-breathing horny toad burn your office down?

I think not. Talk about a one-way ticket to the funny farm. I decided I'd imagined the whole thing and went about forgetting it. Out of sight, out of mind.

The thing about demons is that most people, ordinary people, can't see them. Not because they are truly invisible or anything, but because people don't *want* to see them. Seeing them would mean admitting the monsters are real, and nobody wants to have to admit that.

Granted, there are plenty of demons out there that people can see just fine. That's because they look exactly like you and me. Only one tiny difference: they have no souls. They look human, but underneath, there is nothing human at all. Most of the world's most infamous serial killers were actually demons. Word is, Jack the Ripper was a demon. Which is probably why there is a very specific subtype of demon named after him.

That was the type of demon I was hunting this evening, a Ripper demon. Which kind of sucked. Easy to track a giant red guy with horns and a forked tail carrying a pitchfork; not so easy to track a guy who looks just like every other guy. Until he starts killing.

This particular demon had the bad habit of seducing women and then eating them for lunch. Not all of them. Just their fleshy parts. He'd left a trail of bloody bones across most of Canada. The Canadian authorities were not pleased that I'd taken over the case, but there wasn't a whole lot they could do about it. He was on my turf now.

The sun was just starting to slide down the horizon, streaking the sky with pink and purple as I slipped into the thick shadows of an alleyway down in one of the dingier areas of Portland. The air was thick with the scent of garlic and baking bread, making my stomach growl a little. The narrow alley edged its way between a pizza place and the building where Kabita had told me the demon was nesting.

Unlike vampires, many types of demons like sunlight, and this one had gone straight to the sunniest spot he could find. My plan was to hit the fire escape and head for the top of the building.

My fingers touched cold steel. The fire escape was one of the old kinds that doesn't automatically spring back up after use, and it was all the way down. Somebody up there had me on her nice list.

Technically, Kabita is the demon gal, but hunting demons is a good way to work off some steam and keep the reflexes sharp. Apparently, Kabita thought it was just what I needed. Happy freaking birthday.

Of course, she had a point. Trevor's mysterious message combined with the wait was driving me more than a little crazy.

I pulled myself up onto the first rung of the fire escape. It was one of those old metal ladder things bolted to the side of the building. It looked safe enough, but both the metal and the brick were well over one hundred years old. I proceeded with caution. Last thing I needed was one of the anchors giving way and me plummeting to my death. Or at least to a nasty bunch of broken bones.

I worked my way up, my rubber-soled boots silent on the metal rungs. I made sure nothing metallic scraped against the ladder. Ripper demons aren't known to have enhanced hearing. Still, the last thing I needed to do was alert the demon that he was about to get chopped up into teeny-tiny demon pieces.

I pulled a compact mirror out of my back pocket and held it up over the wall so I could scan the roof without turning into a

Whac-A-Mole. No demon, but there was a small square structure next to the door leading from the roof. It looked like some kind of storage shed. Bingo.

I hauled myself up over the lip of the wall and onto the roof itself. I actually managed not to sprawl face-first. Points for me.

As I made my way cautiously across the roof, a gentle wind teased strands of silky red hair across my face, and the setting sun stabbed hot rays into my eyes. I squinted against the glare, wishing I'd remembered to bring my sunglasses. I am always forgetting those things. They were currently sitting on the dashboard of my Mustang.

I tested the doorknob on the shack door. It turned easily. Obviously, the demon thought he was safe enough on the top of a twenty-story building and hadn't bothered with such mundane things as locks.

I pulled a machete from its sheath across my back, careful not to make any noise, then stepped behind the door to stay out of the line of sight just in case the demon was inside. I'd replaced my favored dao sword with the more demon-unfriendly weapon. It may not be pretty, but it gets the job done.

Ever so cautiously, I turned the knob, testing to make sure it was unlocked. It was. Sword at the ready, I yanked open the door.

The door opened easily. Not a single squeak from the well-oiled hinges. He might leave a royal mess behind him, but this demon knew how to keep house. Then the smell hit me.

Holy crap. What the heck was that? I tried holding my breath, but the smell was everywhere, the cloying stench of rotting flesh and punctured bowels. I tried to breathe through my mouth to avoid the worst of it, but it wasn't easy.

I peered around the door. Yep, I'd found the Ripper's nest, all right. There were human rib cages decorating the walls, and the floor was smeared with dried blood. Leg bones dangled from the ceiling like macabre Christmas ornaments, and skulls lined shelves, bits of flesh still clinging in places. Nasty.

I'd like to be able to say I was sick to my stomach or grossed out or something, because that would make me sound normal, but after three years of hunting vampires and other monsters, my life is anything but normal. I've seen just as bad and smelled worse. I don't know what that says about my life, but probably nothing good.

How he managed to sneak up on me, I'll never know. More than likely, years of hunting humans had honed his skills to the point where even my hunter hearing couldn't pick him up. Or maybe it was the horror of the carnage before me that threw me off-balance for that split second.

It was the rattle of a pebble against the roof that alerted me. I didn't turn. Instead, I hit the floor first. Then I rolled. Good thing, or my skull would have been added to the decor as what looked like the building's fire ax smacked into the doorjamb where my head had been a moment before.

He looked human, all right. Probably would have been considered handsome too, if not for the dark-red blood soaking his clothes and the other bits of goo on his shoes. And then there was the fact that his jaw had unhinged like a snake's, revealing rows of tiny razor-sharp teeth perfect for ripping strips of flesh off a dead body. So not attractive.

I rolled to the side, jumping to my feet as the demon ripped the ax out of the doorjamb. He hissed at me, long threads of pink saliva dripping from his teeth.

The pink was blood. I was hoping his recent feeding would slow him down.

He rushed me, ax in one hand, massive claws suddenly sprouting from the other. Shit, just what I needed; the Ripper was a partial shape-shifter. That hadn't been in the dossier.

I darted to the side to avoid both ax and claws, at the same time slashing him across the back with my machete. Black blood seeped from the shallow cut. His skin was thicker than I'd thought, tougher. His hiss told me I'd pissed him off more than anything.

We danced around the roof, hacking and chopping at each other. I could barely keep up, and I was tiring.

Then he caught me right in the stomach. Fortunately, it was backhanded, so he didn't pierce skin, but I went flying across the rooftop, smashed into the brick wall edging the roof, and slid down into a heap. I hadn't felt pain like that since that night three years ago. The night I died.

I struggled to get to my feet, but my body refused to cooperate. "Gods dammit," I hissed, clutching my right side. I'd bet anything he'd cracked a rib or two. But if I didn't get to my feet, I'd be demon food for sure.

Then the Ripper demon was standing over me, ax raised above his head for the killing blow. This was it. I was going to die right here on top of this building, my bones decoration for a demon's lair. Brilliant.

I closed my eyes and willed myself to find one last drop of strength. Instead, I found the darkness.

It roared up from somewhere inside me, rolling in waves through my entire body, causing me to jerk and spasm like a puppet with a drunk puppet master. It was broad daylight—no actual darkness to channel, but I could feel the burst of energy as Morgan Bailey ceased to exist and became simply a vessel for the darkness.

The darkness screamed, and the demon's eyes widened as he suddenly realized I wasn't alone in my skin. There was *something* in there with me.

That hesitation was enough. With the darkness riding me, I rolled away just as the demon brought his ax down, burying it in the roof.

Before he could yank the ax free, I jumped to a crouch and slashed up and out with my machete. It caught him in the midriff. Talk about spilling your guts.

Black blood poured out of the wound to join the rusty-red human blood on his T-shirt. He screamed, but it was a gurgling sound, which meant I'd hit a lung.

I rolled to the side and, with a quick hack of the blade, took out his Achilles tendon. The minute he collapsed onto the rooftop, I shoved my machete straight through his heart, burying it up to the hilt. Then I hit him full blast in the face with an aerosol can full of holy water.

Good thing we were twenty stories up, because I was pretty sure his shrieking would deafen the hardiest of souls. It was not a pretty sound, and it sent chills down my spine.

The darkness was another matter. It loved that sound, and I felt it throw my head back and scream for joy right along with the dying demon. The laughter spewing from my throat sent shivers down my spine. And not the good kind.

The demon's skin shriveled and blackened, then began to bubble and melt. Holy water didn't work on vamps, but it was like battery acid to demons. I gave him another good spray and stepped back as I watched him scream and gurgle while he sizzled away to nothing.

It was nasty as hell, but the creature was a soulless serial killer and it was my job to stop him. Before he killed more women and used their bones for a little DIY.

When all that was left was a gooey stain on the roof, I closed my eyes and willed the darkness back. It didn't want to go. I'd gotten better at controlling it, but it was still a struggle. It bucked and surged, trying to resist my control, and for a minute, I thought I'd lost it, but it finally faded back into that place inside me where it lived.

I slumped to the roof, completely drained of energy. All I wanted to do was curl up and sleep, but there was no way I was going to call off my own birthday party.

There was only one thing left to do. I'd just have to eat extra cupcakes.

Chapter Three

I was not thrilled about having to wait to open my birthday gift. I've always been sort of an instant-gratification kind of girl. Which has gotten me into trouble on more than one occasion.

I had to admit, though, that the package Kabita had given me looked pretty on my kitchen table. Er, birthday altar.

Kabita had given me a list of items I was supposed to have on my birthday altar. Since I'm not a witch and don't have an altar, I'd used my kitchen table and piled it with candles, photos, and random memorabilia from my life. Particularly life after the vampire attack. That included the dragon scale Kabita's father had given me. Well, not so much given me as shown me, and I'd just kept it.

The doorbell chimed. I frowned. Kabita and Inigo weren't supposed to arrive for another hour.

It wasn't either of them at the door.

"Jack." My stomach clenched and I felt heat rising to my cheeks. Seeing him reminded me of so many things. Some of them wonderful. Some of them painful. None of them I wanted to deal with right now.

"Happy birthday, Morgan," he said in that rumbly Vin Diesel voice of his.

He looked delicious as ever, with his broad shoulders practically making mincemeat out of the seams of his beat-up leather biker jacket. His ocean-blue eyes drank me in.

"Stop it, Jack."

"Stop what?" The innocence in his tone didn't fool me one bit.

I glared. "You know what you're doing. You made your choice." He'd given me up for duty and honor. Bullshit, if you ask me. "And I've made mine."

"So I hear." There was an edge to his voice he had no right to.

"Inigo's a good man," I said defensively. He is more than that. He is an amazing man. Dragon. Whatever. "What do you want?"

"Are you going to let me in?"

Hell no. "What do you want?" I didn't move an inch. I wasn't feeling especially forgiving toward our local resident sunwalker. Never mind the fact that I am quite possibly a sunwalker too. But the idea that I might be an immortal who gains life from the sun like vampires gain life from our blood? Well, that was something I wasn't ready to face. My life had been fucked up enough already without adding that little ray of sunshine to the mix.

Jack sighed and ran his fingers through sun-streaked brown hair. "Fine. I didn't come here to argue, Morgan. I came to give you this." He handed me a small black box, like something you get from a jeweler. "Open it."

I swallowed back panic as I stared at the thing in my hand. It was too big for a ring, thank the gods. But what else would Jack be giving me?

I flipped up the lid. Inside, nestled on a bed of black velvet, was an amulet. The same amulet that had started this whole mess and that I'd given back to him after returning from London: the Heart of Atlantis. *Shit.* That was all I needed.

We'd recovered the amulet together after it had been stolen by a rather nasty piece of work named Brent Darroch. It is an artifact left over from the lost city of Atlantis, and the knowledge and power it holds are unimaginable. And, apparently, it thinks I am its owner.

I started to hand it back to him. I didn't want it. I didn't want what it had given me, the mess it had made of my life. "No, Jack, I—"

He closed his hand around mine, sending little sparks dancing along my nerve endings as he wrapped my fingers tight around the box. "It's yours, Morgan. I want you to wear it."

"No freaking way. This thing has fucked up my life enough already."

His face grew hard. "And your life will continue getting fucked up until you wear it. Until you claim it."

I gave him another glare. "What does that mean?"

He sighed. "It means that it protects its wearer just as it's protected me all these centuries. It will keep you safe, continue to teach you."

I swallowed hard. "It woke the darkness in me, Jack." Not to mention the fire and the crazy-ass dreams.

"And it's the one thing that will help you control the darkness. Promise me you'll wear it."

"Excuse me?" I stared at him. "Did you just say this thing helps *control* the darkness?"

"Well, yes…"

"And you're just telling me this now?" Furious didn't begin to describe my feelings. All this time I'd been struggling to control the power inside me, and he'd had the key all along. And he hadn't bothered to tell me. I'd wear a frigging dog collar if it would help me control the darkness. "Fine. I promise I'll wear it. Fine guardian you are."

"I'm sorry, Morgan. I should have told you."

"Yes, you should have. Why didn't you?"

A muscle clenched in his jaw. "I have my reasons."

The guardian is supposed to protect the Key of Atlantis. The key being yours truly. Some sort of metaphysical link between the two of us and the amulet. His continuing to keep things from me like this does neither of us any good. In fact, it is downright dangerous. I don't understand it at all.

We stood there on my doorstep with the awkwardness of people who were once lovers but have now become strangers.

"Well." He sounded as uncomfortable as I felt. "I'll be going now. I just wanted to wish you a happy birthday."

"Thanks, Jack."

He started to head down the walk, then turned back. "I'll still be around, you know. I have a duty as your guardian. That hasn't changed."

The guardian of the royal bloodline of Atlantis. How could I forget that? It had torn us apart. "I know."

He nodded once, then disappeared into the darkness. I sighed. Gods, I hate awkwardness.

∽

I stood in the middle of the circle feeling ever so slightly ridiculous. It isn't that I don't believe in magic rituals. Heck, you can't kill vampires and demons for a living and not believe in magic. It's just that I've never been much for religious ritual in any form.

The circle itself was made up of Cordelia Nightwing; Eddie Mulligan, my go-to guy for supernatural knowledge; and Inigo Jones, my boyfriend, for lack of a better word. Not that it is the wrong word. It is just that calling him my "boyfriend" makes me sound sixteen.

Before the mysterious text, Trevor had already told me he wouldn't be able to make it. Some work thing. I wasn't sure if it was connected to what was going on with his strange message or not. Gods, how weird is that? I actually have a brother to invite to my birthday parties.

Six months ago, I didn't even know I had a brother. I'd thought Trevor Daly, our government liaison, was nothing more than your run-of-the-mill, pain-in-the-ass suit. But after everything that happened in London, Trevor finally told me the truth. Now I have a brother—a half brother, actually. Talk about crazy.

Kabita was inside the circle with me. She fanned me with a big bundle of burning sage Eddie had brought from his new age shop, Majicks and Potions, and muttered in whatever language it was she used to do her spellwork. The earthy sage smoke tickled my nose, and I let out an almighty sneeze.

Inigo's blue eyes shone with laughter behind his geek-chic glasses. I blew him a kiss.

"Would you two stop? Honestly, I'm trying to purify your aura here," Kabita snapped.

"You could use some purification, Morgan." Cordy gave me an innocent smile. I didn't buy it for a second.

Eddie piped up. "This is a very simple ritual to cleanse the old life and start afresh in truth. I think it's perfectly suited both to the occasion and to your life at the moment."

He had a point. My life up to this point had been shrouded in untruths and half-truths.

"Oh, for goodness' sake. Fine, but hurry it up. I want a cupcake."

Kabita glared at me. "Spellwork shouldn't be rushed," she said in her best schoolteacher voice. "Now, repeat after me:

Bless me, Goddess, for I am your child, daughter of your heart.
Bless my mind that I may be smarter and stronger in my knowledge.
Bless my eyes that they may see clearly the path you set before me.
Bless my lips that I may speak truth and justice.
Bless my heart that I may know love and faith.
Bless my womb that I may know and nurture creativity within and without.
Bless my hands that they may protect the innocent and champion the good.

Bless my knees that I may pray before you.

Bless my feet that I may walk in a more balanced connection to all life."

As I repeated the invocation, I felt a sort of serenity flood my body. I'm not exactly the type to hang around feeling all one with the universe, but it was kind of nice. I managed to stand still through the rest of the ritual, which involved more sage smoke, more invocations, sandalwood oil smeared on my forehead, and a lot of pointing with a very sharp-looking dagger. Finally, Kabita opened the circle, and I released a pent-up breath.

"See, it wasn't so bad," she said, tucking an inky-black curl behind her ear as she carefully laid her ceremonial knife in its box.

I sighed, fingering the amulet that now hung around my neck. "It was OK. Thanks for doing it. Now can I open my presents?"

She grinned. "Only if you open mine first."

Inside the shiny purple box Kabita had given me was an equally purple pair of gladiator stilettos. "Oh my gods!" I squealed. "Are these the ones from Tesselah?"

"You'd better believe it."

Tesselah makes specialized weaponry for the dispatching of supernatural creatures, most particularly vampires and demons. Which meant that secreted in the heels of my new shoes were silver-tipped metal picks sharp enough to stab a vampire through the heart. Freaking fantastic. I practically did a happy dance in delight.

From Eddie, there was a small leather-bound book, no doubt from his shop. Inside were beautiful drawings of dragons along with notes in an ancient, swirling script. It was hard to read, but it appeared to be some kind of history of the dragon race.

Eddie had donned a satin purple-and-cream-striped waist-coat for the occasion. Unfortunately, it clashed rather badly with his mustard-yellow pants and orange-and-yellow-paisley bow tie. Classic Eddie. "I thought such a book might come in useful," he said with a twinkle in his eye.

I laughed. He was no doubt right about that. "It's real?"

"Absolutely. One of the few human accounts of dragons that survives from ancient times. They say it was written by a dragon child. One of the first."

My trip to London had brought me into contact with the dragon clans. My proving them innocent of the murder of an MI8 agent had earned me a sort of place of honor among them. I'd also befriended their current dragon child, Cordy's sister. Dragon children are peacemakers, intermediaries between the dragons and humans. Having a true account of dragon kind from the perspective of a dragon child is unbelievably cool.

Cordelia handed me a hot-pink gift bag. "This is from Bastet and me. She assured me you'll like it."

I barely refrained from rolling my eyes. "Um, thanks, Cordy. And please thank Bastet for me." I honestly couldn't believe such a thing had come out of my mouth.

Inside was a piece of lingerie that was more piece and less lingerie. I blushed bright red and quickly stuffed it back in the bag.

"Perhaps it isn't as useful as the other gifts, but I have a feeling it will come in handy." She gave me a wide smile. Inigo leered.

If only the floor would open up and swallow me whole. "Um, thanks again. Very...nice of you."

As we all dived into cupcakes, it hadn't escaped my notice that Inigo hadn't brought me anything. I tried not to let it bother me. Relationships aren't about material stuff, right?

Right.

"Uh, Morgan," Kabita's voice jolted me out of my pity party.

"Yeah?" I mumbled around a mouthful of cupcake.

"Your amulet. It's glowing."

I glanced down. Sure enough, the stone in the middle of the amulet glowed a deep sapphire blue. *Ah, shit.*

"What does it mean?" Her voice held a mix of fear and wonder.

I had no idea. But with my track record, it probably wasn't anything good. The last time this happened, the amulet had chosen me as the Key of Atlantis, and my life had gone to hell in a handbasket.

Chapter Four

Fringe was packed with writhing bodies when we arrived. Eddie had begged off, and I wished I could have too. It wasn't really my scene. But the rest had been keen to go, so I gave in gracefully.

On the way there, I tried calling Jack about the weird glowing thing, but he didn't pick up. For a man who insisted on shadowing my every move, he sure made himself unavailable at the most inopportune times.

The minute we walked through the door, Inigo was the center of attention, as always. I understood it now, that animal attraction he exuded. It really *was* animal. Or dragon anyway.

Inigo wrapped one arm around me and pulled me close against his side. I snuggled into the heat of him, loving the sizzle that sparked between us. It was the first time we'd been to Fringe since we'd become a couple. I admit it was kind of weird. I was used to seeing women draped all over him, but this time they stood back warily.

"They're scared to death of you," he whispered, his breath tickling my ear.

I laughed. "Yeah, right."

"No, really." He flashed me a wicked grin. "Your reputation precedes you."

I snorted at that. I am a hunter. I kill vampires and demons and other really bad creatures that harm humans. I do not kill supernaturals for the fun of it. Though, I suppose, in this instance, reputation had its use.

Inigo dragged us toward the middle of the dance floor, leaving the others to find their own spots to dance or drink, but something caught the corner of my eye. I could have sworn I saw Jack melting into the crowd. Seriously, was he trying to avoid me? Well, if he was, he had another thing coming. I needed to talk to him about sunwalker business. If he wanted to play guardian, it was time for him to damn well act like it.

I leaned in close to Inigo and spoke directly into his ear. "Hang on a sec; I'll be right back."

He glanced back, an eyebrow raised in question.

"Ladies' room," I mouthed.

With a smile, he let me go, motioning for me to meet him on the dance floor. I gave him a quick nod before worming my way through the crowd of dancers toward the spot where I'd last seen Jack.

I had no idea why I'd lied to Inigo. There was no reason for it. It isn't like he doesn't understand the nature of my relationship with Jack, and I am pretty sure he doesn't have a jealous bone in his body. I shrugged it off. I had enough on my plate without worrying about my sudden bout of untruth.

Naturally, by the time I reached the place I'd seen Jack, he wasn't there. When are things ever that easy?

A couple of pixie girls in ridiculously short skirts and Cookie Monster–blue hair danced closer and tried to do the bump and grind with me. They gave me those pouty looks girls in dance clubs give when they're trying to be sexy. Not my style.

I snarled, which sent the pixie twins packing. It wasn't nice of me, but then, pixies aren't generally known for being nice, either. More like bitchy little trollops. They actually make the sidhe look relatively sane. So I felt somewhat justified.

I scanned the crowded room, catching sight of a blond-streaked head near the bar. With a few well-placed elbows, I managed to clear enough space to get in close. I tugged on the man's leather jacket. He turned around—only, he wasn't a he.

He was a she, and she was enormous: well over six feet tall, with shoulders like a linebacker and skin the color of dark-roasted coffee beans. Her shoulder-length hair wasn't sun streaked like I'd first thought, but naturally striped dark brown, silver, and gold, like the fur of certain animals—wolves, coyotes, badgers. I am pretty sure she was a bear-shifter. How I ever mistook her for Jack is beyond me.

"Yes?" Her tone was polite, or as polite as screaming over the music in a nightclub could ever be, but her expression told me she clearly thought she could squash me like a bug. Probably, she could.

"Uh, sorry. I thought you were someone else."

Her expression spoke volumes. No doubt she didn't hear that excuse very often.

I quickly wormed my way back through the crush of dancers toward Inigo, who was, quite naturally, once again the center of attention. I shook my head slightly as I rejoined him.

Inigo's blue eyes danced with laughter. He knows I hate being the center of attention. I guess I just have to get used to it, because he loves having all eyes on him.

He wrapped both arms around me and pulled me flush up against him. I could feel my cheeks heating. I'm all for a little dirty dancing, but Fringe is awfully public.

"Relax." He nuzzled my ear, sending shivers down my spine. "Forget them. Just let yourself enjoy the moment."

"I'd prefer to enjoy the moment in a really dark corner."

"Later." I swear to the gods he leered at me.

I laughed and wound my arms around his neck, burying my fingers in the silk of his hair as we moved to the music. Heat flooded me as the pounding rhythm took over. It was so primal, so intimate. Everything narrowed down to Inigo and me. I forgot everyone and everything else, lost in the feel of our bodies writhing against each other, our breath mingling.

Until the screaming started.

The club went from crazy to full-out stampede. As the crowd swarmed by us, I grabbed a woman by the shoulders and whirled her to face me. "What is it? What happened?"

"I don't know."

The panicked look on her face told me otherwise. She struggled to get away from me, but she was no match for my hunter strength. "Don't lie to me." I infused my voice with every bit of power I could muster without calling on my new superpowers. The last thing I wanted to do was burn the woman alive. Or worse.

Her expression turned defiant as she continued to struggle. "I told you, I don't know."

She was trying to pass as human, but I could feel her magic pulsing against my skin. I knew what she was, too. I narrowed my eyes and gave her a little shake. "Listen, succubus, you will tell me right now, or I will drain the life force out of you."

OK, so I couldn't do any such thing. Probably. But she didn't need to know that.

"It's the sidhe." She cast a frightened glance behind her as though expecting one of the fae folk to pop up out of nowhere.

"What do you mean?" My stomach lurched. I had a really bad feeling.

"Look for yourself," she hissed, and yanked her arm out of my grasp.

I let her go. It was obvious she was terrified out of her mind. The screams had come from the direction of the bar, so I headed that way.

Inigo and I forced our way against the tide of humans and supernaturals flowing toward the exit until we reached the bar. A sidhe sat on one of the high stools, calmly sipping a glass of glowing golden nectar. He was tall, slender, ice blond, and impossibly beautiful as his facial features shifted and molded into various incarnations. Not something normal humans can see. They just see a basic underwear-model-pretty face. But I am a hunter. I could see his true face. Or faces. Sidhe don't have one face, they have many. And I mean that both literally and metaphorically.

Above the sidhe, suspended in midair, hung Cordelia. The look of terror mixed with anger on her face sent fury coursing through me. The darkness roared to life. My vision narrowed to a pinpoint focused on the sidhe's ever-shifting features.

Usually the sidhe blend with the crowd, letting their powers simmer on low. Humans would completely ignore them. Other supernaturals would know they weren't human, but nothing more. This night, they had released their full power in the middle of a crowded club. No wonder everyone had run for the door in full-blown panic. The power of the sidhe crept across my skin like a million little biting ants.

"Put her down." The voice was mine and not mine. This wasn't the first time the darkness had filled my voice. It seethed inside me, angry that one of its own was in danger. Apparently, it had decided those that were mine also belonged to it. "Carefully."

The sidhe sneered at me. "Or what?"

There is no magic, no creature, more powerful than the sidhe. Or at least there hadn't been. Heck, there still might not be, but it was worth a shot: I let the darkness out to play.

The darkness took over in an instant. My hand flashed out and grabbed the sidhe around the throat, hauling him off the barstool and nearly crushing his windpipe. The golden nectar splashed across the floor as his glass splintered into a thousand glittering pieces. The sidhe tried to call his magic, but the darkness blocked his access to the earth magic he needed. Even his own internal fire magic was no match for my darkness. His facial features stopped shifting as he struggled to breathe.

With the access to his magic cut off, Cordelia came crashing down. Fortunately, Inigo is a lot stronger than he looks. He managed to catch her before she hit the floor.

"Cordy, you OK?" I didn't dare take my eyes off the sidhe to make sure.

"I'm fine, Morgan. Either deal with the cretin or I will." Her voice was a little breathy, but the tinge of anger was obvious. I'd no doubt she'd kick the fairy boy's ass if I gave her half a chance.

A second sidhe flashed into the room. This one was as dark as the one I held was light and just as beautiful. "Release him," the dark sidhe snarled.

The darkness inside me didn't answer.

The second sidhe stepped toward me, murder in his silver eyes.

"Not another move." Kabita stepped up behind the second sidhe.

The sidhe ignored her and kept going.

"I said, not another step." She laid a naked blade against the dark sidhe's throat. He shrieked in agony. "I may not have her power," Kabita said to the creature, her voice deadly calm, "but nothing beats cold, pressed iron."

An iron blade? Go Kabita.

The darkness snatched my attention. It wanted to hurt the sidhe, and hurt them badly. But hurting a sidhe is not a good idea. The fairy court sort of frowns on it, actually. And having the fairy queen as an enemy is never a pleasant experience. Not that I know this firsthand, mind you, but I've heard things.

I struggled to tamp down the darkness, or at least rein it in a bit. It wasn't easy. "Listen to me, sidhe," I hissed into the blond sidhe's ear. "You do not come into my town, to my club, and mess with my friends. You got that?" Shit, who was I? Clint Eastwood?

"We apologize, Morgan Bailey." The second sidhe spoke from a few feet away, where Kabita still had her iron blade to his throat. "It was not our intention to cause offense."

I wasn't surprised they knew my name, but I didn't like it, either. Knowing your true name gives a sidhe power over you.

And I really didn't like that they were being so amenable all of a sudden. "No, you just enjoy torturing those you deem beneath yourselves. Well, this time you picked on the wrong human."

"Again, we apologize. My...colleague will be reprimanded."

Reprimanded? Now, that was a new one. The fairy queen doesn't give a shit whom her subjects harm. Especially if one of those harmed is human. Humans are lower than trolls as far as the sidhe are concerned. At least trolls have magic.

My grip loosened slightly, and the blond sidhe I was holding gulped in air. Still, I didn't let him go. I turned my head toward the dark sidhe Kabita was still holding. "Why?"

"We were sent by our queen to find you. She will be...displeased that one of your friends was harmed in the process."

Weirder and weirder. "What does the fairy queen want with me?"

"She has a gift for you, in honor of your birthday."

Oh crap. Accepting gifts from the queen of the sidhe is never a good idea. "That's OK, thanks. I don't need any more gifts."

The second sidhe's face shifted from a pretty, almost elfin-like incarnation into that of a gorgeous saturnine man. A feral grin stretched across his face. "Oh, but she insists." He held out his hand, palm up. A small blue box appeared.

Kabita raised a brow as she stared over his shoulder at the box. "The queen is giving Morgan presents from Tiffany's?"

The sidhe smirked, but said nothing.

I glanced at his fellow sidhe. The one whose windpipe I was still semi-crushing. His natural scent of peppermint and cloves tickled my nose. They have a very particular scent, the sidhe. One that draws humans like moths to a flame. I wasn't about to get burned. "I'm going to let you go. The minute I do, you had better vanish from this plane. Permanently. Got it?"

He nodded, so I let go. The moment I did, he shimmered out of existence. I wondered whether the queen really would kick his ass for messing with Cordy. I sure wouldn't want to be him if she did. She isn't exactly known for being loving and merciful.

I turned to the remaining sidhe and that damned blue box in his hand. "No offense to Her Majesty, but—"

His features hardened and his voice turned sibilant. "You will accept this gift from my queen, Morgan Bailey, or you will suffer the consequences. My queen does not take such slights lightly."

Crap, crap, double crap. That's all I needed: a pissing match with the fairy queen. Damned if you do. Damned if you don't.

"Fine," I snarled as I strode across the floor and snatched the box out of his hand. "Don't have much of a choice, do I?"

His face was impassive. "None at all. Now may I go?"

I sighed and nodded. Kabita lifted her blade from his throat, and with a small bow, the sidhe flashed out of sight.

I stared at the little blue box in my hand. Shit, this wasn't going to be good. Fairy gifts always come with strings. I couldn't even begin to imagine the kinds of strings attached to a gift from the queen of the fairies herself.

The thought was horrifying.

"Open it."

I glared at Kabita. "You know the minute I open this box, I owe a debt to the queen of the freaking fairies, right?"

She shrugged. "You don't open it, and you'll be at war with the queen of the fairies. Either way, you're screwed."

"Gee, thanks for pointing out the obvious." I carefully placed the box on the polished wood bar. It sat there looking all innocent and pretty, with its little cream-colored bow. Might as well be a scorpion. I so did not want to open that box.

I glanced around the room. The bar was still empty except for my friends. Even the employees had fled, and I doubted they'd be back anytime soon. I turned my attention back to the box.

Inigo reached over and squeezed my hand. "Sorry, Morgan."

"It's not your fault," I said with a slight shrug. "I don't suppose you can sense anything?"

"Not when fairies are involved."

Sidhe magic puts his clairvoyance out of whack. Just great.

My fingers trembled a bit as I carefully lifted the lid off the box. Inside, nestled against a bed of black velvet, was a tiny gold key. I admit to being ever so slightly confused. Why on earth was the fairy queen giving me a key? And what was it for?

"There's a note." Inigo nodded toward the lid.

Sure enough, tucked into the lid of the box was a bit of creamy vellum. I dreaded to think what kind of creature had "donated" its skin for that vellum. I really hoped it wasn't human, because that would totally creep me out.

I pulled the vellum out of the lid and carefully unfolded it. Across the page was written a single sentence in a flowing script of bloodred ink:

This will save your life.

Freaking fantastic.

∽

I felt better once I was buckled into my Mustang. Once I was surrounded by all that metal, there was no way a sidhe could get anywhere near me. Iron would neutralize sidhe magic, possibly even to the point of killing the sidhe, but steel still leaves a nasty mark, and my classic car is chock-full of steel.

"You OK?" Concern flashed in Inigo's blue eyes. I could see little flecks of gold dancing in his irises. The dragon half of him was close to the surface.

I snorted. "Yeah, fabulous. I am now indebted to the fairy queen, all because of some stupid key. Happy birthday to me." It was ridiculous and scary at the same time.

"Yeah, she kind of stole my thunder."

I frowned. "What do you mean?"

He pulled a small box from inside his jacket and placed it in my hand. It wasn't Tiffany blue, but it was small and square and just the right size for a ring. My heart stuttered to a stop before suddenly kicking into overdrive.

"Uh, what's this?" It was a good thing I hadn't started driving yet, or I might have caused a wreck.

My reaction was so visceral and so negative it surprised me. *Why am I so afraid of what's in that box? Shouldn't I be excited? Thrilled? This is Inigo. This is what I want, right?*

"Open it."

"Listen, Inigo—"

"Open it."

I opened it. What I saw took my breath away.

It was a ring, but not some stupid diamond engagement one, thank the gods. I was definitely not ready for that. Instead, strands of intricately wrought silver twisted and turned, the Celtic knots forming a perfect dragon.

"It's beautiful." I could hardly breathe. Terror and excitement warred inside me. Did this mean Inigo wanted some kind of commitment? I've never done well with commitment. Or rather, it has never done well with me. It seems that every time I give my heart to someone, it gets stomped to pieces and thrown back in my face. Kind of makes me a bit skittish.

He took the ring from the box and slid it onto my finger. My right middle finger. Suddenly, I could breathe easier.

"I thought it suited you." He smiled. "And I figured, as long as you wore it, you'd never forget me."

I laughed at that. Inigo is probably the least forgettable person I've ever met.

"Happy birthday, Morgan." His lips were warm and tasted of chocolate and campfires. One of my favorite things about his being dragon.

He drew back and gave me a slightly lecherous wink. "Take me home with you and I'll give you the rest of your present."

I grinned and fired up the engine. I'm pretty sure I broke every speed limit in the city.

Chapter Five

Inigo had his shirt off before we were halfway from the driveway to the house. I saw the neighbor's curtain twitch slightly. I smirked. Mrs. McGillicudy sure got an eyeful. Served her right, old bat. The woman makes Miss Marple look like she minds her own business.

It took me three tries to get the door open. Probably because Inigo's hands were roaming everywhere. And I do mean *everywhere*. Shivers ran down my spine as he started nibbling the tender skin just behind my right ear.

Poor Mrs. McG was going to have heart palpitations.

I finally got the key to behave, and we stumbled into the kitchen, shedding clothing as we went. My shirt joined Inigo's on the floor, followed by my bra. The jeans disappeared somewhere between the kitchen and the bedroom. We made it to the bed just in time for my panties to make their disappearance, followed closely by Inigo's boxer briefs.

I do love a man in boxer briefs. Or out of them.

I slid his glasses from his nose and placed them on the bedside table. It was a safety precaution. We'd busted his last pair of glasses thanks to a particularly passionate evening.

Before I could utter a word, his mouth was on mine, tongue and lips at once, both gently teasing and fiercely possessive. My heart hammered against my chest as warmth flooded my body. His kisses always made my blood pound, my heart race.

His hands skimmed over my body, hands surprisingly gentle. My own fingers explored the tensile strength of his muscles under warm, supple skin, golden against the paleness of my own. Gods, I love the feel of him, the warmth of him. Yeah, he is sexy as hell, but he is more than that. So much more.

I trailed my lips down the side of his throat as he hoisted me up against him. I could feel the hard length of him against my stomach as he laid us both down on the bed, his hand sliding down my thigh. I knew what he'd find. I was wet and, oh, so ready.

"Happy birthday, Morgan," he whispered as he slid into me, stretching me with his hot hardness, pleasure spiking along my nerve endings.

I arched my body toward him, tangling my fingers in his silky golden hair. In that moment, I felt alive in a way I've never been with anyone else.

Happy birthday, indeed.

∽

I stood on a high plateau overlooking the valley below. The hot desert winds teased at my long robes, tangling the heavy fabric around my legs. Perhaps not the most suitable garments for the occasion, but the costly silks that marked me as high priest were also designed to keep my body at ambient temperature. Better whipping skirts than sweating to death under the double suns.

The escarpment fell away beneath my feet to the red earth below, revealing striations of darker red, gold, and purple in the face of the cliff. It was a dramatic landscape like no other I'd seen on any of the many planets I'd visited during my long life. I would miss this place. My heart ached with the knowledge as I turned to my companion.

"You must come with us."

The large man next to me was silent for a moment. His red skin blended with the red of the earth, as it was meant to. This was his home and the home of his people, as it had been for millennia.

He shook his head and crossed his arms over his massive chest. His expression was as stubborn as only the marid's could be. "We cannot. Our place is here."

My jaw tightened, but I shoved down the anger at his stubbornness. I knew I was asking much. I understood his desire to remain, but that was no longer an option. "To stay here is a death sentence for you and your people. Is that what you want? The complete annihilation of your race?"

"Of course not." He shoved a lock of greenish-black hair out of his face, frustration written in every line of his body. "But perhaps you are wrong..."

"We are not wrong. You know we are not. I am sure you've felt the shift. Look." I pointed to another plateau some distance away. At its base was a small settlement of perhaps five thousand citizens. Fortunately, we'd had enough warning this time to evacuate.

The man next to me shook his head. "I see nothing. All is as it should be."

"Wait."

Beneath our feet, the ground began first to vibrate, then rumble, and then it started shaking in earnest. Finally, it began heaving and rolling so violently we would have been thrown off the plateau if not for my magic holding us in place. "Keep watching," I yelled over the roar of the bucking earth.

At first, there was nothing more extraordinary than the quake, and then a giant crack appeared in the cliff face above the settlement. A huge chunk of the plateau opposite us broke off and crashed to the ground, burying the town beneath mounds of dirt and stone. If we hadn't evacuated, five thousand citizens would be dead.

"That is nothing," I told the large man as he stared at the scene in horror. "This will keep happening, and each time, it will grow increasingly violent until it rips the entire planet apart."

"But this is our home. We are tied to this land at a level you cannot begin to understand."

But I did. The very life force of his people was dependent on the planet that was now ripping itself apart. "I will help you and your people tie yourselves to a new land. You know I have the power."

Still, he hesitated.

"We have no choice, Marid," I told my longtime friend. "We must leave Atlantis."

∽

The next morning dawned crisp, bright, and far too early. I managed to prop one eye open and nearly hissed at the light streaming in around the edges of the curtains. I am so not a morning person.

The dream was a little fuzzy around the edges now, but I knew I'd been dreaming about the high priest of Atlantis again, thanks to the amulet. I have no idea why I have to be him in all my dreams. Why couldn't I play the part of a sexy priestess or something?

I frowned as I stared at the ceiling and the little crack near the corner. They were different, the dreams. I was seeing something far earlier in time than I'd ever seen before. I was seeing the destruction of the Atlantean home world.

I wasn't sure whether that was cool or horrifying. Maybe a little of both. What I didn't know was the identity of the new player in my dreams and what his importance would be. But I did know I'd find out. Eventually.

That is how the amulet works. At least so far. It had been that way with the Brent Darroch situation anyway.

Inigo was still snoring away next to me, his head half buried under a pillow, so I climbed out of bed as quietly as possible and snagged a robe off the back of the door. It was one of those fuzzy granny robes Inigo is always teasing me about. It was probably about as far from sexy as you can possibly get, but I didn't care. I was naked, the house was cold, and the robe was warm and cozy. So there.

I tried to send Trevor another text, but it bounced back. I was more than worried; I was downright antsy. Why wasn't he answering?

I somehow managed to get the coffee brewing with only a few minor mishaps. Coffee grounds on the floor is pretty much de rigueur for a morning at my house.

I eyeballed the phone where it sat innocently on the counter. I knew I shouldn't call. Not this early and certainly not before my first cup of caffeinated beverage. Then again, I've never been very good at doing what I'm supposed to do.

I snatched up the handset and dialed Jack's number. The man was going to answer some questions whether he liked it or not.

Apparently, he didn't. The phone rang for ages before clicking over to voice mail. I didn't bother leaving a message.

∽

We hit Highway 26 headed east toward Warm Springs the minute the rush hour traffic was over. The small Central Oregon town is about two hours away from Portland, and I wanted to get there in plenty of time for the meeting.

Halfway up the mountain, I had to stop and put chains on the tires.

The snowplows had been through, but it is still the law. One good thing about having a boyfriend who is half dragon: he could bench-press a Mustang. Inigo had the chains on in a fraction of the time it would have taken me.

People think rain forests are strictly a tropical jungle thing. Tell that to the Pacific Northwest. Rainforests are characterized not by temperature but by annual rainfall. Believe me, we get enough rainfall to qualify. The snow lining the road through the mountain pass was up to my waist.

The highway twisted itself up and around Mount Hood, through a forest of fir trees and frozen creeks, until it finally spilled out onto the high desert of Central Oregon. Flat brown land dotted with sagebrush and juniper trees stretched for miles on either side of the thin ribbon of asphalt. The occasional painted pony grazed on the dead winter grass poking through the snow while ignoring the passing traffic. We were on tribal lands.

Excitement thrummed in my veins. Ever since I was a kid, I've been fascinated by the rich culture of the Native American people, especially the Oregon tribes. Which may have something to do with my uncle having been a cop on the reservation back in the day. Or maybe it is just my own interest in history, particularly the history of my home state.

Years ago, I'd had the good fortune to spend an afternoon chatting with a member of the Warm Springs Tribal Council, thanks to the fact I was dating his stepson at the time. I'd been enthralled by his tales of supernatural things, but I'd thought they were stories made up for entertainment. I know better now.

My phone jangled, jarring me back to the present. Which was probably a good thing, seeing as how I was driving. "Who is it?"

Inigo snagged my phone out of the cup holder where I'd stashed it and glanced at the screen. "Jack."

"Crap." I searched Inigo's face for any hint of jealousy, but there was none. I guess four hundred years gives a person some perspective. Either that or it makes him really good at hiding his feelings.

I pulled the Mustang to the side of the road and hit the call button. No doubt Inigo would be able to hear the entire conversation anyway, but holding the cell to my ear made me at least feel like I had some privacy. "What do you want, Jack? I'm wearing the amulet."

"I just spoke to Kabita. She said you're headed to Warm Springs?"

"Yeah. So?" I barely refrained from rolling my eyes. I was doing way too much of that lately.

"Why didn't you call me?"

Seriously, I wanted to smack him. And not in a good way. "If you check your phone, you'll see I did try to call you, both last night and this morning. If you'd bothered to pick up, I could have told you. Besides, you're my guardian, Jack, not my dad. I don't need to clear every little thing with you." I could feel the steam practically boiling out my ears. The man had ways of getting under my skin.

"Yes, I'm your guardian." His voice turned testy. "You should remember that more often. As your guardian, I'm telling you not to go to Warm Springs."

I did roll my eyes then. I was getting really tired of the whole guardian thing. I get that he is supposed to protect me, the key, from the big baddies, but I can protect myself. Plus, he'd used being the guardian as an excuse to break my heart. I found it hard to forgive or forget that.

"Oh, for crying out loud." I was just this short of yelling, *You're not the boss of me*. But I managed to restrain myself. "Give me one good reason." Not that I would listen.

"It's not safe, Morgan. What you find there will put your life in danger. You need to turn around and come back to Portland."

Like anything in my life is safe these days. I have pretty much been in danger every day since I met him and we found that damned amulet.

"Do you know something specific?"

"No," he admitted. "But I feel it."

Maybe he did, but I couldn't afford to run my life according to Jack's feelings. "Get a grip, Jack. I'm meeting my brother, not some crazy psychopath. I've got a job to do, so let me do it." With that,

I hung up the phone. I'd been so irritated with him I'd forgotten to ask about the amulet and its new glowing trick. Dammit all.

Inigo raised an eyebrow. "What's his problem?"

I shrugged. "He's being his usual overprotective self. I think he's taking this guardian thing way too seriously. You'd think I was some kind of helpless twit."

He laughed. "You are a lot of things, Morgan, but a helpless twit isn't one of them. Jack knows that."

"Well, he sure doesn't act like it." I—just—managed to keep the snarl out of my voice. "He kept going on about how it wasn't safe. That whatever I find in Warm Springs is going to put me in danger. Ridiculous." Danger is pretty much par for the course these days, and Jack's insistence only makes me more stubborn.

Inigo frowned. "Did he say why?"

I shook my head. "Are you getting some kind of vibe or something?"

"No, but Jack's not exactly the overly emotional type."

"Understatement of the year." To all those women out there who think dating Mr. Darcy would be cool: trust me, it's not.

He chuckled a little at that. "True. So, if he says something is dangerous, there's likely a good reason for it."

"Fine, take his side," I grumped as I pulled the car back onto the highway.

"I'm not taking his side." There was still an edge of amusement in Inigo's voice. "It's just not a bad idea to exercise a little caution."

"I'm full of caution."

This time the laughter was full-blown.

∽

We arrived at the café a good hour before the meeting time, which was fine with me. Thanks to my worry about the meeting with Trevor and my hurry to get to the café, I'd missed breakfast. My stomach was letting me know about it.

"Come on. I'm hungry."

"You're always hungry." Inigo shook his head, but followed me inside.

Warm Springs Café was a dinky little hole-in-the-wall with cheap Formica tables and cracked vinyl booths. It was old and dingy, but it was clean. I'd never been there before, but in my experience, such places survive because the food is cheap and damn good. I figured this place was no exception.

I was right.

A middle-aged waitress in a polyester pink uniform brought us plates piled high with food. I dug into my pancakes with gusto. They were divine.

"I can't believe you're eating pancakes."

"Uh, yeah," I managed to mumble around a mouthful of syrupy goodness.

"It's lunchtime."

"So? Pancakes are not a breakfast food; they're an anytime food."

He shook his head and bit into his corned beef sandwich. I had to admit his lunch looked really good, but I was happy with my pancakes. As far as I am concerned, pancakes are the true breakfast of champions. Or I guess lunch in this case.

"Morgan."

I froze, a forkful of pancake halfway to my mouth. "Trevor? You OK?" He looked rough. There were dark circles under his chocolate-brown eyes, and his usually warm latte skin was almost ashen.

He slid into the booth beside me, the vinyl squeaking in protest. "I'm fine. You got my text?"

"Of course. That's why I'm here. Though, I'm not sure why all the mysteriousness. You didn't think to—I don't know—pick up a phone and call me like a normal person? Do you know how many times I tried to call you? I was worried."

He glanced around as though to make sure no one else was listening, then beckoned us both to lean in closer. He was clearly nervous, which was weird. I haven't known my half brother long. While we'd technically worked together for the past three years, it had mostly been Kabita who'd dealt with him. Still, from what I've seen, Trevor Daly has nerves of steel. It is sort of par for the course for federal agents.

"What is he doing here?" He nodded to Inigo. "I told you to keep this quiet."

"And I have." *Mostly.* "But Inigo and I are a team, and whatever it is, it sounds serious enough that we're going to need all the help we can get."

He sighed. "Fine. But I've been ordered to keep things under the radar, so discretion is appreciated."

"Oh, I'm the picture of discretion." Now that I knew Trevor was OK, I could relax and enjoy my meal. I took another bite of pancake. I didn't know who the cook was, but he or she deserved a gold medal. The pancakes were seriously to die for.

"So"—I waved a syrupy fork at him—"tell us why we're here."

"Two days ago, an agent named Daniel Vega was found dead in his hotel room, in Madras." His voice was hardly above a whisper. Fortunately, both Inigo and I have excellent hearing. In my case, it is one of those quirky little side effects of having been murdered by a vampire.

"Madras, as in the little town just down the road?" Inigo asked.

"Yeah, that Madras." Trevor gave the waitress a charming smile as she brought him a cup of coffee. The woman was twice his age, but I swear she blushed like a teenager as she hurried back to the kitchen.

I waited until the waitress left before asking the question burning in my brain. "What on earth was an SRA agent doing in Madras?"

The Supernatural Regulatory Agency keeps itself well hidden within the Environmental Protection Agency. They have limited manpower and aren't in the habit of sending agents to Podunk towns like Madras. That's why they keep people like me around. We get to do the dirty work, and they don't have the expense of sending an agent.

"That's the thing." Trevor leaned in closer. "I don't know. He wasn't there on official business, and he doesn't have any friends or family nearby."

Weird. But not that weird. People visit places for all kinds of reasons. Maybe Agent Vega liked the small-town atmosphere. "OK, so how did he die?"

"The police are claiming it was suicide."

Inigo and I exchanged a look. "Ah. You don't think it was." I kept my eyes on my brother's face. I could see his jaw working.

"I know it wasn't suicide. I just can't prove it."

"I get that he's a brother-in-arms and all that, but why don't you let the agency handle this?" I suggested. "He's their agent. What's this got to do with you?"

Trevor's face hardened. "Daniel was my friend. I'm not about to let them sweep his murder under the rug."

"Whoa," Inigo spoke up. "What do you mean? Are you suggesting the SRA wouldn't thoroughly investigate the death of one of their agents?"

Trevor's expression was bleak. "I'm afraid so. They want this kept very quiet. So they're willing to let me investigate as long as I don't make any waves."

"You're sure?" I hoped he was wrong. I really did. I didn't like the idea that the agency wouldn't come in guns blazing to solve Vega's murder—if it was murder—but then again, I should know better. Like I said, the SRA doesn't like dirtying its hands.

He shrugged. "Sure as I can be. That's why I need your help, Morgan. There's something strange going on, and the agency is keeping quiet about it."

I was getting a really bad feeling. "Strange? What kind of strange?"

"Your kind of strange," Trevor said.

Which meant supernatural wonkiness of the scary kind. "I still don't get why you couldn't pick up a freaking phone and call me like a normal person. I mean, if the agency is willing to let you investigate quietly, what's the big deal? You could have just asked over the phone to meet me."

He shook his head. "There's something really strange going on. I don't know who I can trust and who I can't. Face-to-face was the safest way. Just in case." He gave me a knowing look. "And you can't talk back to a text."

He knows me far too well.

"I need your help, Morgan. Please. I need to know the truth. I owe Daniel that much." There was true pain in his voice. My heart hurt for him.

Six months ago, I hadn't even known Trevor Daly was anything more than an obnoxious midlevel bureaucrat. Now he was begging me for favors that could get me thrown down a deep, dark hole of nasty that could get my ass handed to me by the SRA. But he is my brother. I couldn't say no. Besides, I knew he'd do it for me. Heck, he had already done it for me. I guess that's the joy of family. Kicking bad guy ass together.

I sighed. I had no idea what I was about to get myself involved in, but I was pretty sure it wasn't anything good. "Show me the crime scene."

Chapter Six

Madras is a short drive from Warm Springs through the canyon and up the other side. It is the closest major town to the reservation. And by "major," I mean about six thousand people, give or take. I think it's cool that this tiny little town in the middle of nowhere was named after the exotic city in India. Who knew they were so cosmopolitan back in 1903?

I love the early-twentieth-century buildings that line the main street downtown. It gives the town a sort of vintage atmosphere. Still, the fact is, it is a nowhere town in a nowhere place. What on earth had Daniel Vega been doing here?

It isn't like Madras is a hotbed of supernatural activity. I'd have known if it were. There are no local hellholes or other interdimensional portholes. No ley lines, nothing. Sunnydale aside, the supernatural—whether it be ghosts, vampires, or just random weirdness—tend to collect where there are large numbers of ordinary people. Apparently, paranormal beasties find small towns as boring as humans do.

We followed Trevor's car to a small run-down motel on the other side of town. He pulled into the gravel parking lot and stopped in front of the door marked with a rusted number five. To say the place had seen better days may have been something of an understatement.

"You'd think they'd pay their agents better," Inigo said to me with a nod toward the peeling paint and dirty windows, one of them cracked along the bottom. "There's not much to choose from in this town, but there are better hotels, all of them cheap.

Why choose the crummiest motel? This is barely a step above a pay-by-hour. Unless that's why he was here."

I could hardly imagine Vega coming all the way to Madras for a little action, but who knew? People are strange. "No idea, but I'm probably going to get cooties just from looking at it." I shuddered. "Poor Vega. I can't imagine dying in a place like this."

Inigo leaned over and brushed his lips over mine.

"What was that for?" Not that I was complaining, mind you.

"You had that look."

"What look?"

"That look that says you're thinking of something bad and you need someone to remind you of the good things."

My heart melted just a little bit. How did he know exactly what to do and say at just the right time?

There was a rap on the car window. "Are you two coming? Or are you just going to sit in there and make out?" Trevor was obviously getting antsy.

"We're coming. We're coming. Sheez. Hold your horses."

We made our way across the deserted parking lot. Remnants of crime scene tape still stuck to the sides of the door, fluttering slightly in the chill wind. Trevor produced a key.

"Flashed my badge at the motel manager," he explained. "It's already been cleaned, unfortunately."

The inside of Daniel Vega's hotel room wasn't any better than the outside. The army-green shag carpet was worn down to the nub, and I really didn't want to think about the stains on the bedspread.

"Where did they find him?" Inigo asked.

"In the bathroom. They said he'd slit his wrists." His tone clearly indicated he thought otherwise.

I peered into the tiny bathroom. Odd place to slit your wrists. There was no tub, just a grimy shower stall with a frosted-glass door that didn't shut properly. There wasn't enough room on the floor to lie down. Even sitting would have been a challenge unless you had your butt hanging half out the door. It was certainly not a place I'd choose to end my life if I were so inclined.

"Why would he slit his wrists in here? Why not on the bed?" I frowned and glanced back at the bed. Not that it was a better place to die, but at least it was marginally more comfortable and a whole lot easier to maneuver. "For that matter, why slit his wrists at all? Was there a note?"

"No note." Trevor shook his head. "And they'd cleaned up before I got here. I did see the crime photos, and they didn't look quite right."

I glanced at him. "What do you mean?"

"I don't know how to explain it." He tucked his hands into his pockets. "I've seen a few crime scene photos in my time and it just...it looked staged."

"And he hadn't been depressed? Acting funny?"

"Of course he was acting funny. He took off for the middle of nowhere without a word. But depressed? Definitely not." Trevor ran a hand over his closely cropped curls. "In fact, he seemed really excited. He wouldn't tell me anything, but it was like he was on the scent of something big."

I know that feeling well. I get the same way when I am on a hunt.

Inigo was pacing the room, frowning.

"You get anything?" I asked.

"No." His tone was filled with frustration. "There are too many imprints here. Too many lives have passed through. I can't get a fix on anything."

"Not even a violent death?"

He gave me a look. "There's been more than one violent death in this room. And we're not even sure Agent Vega's death was violent."

"Craptastic."

"Tell me about it." Inigo went back to pacing the room.

Out of the corner of my eye, I caught a flicker. A wisp of something white, like smoke or fog. I turned my head, but whatever it was vanished. A puff of air caressed my cheek, stirred my hair ever so slightly.

I frowned and touched my cheek.

"When did they find his body?"

Trevor spoke up, face grim. "Two days ago. The maid turned up around ten in the morning to do her cleaning. When no one answered the door, she went in. Found him in the bathroom in a pool of blood."

"And before that? When was the last time anyone saw him?" I kept scanning the room, taking in the faded bedspread and the stained carpet, but I was coming up blank.

"Not sure. The desk clerk says she saw him about lunchtime the day before. He was in his car, headed out. She didn't see which way he turned. I can't find anyone who saw him after that."

"OK." I gave the room a last once-over. I could feel it, something tugging at me. I just couldn't put my finger on it.

"Uh, Morgan."

I turned to Inigo. He had the oddest expression on his face. "What?"

"Your amulet is glowing again."

I glanced down. Sure enough, the sapphire was giving off a soft blue glow. Honestly. Do I not have enough crazy in my life without throwing more magical weirdness into the mix?

"Not important." I tucked the amulet inside my shirt to hide the glow. "What is important is focusing on the task at hand. I don't think we're going to get any more information here. Do you know where they're holding the body?"

Trevor nodded. "The local funeral home."

"The funeral home?"

"Yeah. There's no morgue in Madras. The county medical examiner does the initial examination at the funeral home. If he'd ruled it suspicious, they'd have transported the body to Portland for an autopsy. Since it was ruled suicide, there's no investigation. The body stays here until his family claims it."

We headed outside and I waited while Trevor locked up the room. "Can you get me into the funeral home?"

"Shouldn't be a problem. Security around here is a joke."

I raised my eyebrows at that. Both of them, since I can't do the whole Spock thing. "A government agent breaking and entering? I am shocked. Truly."

"Watch it, sis, or I'll dunk you in a snowbank."

I stuck out my tongue at him. "You were ordered not to make waves, Trev. I don't want you getting into trouble." I was a free agent. I could pretty much do what I wanted as long as I was willing to pay the piper. He couldn't. Not if he wanted to keep his job.

"I'll be fine." The look of determination on his face reminded me of someone I knew. Quite possibly me.

"Trev…"

"I'm going with you, Morgan." The tone of his voice told me that was the end of the discussion as far as he was concerned. I barely resisted the urge to growl.

"Fine. Let's go visit the mortuary."

It's not every day you get to say something like that.

∽

The funeral home was out toward the airport on the outskirts of town. It was a chunky redbrick building with cheap wooden columns painted white to give it that Colonial look. I swear every other funeral home in the state has the exact same facade.

"It's broad daylight and you want to break into a funeral home?" Inigo gave me a look usually reserved for crazy people. "Why don't we wait until tonight?"

"Because we're not going to break in. Besides, I need to get back to Portland tonight."

"Why?" He gave me a suspicious look.

I heaved a sigh. "Mom made me promise to come to dinner."

"We're driving all the way back through the snow so you can have dinner with your mom?" The incredulity in his voice was understandable.

"It's my birthday dinner. And breaking a promise to my mother is out of the question."

He raised an eyebrow at that. "I'm sure she'd understand."

"You've met my mother. What do you think?"

He froze for a split second. "Oh, yeah. Good point."

We joined Trevor beside his car. His breath made little white clouds in the chill air. It reminded me of the wisp of something I'd seen back in the hotel room. "How do you want to play this?" He glanced toward the front door.

The place looked closed up tight, but I knew better. This was small-town America, and it was lunchtime. I smiled. "We walk right in like we own the place."

The door swung open easily, and we paraded into the front room. "If anyone asks," I told them, "we're here to pay our respects to our dearly departed relative."

"And if they don't have any dearly departed relatives in the mortuary?" Inigo asked.

"There's always going to be somebody in a mortuary, and they're going to have relatives." I turned to Trevor. "Where would they be keeping Agent Vega's body?"

"In the back where the coolers are."

I nodded and headed toward the back of the building. No one appeared to challenge us. The place was as silent as the proverbial tomb.

The hall was lined with viewing rooms on either side. Some contained caskets and flowers. Others were empty. So far as I could tell, no one was home. No one alive anyway.

"I can't believe they'd just leave the place unlocked in the middle of the day." Trevor kept his voice hushed.

"It's a small town. They're probably having a late lunch or something. It wouldn't be entirely unusual to leave the place unlocked in case of visitors. Who's going to steal from a funeral home?"

"Actually, they're one of the best places to steal from." Trevor's voice was muffled as he poked his head into one of the rooms. "The deceased are often buried with small valuables. No one would notice if a ring or watch went missing."

I repressed a groan. "This isn't New York, Trev. It's Madras. Everybody knows everybody, and nobody is going to steal from the dead unless they want the entire town on their ass. This must be it."

The door was half-hidden by a wall hanging and marked PRIVATE with a small, neat plaque. All very subtle and tasteful.

Inigo tried the door. Locked. "Great," he hissed, "the one place we need to get into is the place they decide to lock."

It made sense, actually. It was one thing to leave the viewing rooms open to the public, but quite another thing to leave the rest of the place open. "You can pick the lock, though, right?"

"Probably. Let me get a look at it."

Trevor tapped his foot. "We should hurry. If we get caught back here, my boss is going to have my head."

"You can go wait in the parking lot if you want, brother mine," I said with fake sweetness.

He just shook his head.

I grinned and turned back to Inigo. "Well, what's the verdict?"

"Easy enough to pick, but if we get caught back there, we aren't going to be able to explain ourselves away."

I shrugged. "Needs must. Do it."

In under a minute, Inigo had released the lock. I turned the knob carefully and swung open the door.

"What are you people doing here?"

The three of us stood in the doorway staring at the man on the other side of the door. He was perched on a stool at one of the tables, munching on a sandwich. Apparently, not everyone had left the funeral home for lunch.

"Excuse me," he said, placing his sandwich carefully on its wrapper. "What are you doing here? This area is for employees only."

"We...ah...the door was open," I said.

"It was not." He jumped off his stool, a picture of outrage. "I locked it myself. Now tell me what you're doing here before I call the police."

"I'm the police." Trevor waved his badge. Unfortunately, the mortician was a little more up with his police procedure than the motel manager had been.

"You're not local PD. And you're not from Portland. Now, who are you?"

"Let me handle this," Inigo muttered. He stepped closer to the man, arms spread slightly from his body, voice calm, almost hypnotic. "Listen to me."

The man turned toward Inigo, whose eyes had started to glow gold. "Who...who...?"

"We're nobody." Inigo's voice had turned almost singsong. "We were never here. Nobody was here."

"Nobody was here," the man repeated.

"You are all alone."

"All...all alone."

"You are going to get in your car and go get a coffee."

"Coffee..."

"That's right. But first, where is Agent Vega's body?"

ഗ

Daniel Vega's body lay neatly tucked inside a body bag, inside one of the mortuary refrigerators.

I frowned. Totally not like what they show on *CSI*.

"You getting anything?" I turned toward Inigo. Sometimes he can sense the souls of the departed. Feel how they died.

"No, still nothing. It's like something is blocking me."

Apparently, this was not one of those times.

"We should hurry up," Trevor said, keeping his voice low. "The mortician could be back any minute."

"So Inigo can put the whammy on him." I swear, sometimes men are so thick.

"Remember, we're on the down low, Morgan."

"Like he's going to remember anything. If he even gets back before we're done."

"Why don't you try, Morgan?" Inigo interrupted our little sibling spat.

I blinked. "What?"

Trevor looked equally baffled, but Inigo just shrugged. "Your abilities have been doing the freaky lately. Maybe you can sense something where I can't."

He wasn't wrong about my abilities. It seemed like every other day something new and weird popped up. I guessed it didn't hurt to try. As long as I didn't start raising the dead.

I had no idea what I was doing, so I just sort of held my hands a few inches from the body, palms facing down. I'd seen Cordelia Nightwing do something similar when working with the tarot. I figured it couldn't hurt.

At first, there was nothing. Reluctantly, I reached down to that place where the darkness lives. I didn't want to go there. I had no idea what I might find, but we needed answers. I could feel it there like a tight little ball of blackness, and next to it, a tiny flame.

Neither seemed interested in the body on the slab, which was sort of a relief. Controlling the new forces inside me is pretty much hit or miss. Mostly miss.

Strands of violet-red hair danced in the breeze, tickling my face. Nothing. I was getting nothing. Wait. What? Breeze?

"Did one of you leave the outside door open?"

"No, babe." Inigo was a warm presence beside me. "Trevor shut it."

"And the door to the room?"

"Shut," Trevor confirmed.

"And you don't feel anything weird?" I didn't open my eyes to look at them, but I could almost feel them giving me dubious looks.

"Weird like what kind of weird?" Inigo again.

"Weird like the fact that there's wind inside this room."

"Uh, Morgan?" Trevor cleared his throat. "There's no wind."

"So neither of you felt any sort of breeze?"

They both assured me they hadn't, which didn't make me feel any better. In fact, it was freaking me out just a little. I would have liked to brush it off as an overactive imagination, but with all the bizarreness in my life lately, brushing things off wasn't an option.

I reached down again, even more hesitant this time. Down into that place where the fire and the darkness live. Still, they didn't respond, which was unusual because I usually have to work at keeping them in.

So I went a little deeper. There. Underneath the darkness and the fire was something else. Something new. I'm pretty sure my heart stopped beating for a split second.

The new thing inside me looked like smoke, swirling in ribbons of pure white, pale gray, and shimmering silver. It wound itself up and over and around the darkness and the fire like strands of glitter, making itself at home.

I watched it, almost entranced by its beauty as it twisted itself into pretty little curlicues. I reached out with my metaphysical hand to touch it, and it danced along my fingers, gently caressing each one. I smiled as the smoke played along my skin, leaving sparkles in its wake.

But it didn't feel like smoke. It felt like—

Without warning, it rushed up and out of me in a billowing cloud, whipping my hair around like I was standing in a hurricane. It felt as if my insides were being ripped out along with it. Terror and panic threatened to overwhelm me as I struggled just to breathe. I was lost in a whirlwind with no sense of direction.

Through a veil of white, I could see Inigo stagger back a couple of steps, clothes plastered to his body, while Trevor very nearly went ass over teakettle, unprepared for the blast. Sheets draped over preparation tables whipped wildly as though lashed by...wind.

Holy crap. The new power inside me was freaking air!

The wind was a visible thing, swirling around the room as it had swirled inside me. It circled around until it hovered over the body of Agent Vega, creating a tiny wind funnel that sparkled in the dim light.

I felt heat on my chest and glanced down. The sapphire in the center of my amulet was glowing again, bright light turning the smokelike wisps of wind spilling from my chest into rich blue clouds.

I caught myself choking on nothing as panic gripped me. Once I calmed down, I realized I could breathe just fine, smoke and all. I let out a sigh of relief.

Then, out of the curls of smoke, a figure began to form over Vega's body. It was shaped vaguely like a man, but I got the impression it was bigger, meatier.

The image grew sharper. Reddish skin drawn tight over bulging muscles. Hunter-green hair spilling over broad shoulders. The image turned toward me, almost as if it were alive and could see me. Its eyes were twin pinpoints of sapphire—reflections of my amulet.

It definitely looked human. Well, other than the coloring. There's not a lot of people with skin the color of a tomato running around.

I would like to say I was freaked out. That would be the reaction of a normal person, right? But frankly, I've experienced so much crazy in the last few years—and especially in the last few months since meeting Jack and discovering the amulet—that I felt confused more than anything. What the hell was going on?

I watched as the man, for lack of a better word, leaned over the body of Daniel Vega. Only, it wasn't the body lying on the table I was seeing; it was a superimposed image. The background looked like the hotel room, and a living Daniel Vega was being held down on the bed by a meaty red hand. The strange man opened his mouth inches away from Vega's, as though about to kiss him. Then he inhaled, his red-hued chest expanding.

Shimmers danced along Vega's body before being swept into the large man's maw and disappearing down his throat. Like an incubus inhaling a person's soul. I stared in horror as the life in Vega's eyes flickered, then died. Then the strange red man turned toward me, teeth bared in a frightening sneer.

I took an involuntary step back, forgetting for a moment that what I was seeing had obviously happened in the past. The image of the red man dissipated in front of my eyes. The smoke and wind stopped swirling madly around Vega's body and began a lazy dance toward me.

Of all the things to be scared over, that did it. I took an involuntary step back, as though I could avoid the inevitable. No luck. The smoke pushed its way through my chest and down into my center, to wrap itself around the fire and the darkness that already live inside me. Only then did it let me go.

My chest rose and fell rapidly as I started to hyperventilate. I grabbed at my chest. I'd had enough. I wanted these things out of me—now.

In full-blown panic, I staggered backward and nearly fell over Inigo. "Whoa, Morgan." He caught me and held me tightly to his chest. "What is it? What happened? What did you see?"

I swallowed hard. "I saw how Daniel Vega died."

"You did? How?" Trevor glanced from the body back to me, confusion written all over his face. Couldn't say I blamed him.

"I don't know. All I know is you were right. Vega was murdered by a supernatural."

∽

The first thing I did after we left the funeral home was call Jack. I might have been pissed at him, but I still needed his help.

"Listen, Jack, is there something I should know about the amulet?"

He hesitated. Telling, if you ask me. I can't understand why he insists on hiding things from me.

"I need the truth, Jack."

He sighed. "What is it doing?"

"Glowing. The damn thing's been lighting up like a Christmas tree."

A pause. "How many times has it happened?"

"Three times. Dammit, Jack—"

"And what were you doing when it started glowing?" he interrupted.

"The first time was at my birthday party. Kabita was doing some kind of ceremony. Cleansing my aura or something."

"There was sage involved?"

I frowned, forgetting he couldn't see me. "Uh, yeah. How'd you know?"

He ignored my question. "And the second and third times?"

I glanced over at Inigo. I'd let him drive the Mustang. I was still a little shaky after the weirdness. "I don't know, exactly." I so did not want to tell him about the whole wind thing. The last thing I needed was him freaking out and going all guardian on me.

"What do you mean by that? Exactly."

I sighed and shoved a lock of violet-red hair out of my face. I really needed a haircut. "I was trying to figure out how someone died."

Jack was silent.

I sighed again. "He died under mysterious circumstances, OK? And the cops are saying it was suicide, so I thought I'd check it out."

"You just thought you'd check out some random stranger's body? Come on, Morgan. Be straight with me."

He was one to talk. "Fine. The person in question was possibly connected to the supernatural, so I thought I'd see if there was more to his death than, you know, normal dying."

"And was there?"

"Oh yeah."

I could almost see Jack frowning on the other end of the line. "So, the amulet started glowing around the dead body?"

"Well, yeah. Once I started channeling air."

A heartbeat. "Excuse me?"

"Um, yeah. It's my new thing. Apparently, I can channel air or wind or whatever, though it looks kind of weird and smoky, or misty, or something."

"I assume you discovered this by accident."

"Yeah. You could definitely say that." Discovering a new superpower had so not been on my agenda.

I told Jack how the wind had swirled out of me, how the amulet had started glowing. Then seeing the red man-thing sucking the life out of Daniel Vega.

"Crap."

"I know, right? Please, Jack, what the hell is going on?"

"With the wind channeling, I have no idea. That's Eddie's department. The amulet…"

"Yeah?" Damn, it was like pulling teeth.

"The amulet has been known to glow when it senses a certain type of magic nearby."

I was getting a really bad feeling about this. "What type of magic, Jack?" I all but snapped.

"Sidhe magic."

Well, damn.

Chapter Seven

Wait. Jack said it glows when sidhe magic is near, right?" Inigo's forehead creased in a frown as he stared at the road twisting into the darkness in front of him.

"Yeah, that's what he said."

"There wasn't any sidhe magic at your birthday party. Not until Fringe anyway."

I rolled my eyes. "Don't remind me. Apparently, the amulet does sometimes respond to earth magic as well, as that's what the sidhe use, more or less." Of course, there is no such thing as "magic," per se. It is all quantum physics, using the energy of the universe around us to manipulate the physical world. It is just that some practitioners, or supernaturals, are more inclined to tap directly into the earth itself rather than the universe in general.

"And earth magic is what Kabita does."

"Yep. That's why Jack asked about the sage." I noticed it had started snowing again. A few little flakes glowing white against the darkness as they drifted slowly on the wind.

"I still don't get why it lit up like a Christmas tree in the mortuary. I think we'd have noticed if there were any sidhe around."

He wasn't wrong about that. The sidhe don't exactly blend in. At least, not to hunter eyes. And Inigo's dragon senses certainly would have picked one up.

"I don't get it either." I frowned. "There's something we're not getting. I need to give Eddie a call tonight."

"After dinner at your mother's."

"Yeah. After that." Oh, the joy. It isn't that I don't love my mother, but she often tries to get rather overinvolved in my life. Particularly my love life. Exhibit A: that gods-awful accountant she'd sent me on a blind date with. Ugh.

Fortunately, I am pretty good at keeping her out of my life. There is way too much she doesn't and can't know about who I am and what I do for a living.

A deer darted in front of my car, nearly sending my heart thumping out of my chest.

Calm down, love. My reflexes are faster than that, Inigo's mind caressed mine. His energy was so soothing I wanted to melt. Sometimes there are benefits to having a boyfriend who is half dragon.

"Either stop that or pull this car over." I was practically squirming in my seat as he continued sending tendrils of warmth through my body.

"Why's that?" His voice was, oh, so innocent, but his blue eyes sparkled with wickedness behind the lenses of his glasses. Gods, I love him in those nerdy glasses. Talk about sexy.

"Pull over. Now."

"If I pull over, we'll be late to your mother's for dinner," he said, his tone calm and logical. But his mind never stopped playing with mine. In a really good way.

"I don't fucking care."

A smile tugged at the corners of his lips. He pulled over.

∽

"You're late. Dinner is practically ice cubes. It would be nice if you let me know when you're going to be late." My mother was the picture of genteel outrage as she laid on the guilt trip. I've always found it a little odd that the woman who'd once bucked society's norms to raise me on her own without a husband is now worried about being proper and acceptable. The two things just do not jibe in my mind.

"And hello to you, Mother." I kissed her on the cheek, breathing in the scent of her. She always smells like cookies for some reason.

"I assume everything is all right." She phrased it as a statement rather than a question, but I heard the worry in her tone and felt a stab of guilt. She worries too much, and I'm not exactly easy on her. Thank the gods she doesn't know what I really do for a living. She'd have a coronary for sure.

"Everything is fine, Mom. Just, you know, snow on the mountain passes. Inigo was being careful."

"Such a good boy." She wrapped him in a hug. "I always know my Morgan is safe with you."

I have no idea what he did to charm her, but my mother has adored Inigo from the get-go. Not something I can say about most of my past boyfriends. I can't even imagine what she would've had to say about Jack. Even though Jack can be perfectly polite and proper when the occasion calls for it, he has a wildness in him, a recklessness, that Inigo doesn't have. A wildness my mother would not approve of in the slightest. The very thought gives me brain freeze.

"You've put on a few pounds." She eyed me critically as I hung up my coat.

"Gee, thanks, Mom." Just what every girl wants to hear.

"You need to be more careful of your figure if you plan on keeping a man's interest. Isn't that right, Inigo?"

"Oh, she's got my interest just fine." He waggled his eyebrows in a lecherous manner that caused my mother to giggle like a schoolgirl.

While Inigo continued his charm offensive, I sneaked off to the bathroom to call Eddie. My mother would have had an absolute fit if she'd known. Not that I was calling Eddie, but that I was making a call, period. Calling one person while visiting another is the height of bad manners, as far as my mother is concerned. Like texting at the table or picking your nose.

I turned on the water so she would think I was washing my hands and then dialed Eddie's number. He picked up on the third ring.

"Majicks and Potions, Eddie speaking." His voice was filled with warmth and good humor. Classic Eddie.

"Hey, Eddie."

"Morgan." His voice took on an edge of concern. "How are you? We haven't been able to speak since that ghastly incident at the club. Cordelia told me all about it. Shocking."

"I'm fine. I just need to have a chat with you about this new case I'm on. Will you be around later tonight?"

"Oh, dear, I'm so sorry. Usually, I would, but I was invited to attend a steampunk convention after-party."

"A what?"

He chortled. "Steampunk. Surely you're not *that* out of the loop, Morgan. You practically dress the part, after all."

"I know what steampunk is." Of course I did. Victorian-era sci-fi, more or less. Hot Topic meets a BBC costume drama. I just didn't know what the heck a steampunk party was. "Eddie, this is important. Please."

"Very well. Why don't you come by the party later? It'll go into the wee hours. I'm sure we can find a place to chat. I'll leave your name with the bouncer."

Eddie was going to a steampunk party that needed a bouncer? "Sounds great."

He quickly gave me the address. Before he hung up, he said, "Oh, and, Morgan, wear your hunting boots. And a corset."

∽

The party turned out to be in one of the huge multimillion-dollar houses in the West Hills. The kind of house that was supposed to look like it came straight out of a fairy tale, with diamond-paned windows and fake turrets. Usually, they just look tacky, but someone had made sure they got the specs on this one right. I'd have been hard put to distinguish it from a real Tudor back in England.

There was an honest-to-gods bouncer at the door. Just like it was a freaking nightclub or something. Except, the bouncer's muscular frame had been crammed into black leather trousers and a sleeveless leather vest that were both way too tight. Over it, he wore what looked like an antique military jacket of some kind. I had to admit it was kind of sexy.

"Invitations." His voice was low and growly and just as sexy as his outfit. It was also not entirely human, which was interesting, to say the least. I was going with shifter of some kind.

"We're here to meet Eddie Mulligan."

"Name."

Not a talkative kind of guy, then. "Morgan Bailey. This is—" I started to give him Inigo's name, but the bouncer cut me off.

"Go on in." He stepped back and let us through the door. All righty, then.

Inside, a girl waited to take our coats. She was pretty and petite and wearing a crimson hoopskirt and matching bustier' with gold braiding. She had what looked like a ray gun from a bad 1950s sci-fi B movie tucked into her belt. I decided to just go with it.

I'd taken Eddie's advice and donned a corset with my jeans and steampunk-style hunting boots. I don't wear a corset often, since it's kind of hard to fight in one, but I have to admit I love them. They sort of nip a girl in and push her out in all the right places. And frankly, they make my boobs look awesome. Something Inigo had clearly noticed, as he gave me a wolf whistle as I shrugged my coat off.

"Thanks. You're not so bad yourself."

And he wasn't. Oh, boy, he wasn't.

He was wearing an ordinary pair of jeans and a white shirt, but over the top, he'd thrown a gorgeous black embroidered waistcoat that would have made Beau Brummel drool. He'd topped that off with a long black duster à la Wyatt Earp. The whole outfit on his well-toned physique was seriously scrumptious.

His eyes twinkled golden. His dragon half was close to the surface, and it liked that it was turning me on. I stepped closer, my lips inches away from his, and trailed my fingers along his right hip. The hip that bears such a uniquely beautiful birthmark. A birthmark he'd been surprisingly self-conscious about until I'd shown him just how beautiful I think it is.

"Come on, sexy beast," I whispered. "Let's do what we came to do and get the hell out of Dodge."

Blue flashed back through his eyes. "You got it, baby." He nodded toward the room down the hall where the party was obviously taking place. I could hear what sounded like a twangy version of Evanescence. "Let's go see what Eddie's up to."

What Eddie was up to was flirting with a group of women who were wearing brass goggles and not much else. I'd no idea he was such a lady-killer. Go Eddie.

"Morgan! Inigo! Come! Ladies, I would like you to meet my lovely friends, Morgan Bailey and Inigo Jones."

He rattled off the women's names, but I hardly noticed. I was too busy watching what was going on around me. It was like the Mad Hatter's tea party got thrown in a blender with a Jane Austen flick and the cast of *Blade*. Holy crap, some guy in a bowler hat was riding a velocipede around the living room.

The women around Eddie were giving Inigo the eyeball. Couldn't say I blamed them. He was pretty tasty. Fortunately for them, I'm not really the jealous type. I knew damned well he was going home with me. They could flirt to their hearts' content, for all the good it would do them.

"Ladies, if you'll excuse me." Eddie straightened his purple-and-yellow-striped waistcoat as he stood, then turned to kiss each of the women's hands in turn. "Follow me, Morgan. I have just the place for us to talk."

I made to follow Eddie out of the room, but just before I did, I turned around and winked at the group of women. I couldn't help myself.

Eddie wended his way through a group of people dressed like they were ready to board a pirate ship. One of them saluted us rather drunkenly with his sword and babbled about an airship raid later, asking if we wanted to join. I politely declined. He appeared devastated for about half a second, until one of the other pirates started a rousing rendition of "Dead Man's Chest."

Eddie led me into the pantry off the kitchen and carefully shut the door behind him. Fortunately, it was a big pantry. How on earth, in a house the size of Texas, was the pantry the only quiet place?

"What do you think of the party? Isn't it wonderful?"

"It's…quite a party." I still wasn't sure whether the partygoers were insane or genius. In any case, their outfits were to die for. "Listen, Eddie. I really need your help. Something weird is going on."

His eyebrows rose at that, disappearing under the brim of his top hat. He looked rather fetching in his turn-of-the-century penguin suit. "As opposed to the usual non-weird stuff that goes on?"

I laughed. "Fair point."

"Tell me."

So I told him about the amulet glowing and channeling air and the wind. Then I described the creature I'd seen kill Agent Vega.

"Wait, stop there. How did the creature actually kill Vega?"

I shrugged. "I'm not really sure, but it looked like it sucked his soul right out of his body. That's crazy, right?"

Eddie yanked off his glasses, polished them, and popped them back on. He looked worried. I didn't like that my usually cheerful go-to guy looked worried. It so wasn't a good sign.

"I'm afraid it's not crazy at all, my dear Morgan. I'm afraid what you're dealing with is a djinni."

Chapter Eight

What, do you mean, a djinni? Like a genie? Like Aladdin or something?" I couldn't help the incredulity. The image of a giant blue Robin Williams sucking the life out of somebody was just way over the edge, even for me.

Eddie's usually cherubic face was grim. "Oh, no. Nothing so Disney as all that. Yes, that cartoon movie made the story popular, of course, but the djinn are nothing so fluffy. In fact, they can be quite deadly."

"OK, so what are they?"

He leaned back against the wall and pondered for a moment. "No one knows for sure where they came from originally. Are they earthen? Or are they creatures from the other side? Perhaps from the demon realms. Fortunately, there are a few things we do know."

"As in?" I prodded.

"Well, first off, it's unusual, to say the least, to find one in the Oregon high desert. They tend to stick to their home turf."

"Which is?"

"The Middle East. Parts of Africa. That's not to say they don't exist elsewhere, it's just not common. Though, the Oregon high desert could be dry enough for them, and they like remote places."

"OK, so what are they, if not genies?"

Eddie shook his head slightly. "That's the thing; no one really knows. They're shrouded in so much mystery. What we do know is that the djinn can temporarily take the form of a human or animal. But they live on another plane of existence most of the time, which is why normal humans can't see them."

And I, as everyone knows, am no longer anywhere near a "normal" human. Dammit. Could things get any worse? "You mean another dimension, like demons?"

He mulled it over for a moment. "Not exactly. It's more like they live in our dimension, but slightly out of phase. Like angels. But they are definitely not angelic."

"OK." It was still a little beyond my grasp, but I kind of got it.

"Sorceresses, magicians, and the like have been known to trap a djinni and use it to perform some truly amazing feats of magic—energy manipulation, if you will," Eddie continued. "But they—the magician or whatnot—have to be extremely powerful. The amount of energy a djinni can channel is far beyond what most humans are capable of handling."

Something clicked over in my head. "Would a sidhe be powerful enough to trap a djinni and use it?"

Eddie frowned and tugged at his lower lip. I couldn't help myself; I reached out and straightened his top hat, which had gone wonky. He gave me a distracted smile.

"I don't know," he finally admitted. "I wouldn't have thought so. The sidhe are powerful, but they are earth and water to the djinn's fire and air. Well, technically, the efreet class of djinn are the fire creatures, but that's not the point. The point is that the sidhe and the djinn would no doubt cancel each other out."

"What about the fairy queen?" There. I said it. No going back.

"Oh, she could trap a low-level djinni, no doubt, but that would start a war with the marid."

"The marid?" Gods, it was like trying to speak Latin or something. I'd heard the term in my dream, of course, but I had no idea what it meant. I felt like I was swimming in circles with no idea which direction to turn, and the waves were getting bigger and bigger.

"The most powerful of all the djinn. Their...king, for lack of a more appropriate word. The djinn would not take kindly to such a thing. And a war between the marid and the fairy queen would not be pretty."

That I could believe. "So who else could control a djinni, if not the sidhe?"

"I honestly don't know, Morgan. As far as I know, there aren't any magi or sorcerers in the area strong enough to entrap a djinni."

"What about clever enough?" More often than not, sheer craftiness works where brute strength fails. I should know. Despite being much stronger than your average human, I am rarely stronger than a vampire.

Eddie shook his head. "They could trap a djinni, but without the power, they couldn't hold it for long. Certainly not long enough to kill someone with it."

Shit. Well, there went that theory.

"And a djinni wouldn't kill Vega on its own?"

"I wouldn't think so, no," Eddie said. "Not unless Vega had offended the creature in some way. But then the djinni wouldn't have sucked Vega's soul like that. He would have tortured the man and then killed him. Left him on the side of the road somewhere as a warning to others. The soul feeding is very specific."

"Specific to what?"

"Ritualistic magic. You suck a person's soul, and you take, with them, their connection to the universe. Their power, if you will."

"So we're looking for someone with enough cleverness to trap a djinni and enough power to hold it and use it to kill Vega and steal his power. Someone who is most likely not a sidhe." Not that I was giving up entirely on the sidhe theory. I just couldn't get past the amulet glowing. Still, I had to keep my options open.

Eddie sighed. "That would be my best guess, yes. Though, of course, I could be wrong. There is much that isn't known about the sidhe."

Fabulous. "OK, one more thing." I told him about the weird wind-channeling back at the funeral home. About the new thing I'd felt inside me where the darkness and the fire live.

"My dear, I don't want to alarm you." Eddie reached out and took my hand, giving it a little squeeze.

"Too late."

He smiled. "It sounds like you're channeling air now."

That was what I was afraid of, and what I'd told Jack was happening. I just hadn't really wanted to believe it. I had enough going on without adding another superpower to my repertoire. "As in the element of?"

"Yes." He nodded. "The ancients often referred to air as smoke."

"So I'm kissing smoke now too." "Kissing" is what the ancients called this ability to channel the elements. And it leads to very, very bad things. Like craziness. And death.

Panic coursed through me. That was all I needed: another freaky superpower to add to the growing list. Granted, they really help out in the hunting department. They make me tougher, scarier, harder to kill. On the other hand, I was really scared about what they were turning me into. I did not want to become one of the monsters I hunted. "Eddie, why is this happening to me?"

His eyes were kind and a little sad. "I don't know, my dear. But there is always a reason for these things. I promise, if there is any way humanly possible to find out, I will do it."

"Thanks, Eddie." I believed him. Eddie hadn't let me down yet.

"Now I should get back to the party before people start wondering what we're doing in here."

I winked at him. "Just tell them I had my wicked way with you."

He laughed all the way back.

∽

Inigo had wanted to stay the night at my place, but I needed time alone. Time to think. There was just too much going on in my head, and I was too used to handling this shit on my own.

I was nearly ready for bed, makeup washed off, silk pajamas on, when I heard something. A slight *thunk* in the backyard. I froze, every molecule of my being focused on that noise.

I couldn't hear anything, but something told me all was not right in my world. Gritting my teeth, I closed my eyes and reached down for the darkness. It raised its head, slowly, almost reluctantly. I beckoned it forward.

It tried to surge then, but I held on relentlessly, only allowing a small tendril to snake out of me and ooze its way along the floor and up and through the window. Through a long, dark tunnel, I could see my backyard, the grass dry and dead now that winter was in full swing. A tree moved slightly in the night breeze, bare branches making a rustling sound. Nope, that wasn't it.

The darkness oozed through the yard, taking my vision with it. It was as though I was becoming part of it. Or it was an extension of me. Two things becoming one entity. I shivered at the thought.

It crept around the corner to the side gate. There it was. A human-shaped shadow.

The darkness tested the shadow, eager for prey. The back of my skull suddenly felt like it was being squeezed in a vise grip as my hunter senses kicked in. I knew instantly what the shadow was: vampire.

What the hell was a vampire doing in my backyard? Granted, this wasn't the first time, but Inigo, Kabita, and I had sent a pretty good message to the local clans when we wasted Kaldan and his entire clan a few months ago.

The darkness wanted out. It wanted to torture and kill. But if there is one thing I've learned, letting the darkness loose is a good way to let it overpower me. From past experience, I knew exactly what would happen if it took over. Without me in control, the darkness would unleash its violence, killing unchecked by any sense of humanity. And that was something I could not allow to happen.

I reeled it back in, fighting it all the way. It seemed like it took hours, but in reality, it was only a few seconds. A few very scary, very sweaty seconds.

Once it was safely tucked away inside me, I focused on prep. I was in my freaking pajamas, for crying out loud, but I didn't have time to change. I needed to get to that vamp and find out why he was there so I could dust the thing.

I yanked on the steampunky boots I'd been wearing at the party and then grabbed the nearest coat-like object I could find. It just happened to be my slinky silk robe. Dammit all to hell and back.

I didn't have time to find anything else. I snatched up the nearest weapon and hit the door running. Fortunately, the nearest weapon just happened to be a really awesome dao I'd bought from Tesselah for my "happy birthday to me" present. The Chinese saber is razor sharp and perfect for a quick beheading or a stab to the heart.

My cell hummed against the bedside table. I wondered vaguely who the hell was calling so late at night, but I ignored it and headed for the backyard. I was on the hunt.

I let a tiny trickle of the darkness back out, just enough so that my vision turned the dark backyard bright as day. My booted feet crunched slightly against the dead, icy grass. Damn, it was cold.

The vamp had made it around the corner and was headed for my back door. He froze when he saw me, then whirled and ran.

So, we were going to play, were we? Excellent. A slight smile crossed my lips, and I wasn't entirely sure if it was me or the darkness. At that moment, I didn't much care.

I gave up all pretenses at silence and let my boots pound out a staccato rhythm on the pavement as we hit the sidewalk. The vamp was running hell-for-leather, but I was right on his ass. I probably could have caught him, but honestly, I needed to work out some frustration.

Fortunately, it was after one in the morning, and the neighbors were sound asleep. I couldn't imagine what they'd think if they saw me running down the street wearing nothing but boots and silk pajamas and carrying a Chinese saber.

The vamp turned a corner and dashed down a street that dead-ended at a parking lot. He was headed into Mt. Tabor Park. He apparently thought he'd lose me among the trees.

In a single bound, he cleared the gate blocking the park entrance. Granted, that sounded impressive, but the gate was only waist high. I followed him with ease; though, being shorter, I had to brace myself with my left hand to clear the gate.

In a flash, he'd disappeared in the deep shadows beneath the thick stands of fir along either side of the footpath. Fortunately, my special hunter Spidey senses were working fine. I could still feel that vise gripping the base of my skull, and I could still "smell" him with that weird psychic thing I seem to have when it comes to vamps.

I cleared a rise in the trail and paused. He was near. I could feel it.

He flew out from the shadows. His body weight sent me crashing to the ground, and my dao went flying. My robe was going to be totally ruined, dammit. And it was brand-new.

I snarled and grabbed the vamp around the throat. I let the darkness curl up my arm so that, with one thrust, I sent him flying.

My fingers scrabbled along the ground, finally touching the hilt of my sword. I snatched it up just in time as the vampire made another rush at me.

This time I was ready. I lashed out with the dao even as I rolled to the side. He missed me, crashing to the ground instead. Unfortunately, I only nicked him. I could smell the old copper tang of his blood, but it wasn't anything that would keep him down.

I jumped to my feet and ran at him, but he somehow managed to grab one of my boots and yank my feet out from under me. I slammed to the ground, the air rushing from my lungs, my vision going dark around the edges.

In one pounce, he was on me, flipping me onto my back. His legs straddled my waist as he grabbed my chin in his right hand and yanked my head to the side, baring my throat. That pale column of smooth skin over throbbing vein, it's like crack to a vamp. And I couldn't stop him.

He was far too strong. Stronger even than my hunter strength. His fangs were just a kiss away.

A sudden roaring filled my ears, and a pale, silvery column of smoke billowed out of the center of my chest. It wrapped itself around the vampire like a snake.

He froze, eyes wide. "What the hell?"

The smoke lifted the vamp up and off me, almost like it was a third arm. A very strong arm. Only, I wasn't controlling it. My brand-new air ability was playing all on its own. All around me, dead leaves and bits of twigs and old candy wrappers whirled around as though caught in a mini tornado.

"Put me down," the vampire screeched, thrashing against the hold of the air pouring out of my chest. To no avail. The air didn't budge. The vamp's eyes were wide with terror. Couldn't say I blamed him. I was more than a little freaked out myself.

I scrambled to my feet, heart beating like a wild thing in my chest. The whole situation was way beyond me, but I tried to play it cool. "Why were you at my house?"

"Put me down," he begged. "Put me down and I'll tell you."

I raised my eyebrows at that. "Do I look stupid? Tell me why you were at my house."

"Will you put me down if I tell you?"

A very unpleasant smile flitted across my face. "Oh, yes," I purred. "Of course I will."

"Promise me."

I stepped closer, caressed his cheek with one finger. "I promise."

"OK. There's a contract out on you."

"A contract?" Someone wanted me dead? Huh. Wouldn't be the first time. Though, as far as I knew, this was the first time somebody had actually offered money to get the job done.

"Yeah, yeah. Ten thousand dollars."

"Is that all?" In a weird way, that pissed me off.

"Hey, that's a lot of money in this economy."

"All right, then. Do you know why someone issued the contract?"

He shook his head vehemently. "No idea."

"Now for the million-dollar question: *Who* issued the hit?"

"I don't know. Really, I don't. I just found it posted in a chat room."

"A chat room? Seriously?"

He shrugged.

"Give me the address."

He babbled off the website address, which I committed to memory. Or hoped I had.

"You promised you'd let me down."

I sighed. "Oh, yes. Of course."

Slowly, the tendrils of smoke lowered him to the ground, though the air still swirled around him. With a single thrust, my dao sliced through skin and muscle and bone until it pierced the heart.

His eyes widened, dark blood spilling from his lips. "You promised." His voice was a whisper.

"And I kept my promise," I whispered back. "But I never promised not to kill you afterward."

With a final twist meant to destroy the heart, I pulled the saber back out. The vamp's body crumpled to the ground and then burst into dust.

The air did one last swirl around me, scattering the ash to the winds. I smiled a little. So, someone wanted me dead and was willing to pay for it. That would be the last stupid move they'd ever make.

Darkness lurked in my eyes as I started down the hill.

Chapter Nine

I headed back down the hill toward home, my boots making good solid thunks against the pavement. I felt amazing. Energized by the kill.

My feet stumbled as I realized what I was thinking, feeling. What I'd done…that wasn't me. Hunting, I enjoy. Killing is just part of the job. And yet…

I closed my eyes, breathing in deep. This wasn't me. I'm not the kind of person who takes pleasure in taking life. Even that of a vampire out to kill me. No, the thrill I felt wasn't mine. It was the things living inside me. And it made me feel sick.

I opened my eyes. There was nothing I could do about it at the moment. Nothing but try to control the powers that live inside me, keep the monsters at bay.

I suppose I shouldn't have been surprised to find Jack on my doorstep when I got home, but I was. I also shouldn't have been surprised to feel a stab of longing mixed with regret as my eyes scanned the physique that would put Michelangelo's David to shame. That was a dark path I was not about to go down. He'd caused enough heartache without adding any more. I brushed those feelings aside.

I would like to say it was easy. That would be a lie. Because, as sexy as Jack is and as great as our physical relationship had been, there is more than that. A visceral connection that goes far beyond anything I've ever felt. Even with Inigo. I don't know if it is because Jack is my guardian or because of the Atlantean blood, but there is something between us. There will always be something between us.

"It's late, Jack." I didn't really have to ask why he was standing on my doorstep in the middle of the night. He was the guardian, after all. My guardian.

"You didn't answer your phone." His voice was grim and just a little angry. I could sense he was trying to keep his temper in check.

"Let me guess," I said, letting myself in through the kitchen door I hadn't taken the time to lock. I didn't bother turning on the overhead light. "You were calling to warn me of impending danger. Thanks, but I'd already figured that one out." As the guardian of the Key of Atlantis, he has some sixth sense thing going on when it comes to me and danger.

"What on earth are you wearing?"

I glanced down at myself. I must admit I was a bit of a sight. "My pajamas. What does it look like?"

"Morgan—"

"Thanks for the heads-up," I interrupted, "but as you can see, I'm fine."

"Morgan," his voice was nearly a snarl, "how can I protect you—"

"I don't need your protection, Jack. Don't you get that? I can take care of myself. Obviously. I killed the big bad vampire all by myself." I didn't mention the contract on my life. The last thing I needed was to give Jack more of an excuse to play guardian.

"I know you can take care of yourself, Morgan, but I'm your guardian. I'm supposed to watch out for you."

"Then how about you do it from a distance?" It was mean, but I couldn't help it. I didn't want to deal with Jack. Maybe I couldn't deal with Jack. "Now, it's late and I'd like to go to bed." I glanced pointedly at the back door.

"Fine. But I *will* be watching."

I had no doubt of that.

∽

"Someone has a hit out on you? You've got to be kidding me." Inigo's voice on the phone had lost all sound of sleepiness the minute I'd told him about the vampire attack.

"No, I'm not kidding. I'm staring right at the advertisement." The vamp hadn't been lying about that. It was right there on the website in black and white. Or black and red, actually.

WANTED DEAD: Hunter Morgan Bailey.
REWARD: $10,000.

And below that was a photo someone had snapped of me standing in line at Voodoo Doughnut. My blazing red hair stood out against the Pepto-Bismol-pink walls of Portland's famous doughnut place. It could have been taken anytime, since I visit Voodoo on a semiregular basis. But the fact was someone had been following me. Someone knew my routines and knew where to take that picture.

And the biggest, scariest fact of all? Somebody wanted me dead, and they wanted it bad.

Welcome to my life.

"I'm coming over, Morgan."

Part of me wanted to argue. That old independent streak rearing its head. But a bigger part of me just wanted to curl up in his arms and hide from the world for a while.

And he was a freaking half dragon, for crying out loud.

I figured I might as well make coffee. I sure as hell wasn't going to sleep.

I closed my eyes on a sigh. I fingered the Atlantean amulet that hung around my neck. There was no use denying it anymore.

Ever since I'd come into contact with the amulet, my life had been turned upside down and sideways. That includes the fact that I am now some kind of human conduit for every superpower the people of Atlantis ever concocted.

Shit.

Fortunately, Inigo arrived before my thoughts could get too maudlin. He tsk-tsked over my ruined robe and promised to buy me another. I didn't doubt it, though I was a little scared about what he might buy. With my luck, it would be sheer. And pink. I shuddered at the thought.

He hauled me off to bed, not for sex, just to cuddle. Having a boyfriend who can read your every mood is sometimes a really good thing. I snuggled into his heat, inhaling the chocolatey campfire smell of him. Sometimes I wonder what I'd ever done without him in my life.

His arms were deliciously warm as they wrapped around me. I could hear his heart under my ear, its strong beat lulling me. Before I knew it, I'd slipped off into dreamland.

ᔕ

"*You owe us, Marid.*"

"*We owe you nothing, Priest,*" the giant man snarled. His over-developed muscles bulged and shifted under reddish skin. His enormous frame completely dwarfed me.

"*We brought you here,*" I reminded him. My tone was calm, but inside, my heart was beating furiously. For all my power, I knew the marid could kill me with the snap of a finger. "*We saved you from certain death. Without us, you would have died along with our sun.*"

"*You should have let us die with our world,*" the marid spat. "*This place is not a place for us. It cannot sustain us. We will die here, despite your meddling. I should kill you for that alone.*"

Fire danced at his fingertips and the wind kicked up, swirling around us until my heavy silk robe flapped around my frame. It snapped so hard I would no doubt have welts afterward.

I swallowed. The marid were the most powerful of the djinn. Even on our home world, they were difficult to control. Here...it was beyond difficult.

"Listen carefully, Marid. There is a way."

"To save my people? Impossible," he snarled. "Half my clan has already perished. What can you do, Priest?"

I smiled at that. Despite his hatred of me, he was still afraid. I could see it written clearly in the lines of his face and the shadows in his eyes. In this instance, fear was good.

"Give me what I want, and I vow by all the gods your people will survive."

The giant man pondered for a moment. "You fail me and I will destroy you and all you hold dear, Priest."

He could try. But I kept silent and let him have the last word. "So shall it be."

∽

I woke with my face smooshed into my pillow and Inigo's arm wrapped around my waist. At some point in the night, I'd turned and we'd ended up spooning. My favorite.

The dream came back to me in bits and pieces. I'd been the high priest again. Freaking fantastic. Well, at least I hadn't gone crazy and murdered anybody this time.

I frowned. Something had woken me. I just couldn't—

The first few perky bars of Caro Emerald's "That Man" filled the room. Phone. That's what had woken me up. I squinted at the clock—4:00 a.m. Somebody had better be dead. If not, they would be.

"'Lo?"

"Morgan, it's Trevor."

I sat up in bed. Inigo grunted in his sleep and tried to pull me closer. Men.

"Trevor, what's wrong?" I could hear it in his voice. All was very definitely not well.

"I'm in the hospital. In Bend."

Bend is about an hour's drive south of Madras on the edge of the Deschutes National Forest and the closest hospital to the small town. I didn't like the sound of that. "What happened? Are you OK?" I must have sounded half-hysterical, because that woke Inigo up quickly.

"I will be." My brother's voice was a little huskier than usual, but he didn't sound too bad.

"What do you mean, you will be?"

"Morgan, I'll be fine."

"Trevor." I couldn't help if I sounded a little testy. The man was trying my patience. "You do not call a person at four a.m. just to tell them you're fine."

"I was attacked last night. In my hotel room. Fortunately, somebody anonymously called the cops and the attackers ran off, but they gave me a pretty good ass kicking. I've got a cracked rib, some contusions, and they're insisting on keeping me for observation. It's no big deal."

"You've got a concussion, don't you?" Why else would they keep him for "observation"? No big deal, my ass.

He sighed. "Yeah. A little bit."

"Dammit, Trev."

"Morgan, I'm fine."

"Were they human?"

"I think so." He lowered his voice. "They seemed human. But..." His voice trailed off.

"But you think somebody else was pulling their strings."

"Yeah, I'm sure of it. One of them said something about not getting paid if they didn't finish it."

Meaning finish him. Another hit. It wasn't just me. They were after my brother too. What the fuck was going on?

As if sensing my distress, Inigo wrapped his arms around me, pressing his chest against my back and rubbing his cheek against my hair. It felt good. And a little distracting. I probably should have shoved him off so I could concentrate, but I liked his touch, and I think he needed to touch me as much as I needed him to.

"OK, Trevor, you stay in the hospital and do what the doctors tell you. No being macho, OK?"

There was laughter in his voice. "OK. What will you be doing while I'm getting waited on hand and foot?"

My own voice was grim. "Finding out who did this to you and ripping them limb from limb."

∽

OK, maybe I had gone a bit overboard, but I get a little pissy when one of my people is threatened. And Trevor Daly is very definitely one of my people. He isn't just my half brother; he'd helped me save Inigo's life.

I frowned. Of course, there'd been more to it than that. The anger that burned inside me was so much deeper it was almost as if it wasn't mine.

Of course, that was ridiculous. I gave myself a little mental shake and focused on the task at hand.

We were headed back over the mountains toward Madras and Trevor's hotel room. I was hoping we'd pick up on something. Something that would lead us to the people who'd hurt Trevor—and hopefully whoever had hired them to do the job. I had no idea whether the hit on Trevor was related to the hit on me, but it was just one too many coincidences for my liking.

I was staring glumly at the road in front of us, the towering, snow-dusted evergreen trees dark shapes against the predawn sky. Suddenly, The Cure blasted from the stereo.

You need thinking time, Inigo's mind touched mine. *Music always helps you think. I'm here when you need me.* Then he withdrew from my head, a smile hovering as he drove my car deeper into the mountains.

I was a little overwhelmed at his thoughtfulness. Sometimes I think he is way too good for me. How could I ever possibly deserve him?

I reached across and took his hand, tangling my fingers through his before letting my thoughts drift away. I'm telling you, every girl should have a mind-reading, clairvoyant half dragon for a boyfriend.

ဢ

Trevor had been staying at the nicest of the three hotels in town, which wasn't saying much. It was pretty basic, but it was clean and tidy and the manager was no-nonsense. Which was actually sort of a downside. There was no way he was letting us in Trevor's room.

When I told him I was Trevor's sister, he gave me a look that plainly said he didn't believe me. He was very clear on one point: he didn't care if I was the frigging queen of England; I wasn't getting in that room. A badge might have done it, but the SRA doesn't exactly go around handing out shields to their subcontractors. Having met a hunter or two, I can't say I blame the SRA. Most hunters aren't exactly pillars of the community. In fact, most of them make me look downright normal.

Once out of sight of the manager's office, we headed toward the back of the motel. We hugged the building, keeping the cars between us and anyone who happened to wander through the parking lot. Not that there were many cars to use as cover, just a beat-up reject from the seventies that was the size of a small boat and a two-door hatchback that had seen better days. Plus, a plain black Ford sedan that I knew was Trevor's.

We eyeballed the door to Trevor's room. I was getting in there one way or another, even if I had to crawl through a window. Fortunately, I didn't have to resort to such drastic measures. A little bit of outrageous flirtation with the maid and we were in. I should probably point out the flirtation was done by yours truly. Apparently, Inigo wasn't quite the maid's type.

Although it was obvious there'd been a fight in the room, it didn't look as if anything had been taken or rifled through. They'd definitely been after Trevor, not robbery. Dammit. This was not looking good for either of us.

"They were human."

I glanced over at Inigo, who was prowling around the room. "You can sense them?"

"Hell no." He laughed. "I can smell them. They all seriously need to bathe. And I think they're on something."

"Tweakers?"

He shrugged. "Can't tell for sure, but probably. They were definitely drinking heavily. You get anything?"

I frowned. "No, but I think there's a lot more to this than a bunch of druggies who need a bath."

"I agree. Next step?"

"We find them." Yeah. So easy.

Needle. Meet haystack.

Chapter Ten

Thanks to Inigo's sense of smell, tracking Trevor's attackers wasn't as hard as I had thought it would be. I guess I hadn't realized the extent of a dragon's olfactory senses. We found them—or rather, one of them—in a run-down apartment block on the outskirts of town. The place made the motel Vega had stayed in look like a palace.

Several shingles were missing off the weathered siding, and the steps looked like they'd crumble at any minute. Rusty screen doors, minus their screens, squeaked slightly in the breeze. Inigo nodded at a unit in the middle of the building.

I rapped on the door, which looked like it had once been painted bright blue but now was more grayish than anything. There was a shuffling inside, then a sleepy voice: "Who is it?"

"Pizza."

"I didn't order any…oh." The young man who opened the door was scrawny, bleary-eyed, and wearing nothing but a pair of tighty-whities. Minus the tighty. And the whitey, actually. So not attractive.

"Yeah, *oh*. What's your name, kid?" I kept my voice firm, professional, but with just an edge of good humor. No use freaking him out. He was obviously half strung out already.

"Uh…uh…Mikey." He peered at me through long strands of dirty-blond hair. His eyes were red rimmed and a little glassy.

"Mikey, huh. Listen, Mikey, I've got some questions for you. Mind if we come in?" I slid one booted foot across the doorframe so he would be unable to slam the door on us if he decided to be uncooperative. Which looked likely.

"Why? What questions? I don't know anything." He was starting to panic, beads of sweat popping out across his forehead, skinny body trembling so hard I was half-afraid he'd snap a rib.

"Listen, we just want to come in and talk to you for a minute. No biggie." I kept my voice light and cajoling. I was afraid it wasn't going to work. I was right.

Mikey slammed the door, which bounced right off my boot. Then he took off running toward the back door, with his drawers sagging halfway down his butt. I so did not need to see his pasty-white cheeks. I'd have nightmares for a month.

"I'll get him." Inigo flashed a grin and took off after the kid. Two bounds and Mikey was laid out flat on the floor, with plenty of crack showing.

I stared down at Mikey curled up into a fetal position. He couldn't have been much more than sixteen. He should have been flirting with girls, going to senior prom, playing football, driving cars too fast. Not strung out on who knows what in a crappy apartment in nowhereville. Gods, this world can be so fucked up.

"Not the face."

"What?" I stared down at Mikey, then glanced up at Inigo, who gave me a shrug. "What are you talking about?"

"Please. Beat me up. Take what you want. Please just don't hit me in the face." He was practically sobbing.

And that's when it hit me. There are a few professions where the face is an important part of the package, but I doubted Mikey was an actor or a model for Calvin Klein. My stomach turned sour and I wanted to throw up. "How old are you, Mikey?" I kept my voice soft, my body still. I didn't touch him, but I didn't back away, either.

Tears trickled down his face, but he didn't bother to wipe them. "Sixteen."

Shit. Shit, shit, shit. "Where is your family?"

"Ain't got one."

And knowing the way the foster system works, he was probably worse off in the system, believe it or not. Double shit. I felt sorry for the kid, but he'd been involved in beating up my brother. Maybe even in murder. I couldn't let that stand, no matter what kind of shitty life the poor kid had lived.

Still, he didn't strike me as the type who could take down a man like Trevor Daly. Not even on a good day. There was more to all this; I could practically smell it.

"Listen to me, Mikey." I didn't let a hint of anger slip into my voice. He was freaked out enough. I needed him calm. "I want to help you, I do. I want to make sure you don't have to..." My voice thickened, and I had to clear it. The kid did not need my pity. He needed strength. "I don't want you to ever have to do that anymore. You got it?"

"You can't help me."

"Yes. Yes, I can. You help me and I promise. I promise I will help you." I had no idea whether I could keep that promise, but damned if I wouldn't kill myself trying. Nobody deserves this kind of shitty life.

"What...what do you want?" His voice trembled.

"Last night you were there at the Madras Motel when a man was beaten up. Beaten so badly it put him in the hospital. That man was my brother."

Mikey squeezed his eyes shut. "I'm sorry. I'm sorry. I didn't want to."

"Listen to me, Mikey. I need to know what happened. I need the truth, OK?"

He nodded a little, his cheek smooshing against the carpet. "OK."

Inigo handed me a thin blanket he'd grabbed from somewhere. I gave him a grateful look and turned back to Mikey. "Mikey, I'm going to put this blanket around you, OK? Hard to have a serious conversation with you in your Hanes."

He opened his eyes and gave me a wry grin. Good, there was someone home.

I draped the blanket around him. "Now, can you sit up?"

He nodded and slowly sat up. I didn't help him, didn't touch him. What he'd been through, he probably wouldn't have let me if I'd tried. "OK, Mikey, tell me about last night."

He squeezed his eyes closed, then opened them again. "I was hanging out down at the bar with a couple guys I know, and this man came up to us. Said he had a job. Said he'd pay us good. I thought…" His voice trailed off.

I knew what he'd thought. He'd thought the man had wanted his special services. "But the man wanted something else?"

Mikey nodded, his stringy hair flopping in his face. "Yeah. He said there was this…" He slid a look toward me. "He used a bad word for your brother. About him being black. I'm sorry, miss."

Miss? I nearly rolled my eyes, but I kept my expression neutral. "I get it. Go on."

"Well, he said that your brother didn't belong here and needed a lesson. He'd pay us to teach him that lesson. I didn't want no part in it, honest. But the others…" He shrugged his skinny shoulders. "And I needed a fix real bad. I'm so sorry…" Sobs racked his body. "I didn't touch him, I swear. I just stood lookout. But when I saw…when I saw…"

"Calm down, Mikey. Calm down. When you saw what?"

"They beat him pretty bad, miss. I knew they were gonna kill him, and I begged them to stop. They gave me my money and told me to leave and let them finish up. That they'd kill me if I told."

There was a look in his eyes, and I knew without a shadow of a doubt there was still something in Mikey worth saving. "You called the cops, didn't you?"

"If they knew, they'd kill me. Please don't tell."

"I won't. Promise."

A look of relief spread across his face. "I'm really sorry...I just...I needed..." He hung his head in shame.

He was a junkie. He needed a fix. Gods, this world is fucked up. "Mikey, tell me about the man. The one that hired you. Did you know him?"

Mikey shook his head. "Never seen him before. Honest."

"What did he look like?"

He frowned and scrunched up his face as though trying to pull a memory from the dregs of his drug-addled brain. "He was kind of scary. Tall, thin, really pale. Had this spooky voice."

Inigo and I exchanged looks. Sounded like a vamp to me. "He give you a name?" I prodded.

"No, but I was kind of out of it. Maybe he told the others."

"You got their names? An address, maybe?"

He had, and he gave them to me almost eagerly. Atoning for his sins. But I knew he'd never get straight without help. A lot of help.

"Mikey, you've been very cooperative," I said. "But you owe me for what you did to my brother."

His shoulders slumped even more than they already were. "I know." His voice was barely above a whisper.

"So here is what you're going to do. You are going to take this card." I scribbled down a name and number on a scrap of paper and handed it to Mikey. I have a cousin who helps people in difficult situations, and I knew she'd be able to help him. "You are going to call this number, and you will tell the lady who answers that Morgan Bailey sent you to her. You got it?"

He turned the card over and over in his hands. "Yes, miss."

"You will tell her the truth. About your drug habit, what you do to support it. The truth, you understand?"

The look of shame on his face was so profound it broke my heart.

"She won't judge you, Mikey. I promise you that."

He finally nodded. "OK, I'll call."

"Good. And you will do everything she tells you to do. Everything. You got me? Because if I find out you haven't, I will hunt your ass down."

A look of absolute panic crossed his face. "I'll do it, I promise."

I smiled for the first time. Maybe there was hope for the kid yet. "Good. And, Mikey?"

"Yeah?" He gazed up out of big tear-stained eyes like I was some kind of freaking savior.

"Take a shower."

∽

Beau and Benedict Radnor lived in a run-down mobile home in the local trailer park on the outskirts of town. It was the sort of place where hope goes to drink itself into oblivion, and the Radnors' trailer was the worst of the lot. The cracked pink siding, plastic grass, and piles of empty beer bottles screamed white trash. No surprises there.

A half-rusted pickup truck was parked haphazardly across the narrow drive. The gun rack in the back window was empty.

"I don't think we should knock," I whispered to Inigo.

"No kidding. They're probably armed to the teeth."

He didn't look at all nervous, which was good, because I was nervous enough for both of us. I know, I know. How stupid is that, a vampire hunter scared of a couple of rednecks? What can I say? I'm not used to going up against creatures I can't kill.

Not that I couldn't kill the hillbilly brothers—I totally could. But that would get me thrown in prison for a very long time. And I don't look good in orange.

"OK." I sucked in a deep breath. "Ready?"

Inigo gave me a nod; then, with one little push, he sent the door flying right off its hinges. It crashed into the opposite wall of the single-wide trailer, then bounced back, hitting the floor with a bang.

"Oh, way to be subtle, babe."

He flashed me a smile before leaping over the fallen door in a graceful bound. Show-off. I climbed over it somewhat less gracefully.

We needn't have worried about the noise. The Radnor boys were sprawled out on the shag carpet of the bedroom floor, dead to the world and reeking of booze. They hadn't even made it to the twin beds in the trailer's only bedroom before passing out. Gods, I hate drunks.

My ex-fiancé, Alex, had discovered a taste for hard cider after we'd moved to the UK. And when he got drunk, he got happy, then suicidal, then abusive. Just another sin to tag onto his long list of many.

Inigo knelt down next to one of them and yanked the guy's head up by the hair. Nothing but a snort and some drool.

An evil smirk crossed my face. "I have an idea." I tromped out of the room, rustled around the kitchen a bit until I found a plastic garbage can overflowing with empty beer cans. I dumped them out on the floor—I figured those two were far enough gone the noise wouldn't wake them—and filled the garbage can with water. Really cold water. Which I proceeded to dump straight in the faces of the Radnor brothers.

They came sputtering to life.

"Hello, boys." I sat down on the nearest bed, making a mental note to call my doctor for a tetanus shot later. And maybe a rabies one while I was at it. Who knew what kind of nasty things were crawling around in the bedding? "We need to have a little talk. Somebody was very naughty last night."

They blinked at me through identical bloodshot eyes in identical puffy faces. They looked close to thirty, but it wasn't a good thirty. Huge bellies hung over their saggy jeans, and their noses were already red and veiny. Career drunks and assholes. Goodie.

"What'choo talkin' 'bout, bitch?" the one on the right snarled nastily.

Inigo got all up in his face. I could sense his dragon rising to the surface and knew the Radnor brothers could see the gold fire dancing in Inigo's eyes, though it was doubtful they understood what they were seeing. "Listen, you waste of human flesh." The dragon was in his voice too. "Show the lady some respect, or I will remove your oh-so-valuable manhood from your body before I flay you alive."

The Radnors looked ready to piss themselves. I grinned. Playing good hunter/bad hunter with Inigo was hella fun. And even if the two rednecks told anyone about the two people who'd busted down their door and threatened their lives, no one would believe them. Everyone would just assume they'd been hallucinating thanks to the booze and the drugs.

"Thank you, my love. Now, boys, I want to know all about the man who hired you to beat up a federal agent last night."

"What do you care?" the Radnor on the left spat out. "That fed was just some…" The word that came out of his mouth is not one that I will repeat. Ever.

I am not a violent person. OK, you can stop laughing. I am not a violent person against humans, but that asshole had me planting a fist straight in his face. It hurt like hell, but it was, oh, so worth it.

"That's my brother you're talking about, asshat. Now I want the truth, or I let my boyfriend here turn you inside out. Literally. Got it? I want to know about the man who hired you."

There was some howling and carrying on, but eventually, I got the answers I needed. An address for a farmhouse out near Culver.

"What should we do with them?" Inigo asked.

I gave the Radnors a rather nasty grin. "Tie them up with a pretty red bow and leave them for the police."

Which is exactly what we did. Minus the red bow. Amazing what you can do with a roll of silver duct tape.

Chapter Eleven

Y ou have got to be kidding. This place is a dump."

I couldn't disagree. The farmhouse we'd been directed to by the Radnor brothers was just this side of falling down. I gave Inigo a little nudge with my elbow. "Want to go in first?"

"I thought you were the big badass vampire hunter." Humor laced his tone.

"Yeah, and you're the big badass dragon boy."

That made him laugh. Which made me grin. His laugh has a tendency to hit me right in my yummy spot.

The tingling at the back of my skull sobered me up. "It's a vamp nest."

"You sure?"

I gave him a look. He had the grace to look embarrassed.

"Sorry. You're sure."

I crossed my arms and studied the run-down house. Getting in without attracting attention was going to be tough. Too much debris. Too many loose and rotten boards.

"The only thing that's on our side is that it's full daylight. We'll have the upper hand."

"We could burn them," Inigo suggested. "Light the place on fire and leave it."

I shook my head. "We need answers. Hard to question a pile of ash." A vamp hiring rednecks to beat up a federal agent was so far beyond the norm it was mind-boggling. If a vamp wanted someone dealt with, it would just go and suck the person dry or rip out their jugular or something. It would not hire a bunch of drunks to play enforcer.

"I can't tell how many are in there, can you?"

I couldn't. "We can't risk pulling the boards off the windows, either. We don't want to accidentally fry the guy with answers. Dammit." I went around to the back of the Mustang and popped the trunk.

I began pulling out various blades and bottles and stashing them about my person. When in doubt, load for bear. Figuratively speaking.

Inigo was more conservative. He chose a UV gun and a single blade. Then again, he has abilities far beyond mine. Like, say, shifting into a dragon the size of a large horse. Trust me, that is way more of a shock to the system than a UV gun. Though, damned if he isn't pretty when he does it.

"Ready?" I asked. He nodded, and we slipped into the house as fast and quietly as possible.

The minute we stepped through the front door, I knew the vamps weren't in the house. "They're underneath," I whispered.

Inigo nodded and headed for the kitchen, with me hot on his heels. He pushed at one of the doors that led off the kitchen. It resisted, but finally gave in with a squeak and a groan, revealing a large pantry.

I got the next door. It swung open easily, if a bit creakily. Steps led down into the gloom of a basement.

The grip at the base of my skull tightened. There were definitely vampires in the basement, but I still couldn't get a fix on how many. And my stupid amulet felt like it was burning a hole in my skin where it lay against my breastbone.

I had no idea why the Heart of Atlantis would flare to life in the middle of a vampire nest. The thing has a mind of its own. I was half tempted to take it off and stick it in my pocket, but I didn't have time for screwing around. We had vamps to interrogate.

"Did you see any windows leading into the basement?" I asked. I hadn't seen any, but it's always good to double-check.

"Nope. It looks like this one's completely underground. Probably why they chose it."

Damn. Without a way to let in the sunlight, we were at a disadvantage. Even though vamps are usually forced to sleep by the rising sun, they can still wake up: something I learned from a vampire named Terrance. And being completely underground, they'd still be deadly.

I clipped my flashlight onto my UV gun. The flashlight was a special Tesselah edition with a full-spectrum lightbulb. It wouldn't do the same damage as the sun or a UV gun, but it would hurt the suckers like a hot stove to bare skin. Probably not what the original inventors of full-spectrum lighting had in mind.

I crept down the stairs, Inigo hot on my tail. At the bottom, we both stopped and gaped in surprise.

The basement floor was covered with sleeping bodies. There must have been about thirty of them. And they weren't all vamps. There were demons in the mix.

What the...?

"Demons and vamps don't work together," Inigo hissed in my ear.

"No shit," I whispered back. I had no idea what was going on, but I *really* didn't like it. Anything that got vampires and demons working together in harmony was not going to be good for the human race.

"I think we should get out of here and just burn the place. We can figure out what's going on some other way."

I opened my mouth to agree with him, but it was too late. We hadn't noticed a demon clinging to the dark ceiling. Slowly, it unfurled its wings and let out a low keening sound. Before we could bat an eyelash, the entire place was thrumming with waking monsters.

"Up the stairs!" I yelled, training my gun on the nearest vamp and firing off a ray of pure UV light. The vamp dusted, but there were more coming. Way more than we could handle in such a tight space on our own.

Move your ass, Morgan. Inigo's voice in my head was practically a yell.

"Believe me, I am." I dashed up the stairs after him, another vampire just a breath away.

I hit the kitchen just as Inigo smashed the boards off the window, spilling hard winter sunlight into the room. The vampire that had been milliseconds from snacking on me burst into dust.

Sunlight would stop the vampires, but not the demons. Two more vamps dusted before they wised up and sent the noncombustibles instead.

Not good.

Inigo and I backed up in the kitchen as far as we could from the basement door. We'd both switched from guns to blades, as UVs are useless against demons.

The first one that crept through the door was about four feet high and covered in greenish-brown scales. It was snarling like a mad dog and just as friendly. What really had me worried were its talons. Razor sharp and twice as deadly.

I eyed the thing warily. "Dammit, why isn't Kabita here? She's the demonologist, not me. What the hell is that thing?"

"Looks like a sonne demon," Inigo said. "They look nasty, but they're low-level. Easily manipulated by anyone with more psychic power."

"Oh, good, then you can control them."

"Afraid not." A frown creased his forehead. "This one's already being controlled by someone else."

"The vamps?"

"No. Something stronger."

The demon snarled and charged at us, its deadly talons flashing. One swipe of Inigo's blade declawed the demon. I finished it off with a dao across the throat. The head went toppling off and rolled across the floor, to stare up at us blankly. Bye-bye, demon.

"That was easy and painless."

I had spoken too soon.

Demons came pouring out of the basement as if from the bowels of the hell dimension itself. Inigo and I had no time to think, let alone speak. We only had time to hack and stab and slice.

The floor under my feet was slick with demon blood. My boot slid out from under me, and that was all one of the demons needed. It jumped on my back, taking us both down. I hit the floor hard. Fortunately, my training kicked in, and I rolled with the fall, shaking off the demon and coating myself in blood in the process.

As I lay there, flat on my back, the demon made another run, talons flashing in the sunlight. Fortunately, I was in the perfect position. I raised my legs, bending my knees, and caught the creature in the chest with my feet. One heave sent it flying across the kitchen, nicely impaling it on Inigo's blade.

"Oh, well done."

"Thanks, babe." I flashed him a grin.

We stayed braced for battle, but nobody else popped up from the basement. "Guess we got all the demons."

"Damn, you're a mess. I think we should hose you off after this."

I looked down at my clothes. Ruined, no doubt. Shit. That meant I'd have to go shopping. I hate shopping. "We got some vamps to dust first." I glanced over at the basement stairs. I so did not want to go down there. "Ideas?"

"Nothing comes to mind."

I mulled it over a bit. "OK, so we got the demons cleared out. There can't be that many vampires down there, right?"

"I still can't get a read on them, but yeah. Maybe a dozen."

Crap. A dozen vampires in an underground, enclosed space. This was so not my day.

And then an idea hit. It was so ridiculously over-the-top it might just work. "I'll be right back." I dashed out to the car, rummaged around in the trunk, and came back with an ax. Axes aren't my weapon of choice, but they have their uses.

Inigo eyed the ax, then me. "You going to take up lumberjacking?"

I rolled my eyes. "Don't be an idiot."

Moving around the living room floor, I felt the floorboards under my feet until I found just the right spot. Then I heaved the ax and slammed it into the floorboards, my hunter strength sending it deep into the brittle wood.

"Shit, Morgan."

I ignored him and swung again. And again. Until a hole began forming right in the middle of the living room floor.

Inigo smiled and held out his hand. "Damn me, you're a genius. Here, let me have a turn."

My shoulders were aching, so I handed him the ax and let him whale at the boards for a while. I am woman enough to admit my hunter strength is no match for his dragon half.

Before long, there was a huge hole spilling sunlight straight down into the basement. Hissing and snarling and poofs of dust told us at least some of the light had hit its mark. Hopefully we hadn't accidentally dusted the wrong vamp, but we could no longer play it safe. There were just too many of them for the two of us to handle alone, and there wasn't time to bring in reinforcements.

Replacing our blades with UV guns, we headed back downstairs. Amazing how light really opens up a space. There were only a couple of corners left that were dark enough for the vampires to hide.

I strode up to the first corner. There were two vamps hissing at me like a couple of feral cats. They felt young. Newly turned.

No more than a couple of years, and neither of them matched the description of the man in the bar. I knew without a doubt they wouldn't have the information we needed.

"Sorry, guys. End of the line." And I dusted them both. UV ray straight to the heart.

The other corner held what appeared to be the last vampire. He definitely matched the description given to us by Mikey. He was older than the other two vamps. Much older. I could feel the age of him pressing against the back of my head. And yet, strangely, he looked afraid. I was pretty sure it wasn't of me.

I rubbed absently at my breastbone. I'd forgotten all about it in the fight, but now it felt like the bloody amulet was on fire.

"So, you like to hire redneck asshole idiots to do your dirty work, do you?"

His jaw worked. Finally, he spat out, "I don't know what you're talking about."

"Oh, I think you do. My brother. Trevor Daly. You paid three men to attack and kill him. Why?"

The vamp's mouth worked as though he wanted to say something, but nothing came out. He doubled over, as though in pain.

I grabbed him by the hair and yanked him back up. "Listen, you undead freak. I want to know why you had my brother beat up."

It looked almost as if he was struggling to breathe. "Not me." His voice was barely above a whisper. Strangled. "Not me."

And then he burst into so much smoke. Ash drifting to the floor.

"What the fuck?" I stared at the space where he'd been standing and then whirled to face Inigo. "I barely even touched him. What on earth is going on?"

Inigo shook his head. "Some kind of magic. Same as what I felt controlling the demon upstairs. It dissipated when the vampire dusted."

Magic. Earth magic. I suddenly realized that the amulet, which had felt like a hot coal against my skin, now felt cool to the touch. I yanked it out and stared at it. No heat. No glow. But I knew without a doubt it had been glowing a minute before.

What the hell was going on?

Chapter Twelve

What the hell is going on?" I stormed out of the farmhouse, practically slamming the door behind me. Anger rode me hard, digging its claws deep into my soul. The darkness stirred. It liked the anger.

I put a lid on it fast. The last thing I needed was for the darkness to get out of control. Especially since I could feel the fire hot on its heels and that new thing swirling inside me. What was I? Some kind of godsdamned Fifth freaking Element?

I turned toward Inigo, and if the look on his face was anything to go by, he was just as pissed as I was. "No idea, babe. But something or someone was controlling those creatures, or they would not have been working together."

"Yeah, and I'll bet dollars to doughnuts whoever it was immolated that vamp so it couldn't lead us straight to its master." I'd never heard of any creature that could dust a vamp remotely. I couldn't imagine the power that would take.

I was also pissed off. I really wanted to throw something. A rock, maybe. There were plenty of them lying around, but I refrained. Instead, I dug around in the trunk for a change of clothes and some wet wipes. It was way too cold for stripping to my underwear, but I'd rather freeze my ass off than spend another minute covered in demon goo.

I yanked a clean shirt over my head, then pulled out my phone and dialed Kabita. She answered on the third ring.

"Yeah?"

"You ever hear of demons and vampires working together?"

There was a pause. "Does this have to do with your little field trip to Warm Springs the other day?"

"Yep."

Another pause. "No, can't say I have. Demons and vamps tend to be a lot like baking powder and vinegar. They would never willingly work together. How many are we talking?" she asked.

"Thirty or so."

Kabita let out a deep sigh. "That would take a lot of power. A witch practicing the dark arts might be able to hold one or two of each, but thirty? No idea."

"Shit. OK, thanks. Wait, one more thing. Kabita, can you get me information on the owner of a property out near Culver?" I gave her the address.

"What are you up to, Morgan?"

I could hear her fingers already tapping away at her keyboard. "Not sure, K, but somebody attacked my brother last night." I gave her a quick rundown.

"Wow."

"No kidding."

"OK, it looks like that address you gave me has been empty for several years, but it's owned by a guy named Albert Fey."

"You got an address for him?" I asked.

"Sorry, all I can find on him is a post office box in Portland. He could be anywhere."

"Great. OK, thanks."

"Now what?" I turned to Inigo as I hung up. "How the hell are we going to figure out who's behind this? The nest was our last lead."

"No, it wasn't."

I must have looked completely lost, because Inigo laughed.

I scowled. "Don't you dare laugh at me."

He shook his head. In two strides, he was at my side, pulling my unyielding body into his warmth. I couldn't help it. I melted.

Some tough vampire hunter I am. One hug from her boyfriend and she melts like butter.

"We have one card left up our sleeves, Morgan. Have you forgotten?"

Apparently, I had. I burrowed my face into his neck and breathed in his scent. It calmed me enough that I could think semirationally again. "Remind me."

"Trevor."

I leaned back so I could see his face. "But Trevor only saw the hillbilly brothers and the kid, Mikey. How could he possibly lead us to whoever is behind all this?"

"I'm thinking your new little trick might be able to help with that."

"You mean my sudden ability to create mini tornadoes? How is that going to help?"

He smiled. "Have you forgotten? The last time you channeled air, you saw a djinni kill Agent Vega." He shrugged. "Maybe if you do it around a living person, someone still affected by the magic, you'll pick up more."

"Hell, it's worth a try. With the nest gone, we don't have much else."

Minus finding one Albert Fey, Trevor really was our last lead. So after tossing my dirty clothes into the trunk, I climbed into the Mustang and cranked up the stereo. Loud. I needed a little rock music, and Evanescence was just the thing. Inigo didn't even crack a smile as I sang at the top of my lungs all the way to the hospital.

∽

I have always hated hospitals. I think most people do. They're kind of creepy and depressing and reek of chemicals.

"Shit, I hate hospitals."

I glanced at Inigo in surprise. He can't read my thoughts. My emotions, maybe, but not my thoughts.

"I'm clairvoyant, remember? Hospitals hold lots of bad juju. I hate when they want to talk to me." By "they," he meant ghosts.

We'd never really talked about it before. At least not on the whole "I see dead people" level. I guess I'd just thought of him as being like Cordelia. Communicating with the other side and whatnot. I reached out and took his hand, threading my fingers through his. "Is it bad?"

His smile was a little forced. "Not if I ignore them."

I stopped, tugging at his arm. "Why don't you go back to the car? I can talk to Trevor." I so didn't want him in pain, and I could see just being there was hurting him. His eyes were haunted like I'd never seen before. It tore me up.

He squeezed my hand. "Morgan, I'm fine. I don't break so easy. I'm not as weak as all that."

"That is not what I meant…"

"I know what you meant," he shushed me. "And I love you for it. But I'm fine. Let's go talk to Trevor, and then we can get out of here. OK?"

"You're the boss."

That made him laugh. "Oh, right. That'll happen."

Trevor was propped up in bed, being fussed over by an extremely pretty blonde nurse. It was pretty obvious she was smitten, which amused me to no end.

"Hey, Trev."

The nurse whirled on me. "I'm sorry, miss." Her tone was just this side of snarky. "Visiting hours are for family only."

She was full of shit, of course. It was still well within visiting hours, but her narrowed eyes screamed jealousy. I'd have loved to have played with her, but time was of the essence. "I *am* family. I'm his sister."

By her expression, I could tell she didn't believe me. She opened her mouth, but Trevor jumped to the rescue.

"It's true, Emily. Morgan is my sister."

That seemed to placate Nurse Emily, and she reluctantly toddled off to tend to her other patients.

"That one has the hots for you, big brother." I couldn't help teasing him just a little.

He rolled his eyes. "She is driving me insane. They'll need to check me into the psych ward after this."

I raised my eyebrows. "Not your type?"

"Definitely not."

I crossed to the bed and leaned down to give him a hug. "I'm so glad you're OK." He looked a little worse for wear—black eye, bruised cheekbone, arm in a sling—but he seemed chipper enough.

"You should see the other guys," he joked.

"I did. Trust me. You definitely got the worst end of it."

Trevor frowned. "They caught me off guard." He said it like it had never happened before. Probably, it hadn't. Weird powers run in the family, after all.

"We think they had a little magical help," Inigo spoke up.

"No kidding?" That got Trevor's attention.

"The guys who attacked you were hired by a vampire." I settled myself on the chair next to the bed. "Which is weird enough, but we found the vamps' nest. They were working with a bunch of low-level demons."

Trevor frowned. "That's unusual."

"I know, right? On top of that, when we tried to question one, it dusted. On its own."

"Not exactly on its own," Inigo pointed out. "There was magic involved. We just don't know what kind of magic."

"The place where they were hiding is owned by some guy called Albert Fey. Ever heard of him?" I asked.

Trevor shook his head. "Sorry, no. Doesn't sound familiar."

Inigo and I exchanged glances.

"We were hoping that if Morgan uses her new abilities on you, she'll see something like she did with Vega," Inigo suggested.

"It's a good idea," Trevor agreed, "but I was attacked by humans. Not supernaturals. I don't see how Morgan can pick up anything."

"There is one more thing," I said.

Two pairs of eyes turned toward me.

I felt a little nervous and kind of dorky saying it, but it had to be said. "The amulet was glowing again."

"What? Why didn't you tell me?" Inigo was pissed.

I shrugged. "There wasn't time. We were fighting more than two dozen demons and vamps. And then there was the dusting business." I shook my head. "But the amulet got so hot it nearly burned my skin. And you know what Eddie said."

Inigo nodded, but Trevor looked confused. "What did Eddie say? Why was your amulet glowing?"

I sighed. I didn't want to say it out loud, because it freaked me out to no end, but Trevor had to know. "Sidhe magic. The Atlantean amulet glows in the presence of sidhe magic."

Trevor gaped at me a moment. "The sidhe would never work with vampires. Or demons, for that matter. It's...anathema. Not to mention a death warrant should the fairy queen find out."

"Eddie said the fairy queen was the only one who might have enough power to control one of the djinn, but only a low-level one. He doesn't think we're looking for one of the fae. He thinks the amulet could have been triggered by earth magic. But with all this sidhe magic going on, I'm not convinced they're so innocent. Are you sure the sidhe aren't up to something?" It would be just like them too. They do like to cause trouble.

Trevor shook his head. "In all my years with the SRA, I've never once heard of the fae dealing with such creatures as the djinn. I find it very hard to believe they'd start now."

"And you're sure you saw nothing else when the guys attacked you?"

"Sorry, Morgan. No."

I sighed. "You mind if I do that wind thing again?" It wasn't that I wanted to, but I couldn't see any other way.

He looked a little hesitant, but he agreed. I wasn't sure if it was because he was my brother or just a good agent. Maybe a little of both.

Inigo went to guard the door while I stood up and held my hands over Trevor's body. I felt like a dork, but what else was new? Closing my eyes, I reached down into that place where the fire and darkness live, down to that new power that curls and wraps around them.

Air.

I honestly had no feel for whether it was good or evil. Maybe it was neither. Maybe it was both. What I did know was that it was sneaky and could turn on me in a moment.

It played coy at first, but I coaxed it until it began to gently unfurl up and out of my center and through the middle of my chest. It wrapped itself almost lovingly around my brother. Almost as though it channeled my own love for him.

Then, as if waking up, it began whipping around the room like it had with Vega. Faster and faster, until Trevor and I were caught in the middle of the vortex. The curtains thrashed wildly against the windows, and the chair I'd been sitting on spun across the room until it crashed into the wall.

In my peripheral vision, I saw the nurse run into the room, eyes wide. She yelled something, but I couldn't hear her over the roaring in my own head. Inigo grabbed her and held her still, so I turned my attention back to what I was doing.

The palms of my hands grew warm as they hovered above the bed. My vision tunneled down until it was just my hands, and

Trevor, and the air. And then another shape began to take form within the silvery smoke.

This time it wasn't human shaped. It was something else. A tattoo on a man's arm. A symbol. A symbol I know very well, indeed.

The same symbol my brother wears around his neck. The symbol of the ancient Atlantean royal house.

Chapter Thirteen

M organ, no one with any connection to that symbol would ever harm me," Trevor insisted.

Once I was done with my little stage act, Inigo had put the psychic whammy on the nurse and sent her on her way. Before the guy at the mortuary, I'd had no idea he could do that, and now he was wiping people's brains left and right. Made me wonder what else he had up his sleeve.

"So, there really are people out there with the crest of the royal house of Atlantis tattooed on their bodies?" I was pacing back and forth in front of Trevor's hospital bed.

"Yes, of course." He nodded. "My father—*our* father—told me about them when he gave me the amulet. They are descendants of the Atlantean sentinels. Sworn to protect the bloodline."

That stopped me in my tracks. "Say what?" This was the first I'd heard of any sentinels. And if they'd been sworn to protect the royal bloodline of Atlantis, where were they when I was getting murdered by a vampire three years ago? "Is that like a guardian?"

"Not exactly. From what I understand, there is only one guardian chosen by the Heart of Atlantis"—he nodded to where the amulet lay carefully tucked under my shirt—"to protect the key. You."

"Yeah, got that."

"Sentinels were the elite of the Atlantean royal guard, chosen to guard the heirs to the throne. Modern-day sentinels claim direct decent from their original Atlantean counterparts. Kind of a secret society." He shifted in bed a bit, wincing as he jarred his injured arm. "I don't really know much about it. Dad just said that if ever I met a man with a tattoo matching the amulet, I was to trust that man with my life."

"And have you met anyone with that tattoo?"

"About a year after Dad died, yes." He rubbed absently at his forehead. He probably had a throbbing headache, and I had no doubt little Nurse Emily would be in to throw us out at any minute. "I was hanging out with some friends at the mall after school, and this old Native American guy came up to me. Said he knew my father and he was sorry. Usual stuff. I shook his hand, and that's when I saw the tattoo on his inner forearm."

"Did you ask him about it?"

"Of course, but he wouldn't say much."

"So he was what? Letting you know he was there? Watching over you or whatever?" It made sense. If there really were some super-secret society of sentinels out there. Say that three times fast.

"Yeah, that's my guess." Trevor nodded, fatigue beginning to show around his eyes. His normally rich latte skin had a decidedly chalky cast to it. I was betting he was more hurt than he let on. Men and their machismo.

"OK, we're out of here. You get some rest." I leaned over and gave him a sisterly peck on the forehead. "I don't suppose the old guy is still alive?"

"Sure. His name is Tommy Waheneka. He's a tribal shaman, and he still lives somewhere on the Warm Springs reservation."

∽

My cell rang as we left the hospital. I barely refrained from groaning when I saw the caller ID.

"Hi, Jack."

Inigo shook his head, clearly amused.

"What's going on, Morgan?"

"What do you mean?"

"Don't play dumb with me," he snapped. "I know when you're in trouble. Where the hell are you, and why aren't you answering my calls?"

"Geez, snap my head off, why don't you? I was in the hospital. I had to turn my phone off."

He let out a string of colorful words in at least three different languages. "Who hurt you? Is Inigo with you? Why did he let you get hurt?"

"Gods, Jack, relax. I'm fine. Trevor's the one that got beaten up, not me. I was just visiting him."

"Oh." That shut him up. "So you're OK, then."

"Of course. I had a little run-in with some vampires and demons, and my amulet did that glowy thing again, but other than that, everything is fine."

"Good. Then you're headed back to Portland." It wasn't a question.

"Actually, no. I have stuff to do first."

"Morgan—"

I hung up on him.

"Are you sure hanging up on Jack is the best thing to do?" Inigo asked, still clearly amused. "You know that's only going to piss him off even more."

"Do I look like I care? I have a job to do, and I don't have time to coddle his ego." It wasn't fair, and I knew it. Jack was doing his job too. It was me who had the delicate ego, still hurting over him choosing duty over me. It was me who had way too many unresolved issues. It was me who felt guilty about said issues when I had moved on to someone else.

"He's only trying to protect you."

The weirdness of my new boyfriend defending my old one did not escape me. I sighed. "I know. But he really gets on my last nerve sometimes." I shook off the irritation, along with the guilt, and changed the subject. "Now let's go find Tommy Waheneka."

ဢ

Trevor hadn't known exactly where Tommy Waheneka lived, so I decided the place to start was back at the Warm Springs Café. I'd have bet anything our waitress from the other day knew everybody within a twenty-mile radius. She was bound to know where Tommy lived. The challenge was convincing her to tell me, a complete stranger.

We slid into the same booth we'd sat at before. The waitress who came to take our order wasn't our original waitress. This one was a good three decades younger and forty pounds lighter. Her name tag read *Anna*.

I gave Inigo a slight nod. It was his cue to turn on the charm offensive. A little light flirting never hurt anybody, and I've yet to meet a woman immune to Inigo's charms. Not counting the hotel maid, of course. By the time Anna brought our meal, he had her hooked.

"Anna. That's such a pretty name. I don't remember seeing you the last time we were here."

"Oh." She blushed bright red and gave her glossy dark hair a little toss like women do when they're trying to appear attractive to a man. "I only work weekends and during the summer, when it's really busy. Patty works during the week."

"Patty." He swirled his spoon around in his coffee mug. It was almost hypnotic. "She must have been the one who served us. Do they make you work weekends all by yourself, then? That must be really stressful."

"Oh, no, Patty comes in for a few hours during the lunch and dinner rush."

"That's good." His voice was sympathetic. "I'd hate to think they overworked you."

She blushed an even deeper red. "Oh, they wouldn't do that. My uncle is the owner. He's really good to me."

"It's good to have family and friends to care about you. I have a friend who lives around here. Maybe you know him? Tommy Waheneka."

She frowned. "Oh, yeah, I've seen him around. He sometimes stops by for coffee and pie on his way back from Madras or Portland. He keeps to himself mostly, but he's pretty important in the tribe."

Inigo nodded. "I'd like to stop by and say hello, but I've never been to his house before. Does he live nearby?"

"Oh, no." She topped up our coffee mugs from the carafe she held. "He lives way out somewhere in the woods. Patty would know. She'll be in soon if you want to ask her."

"That'd be nice. You've been such a help." Inigo really poured on the charm.

"Sure. No problem. If you need a refill, just wave." With that, Anna sashayed off with an extra swing in her step.

"Wonder if that charm of yours will work on Patty?" I teased Inigo just a bit.

"Oh, just you wait and see."

Initially, Patty seemed flattered by Inigo's charm offensive, but when we started asking questions, she clammed up. I finally decided I had to tell her the truth. Well, part of the truth.

"Listen, Patty, that man who was in here with us yesterday? Remember him?"

She gave me a look that clearly told me I was an idiot. "Of course. I remember all my customers."

"He's my brother. A couple of assholes put him in the hospital last night."

"I'm sorry to hear that," she said, "but I don't see what that has to do with Tommy."

"Tommy and our dad were good friends before Dad died, and Tommy kept an eye on Trevor when he was younger. Trevor asked me to find Tommy for him. That's all. I'm just trying to find our father's friend for my brother."

Patty eyeballed me for a minute. "You're not telling me everything, of that I'm sure. But you have honest eyes, so I'm going to tell you how to find Tommy. You do anything to hurt that man and I swear you will wish you'd never come here. You understand me?"

"Yes, ma'am." I truly believed she meant it too.

"Hand me a napkin, and I'll draw you a map."

Tommy Waheneka lived beyond the last outpost, and then some. Seriously, his cabin gave new meaning to the word *rugged*. I was halfway to hearing dueling banjos in my head by the time we finally arrived at his front door in a cloud of dust and screeching chickens.

Tommy looked about a thousand years old, leathery face worn and creased by sun and time. His eyes, they were ageless. Bright and new and filled with humor that mocked the world. I liked him instantly.

"Nice car." He glanced at the Mustang and went back to rocking gently on his front porch and whittling a stick into what looked like some kind of animal.

"Thanks. Tommy Waheneka?"

He didn't say a word, just kept rocking.

"Stupid me. Who else would you be, out here in the back-ass of nowhere? Can I see your arm?" When in doubt, be blunt.

Tommy's fingers stilled. So did the rocking. I thought for a moment he'd refuse. Instead, he held out his left arm and then slowly turned it over and pulled his jacket sleeve up to expose the inside of his forearm. Tattooed on the coppery skin was the same symbol Trevor wore around his neck: the symbol for the royal house of Atlantis. The symbol I'd seen in my vision.

"Took you long enough." His voice was scratchy and rough, but surprisingly strong for such an old guy.

"You're a sentinel."

"Not exactly," he said with maddening calm. His fingers went back to whittling, and he went back to rocking.

"What do you mean, not exactly? Trevor Daly told me the sentinels bear the mark of the royal house. He told me you were a sentinel."

He was quiet so long I thought he wouldn't speak. "I knew your father."

I had expected it, but it still kind of floored me. "How?"

"He was a good man, Alexander Morgan."

It didn't exactly answer my question, but it was pretty clear that pushing the man wouldn't get me anywhere, so I kept my mouth shut. Not a common occurrence for me, but I was trying.

The rocking chair squeaked over the porch boards; the knife scratched against the small bit of wood in Tommy's fingers. The old man was silent for what seemed like ages. "You look a bit like him around the eyes. A little like his son too."

"Yeah?"

"You're stronger than him, though. Your father."

"What do you mean?" I couldn't imagine that.

"How many do you carry inside you now?"

My heart stopped. Then it pounded in my throat so hard I couldn't breathe. "What?" I glanced over at Inigo, who shrugged. Obviously, he was completely baffled. Unfortunately, I was not.

"Elements." Tommy's voice was so calm. So quiet. As though nothing could ruffle the man. "How many do you carry inside you?"

I swallowed hard. How on earth did he know? "Three."

He nodded as if it all made perfect sense. "Three more."

"What? Did you say there are three more?"

He nodded placidly, still intent on carving whatever it was in his hands. "There are six in total."

"Six? Are you fu—freaking kidding me?"

His face remained placid, but I could almost feel the laughter coming off him in waves.

"What are the other three?"

Tommy rocked gently as he whittled away. "What do you think?"

More riddles. Lovely. "Well, going with the whole elemental theme, I'd say water and earth. But the sixth? No idea."

"It'll come to you. In time."

"How do you know all this if you aren't a sentinel? Why do you have the sentinel mark? How did you know my father?" The questions spilled out. I couldn't stop myself.

Without a word, Tommy got up out of the rocker and went into the house, leaving the door open behind him. I just stared. What the hell?

Inigo gave me a little nudge. "I think he wants us to follow him."

"How can you tell that?"

"He didn't slam the door in our faces."

Good point.

The cabin was a single room, warm and dim. Shadows swam in the corners, and the air smelled of burning sage and wood smoke. Dried herbs hung from the rafters. Small bottles of various powders and liquids lined the shelves along one wall.

Tommy was stirring a pot of something on the woodburning stove. "Sit."

The only place to sit was at a well-worn oak table against one wall of the cabin. "Are those for brewing magical potions or something?" I pointed at the wall of bottles.

Tommy gave me a look. "They're cooking spices."

"Oh."

Inigo looked like he was holding back a laugh. I glared at him.

"Do you even know what a shaman is?" Tommy placed two bowls full of some kind of stew in front of us. It smelled divine, and my stomach let out an embarrassingly loud growl.

"Um, no. I know witches and hunters and, you know, stuff like that. I've never met a shaman." I felt like a freaking idiot admitting my lack of knowledge, but there was no point denying it. I'd already made a major faux pas with the herbs.

Tommy joined us at the table with his own bowl of stew. "There is power all around us. In the sun. The moon. The trees."

This I know. Kabita has drilled it into my head enough times. In the old days, they called it "magic." Some still do because it's easier, simpler, but it is really quantum mechanics.

"Anyone can draw on this power for their own purpose. A small amount to aid in the hunt, or for good luck, but only a shaman can draw large amounts of this power for the good of his or her people. To heal. To defend."

It made sense. I know from my own experience that anyone can draw power from the universe. Some call it Reiki. Others, prayer. Whatever. Energy is energy.

And then there are those who can channel enough energy to do some seriously scary shit. People like Kabita. People like me. Though I'm not sure I count, since my abilities come from channeling weirdness.

I wondered if that meant we are shaman too, in a way. Using our abilities to protect our people. Except our tribe is the entire city of Portland. In the long run, the only thing that truly matters is that, whatever the label, Tommy, Kabita, and I all do what needs doing.

"So you're a healer." I took a bite of stew. The savory juices of the meat exploded on my tongue, mingling with the zing of herbs and the freshness of the vegetables. It was divine.

"One of my talents, yes. That was the reason your father came to me."

I paused midbite. "He came to you?"

Tommy chewed thoughtfully. "I don't recall when it was. Time isn't important. But he came to me. He was dying."

"What do you mean? Trevor said he was murdered."

"Yes."

I wanted to scream in frustration. "Then how was he dying?"

"We are all dying."

Dear gods, the man should win a medal for cryptic. "Listen, I just need to know about my father. And Trevor. Do you know why someone is trying to kill my brother? Why someone killed his friend Agent Vega? Can you tell me—"

The old man waved a hand. "So many questions. All in due time. Eat your stew."

He shut up after that and refused to answer a single question. My stomach was in knots and my fuse about to blow.

Patience, love. If we want answers, we have to let him give them to us in his own way. I felt Inigo's soothing voice in my mind, but I was in no mood to be soothed, so I sent him a death glare. It didn't faze him a bit. Sometimes it is a wonder he puts up with me.

The rest of the meal passed in silence. Even the washing up was done quietly; Tommy Waheneka refused to speak until every dish was washed, dried, and put away. By the time we were finished and gathered around the woodstove in the world's most uncomfortable chairs, I was about ready to blow a gasket.

Tommy sat for the longest time, staring into the flame dancing in the window of the stove door. I was just about to start demanding again when his voice broke the silence. "I met your father on the day he died."

Chapter Fourteen

I wondered if I looked as shell-shocked as I felt. "What? Did you say you met my father the day he died?"

"That is how I was able to see him, of course," Tommy said, as if that explained everything.

How he thought that explained anything, I did not know. I was about to tell him so in no uncertain terms when Inigo gently preempted my tirade. "Shamans are like me, Morgan. They can often see the spirits of the dead, the dying. Sometimes they can even communicate with them."

I glanced over at Tommy, who nodded in confirmation. My mind was a whirl. "So, you saw my father's spirit when he was dying?"

"Yes. He came to me," the old man said. He stared off into the distance so long I was afraid he wasn't going to continue. "He was worried about his son. His daughter was safe, but his son...not so much. I promised to keep watch over the boy."

My brain ticked over. "You had yourself tattooed so Trevor would know our father had sent you."

"Yes. Your father showed me the symbol. Told me what I should do."

Well, shit. Could this get any weirder? Oh, don't answer that.

"Trevor said our father was murdered."

Tommy shook his head. "We spoke of many things, but never of that."

Damn. I'd hoped he could shed some light on my father's death. "But why you? Are you sure you're not a sentinel?"

He cracked a laugh at that. "Not a drop of Atlantean blood." More staring off into the distance. "We spoke many times about things not of this physical world after he died. Interesting man, your father. Keen mind. Troubled soul. Although we never met in person—at least with both of us on this side—we became friends. When he had nowhere else to go, he came to me." The old man shrugged.

I was about to open my mouth and ask why when it hit me. Shamans protect their people. From the moment my father asked Tommy Waheneka to watch over my brother, Trevor became one of Tommy's people. To guard. To protect.

"So you've been watching over Trevor all this time."

"Since he was fifteen years old."

"And you still watch over him now."

The shaman gave me a shrewd look. "As promised."

"So you can tell me why he was attacked the other night. And why you didn't stop those assholes."

"Morgan." There was warning in Inigo's voice.

I wasn't surprised. I was walking dangerously close to being disrespectful. But if you want to get cliché about it, sometimes you gotta break some eggs. Or walk where angels fear to tread. Or something.

Tommy waved Inigo's warning aside. "She's her father's daughter. Can't help herself." Those shrewd brown eyes bored into mine. "I can't tell what I don't know, but I do know this: it wasn't Trevor Daly they were after."

That got me. "What do you mean?" I was getting a bad feeling.

He leaned back in his chair and gave me the silent treatment. Naturally, I wanted to get all up in his face, but I had the oddest feeling he was testing me. Fine. I leaned back in my own chair with my arms crossed over my chest.

We sat like that for what seemed like ages as I let my mind click through everything that had happened. I squirmed first.

Damn, but those chairs made a person's butt sore. I had no idea how a man old as dirt could stand it. I made a mental note to buy nothing but cushy chairs.

Then something else hit me. "They could have killed Trevor. Easily. But they didn't. Instead, they—whoever 'they' are—sent a couple of bumbling rednecks after him. Why? I mean, they killed Agent Vega with a djinni. Made good and sure he was dead. Obviously, the two attacks are connected somehow."

Tommy Waheneka gave me a look of approval, but remained silent. Obviously, I was on to something.

"OK, so if they weren't actually worried about killing Trevor and there was no obvious reason for beating him up, like say interrogation or something, there has to be a less obvious reason." I mulled that over for a while.

"Who was the first person Trevor called when he got to the hospital?" Tommy's voice was peaceful, nonchalant.

"Me. But that's natural; I'm his sister..." My voice trailed off. I am his sister. I also work with him. He is my SRA contact. My "handler," if you will. And I am the only hunter within hundreds of miles, the first person the SRA would send even if I hadn't come on my own.

"Me? They want me?" I could have smacked myself in the head. There was a hit out on me, for crying out loud. Why wouldn't they be after me? But I'd been so focused on this whole sidhe/djinn business, I hadn't stopped to think.

A slight smile quirked the shaman's lips. "Yes, Morgan. You."

"But who are they? And why me?"

Tommy heaved himself out of his chair and went to tinker at his stove. "As to the who and why, I have no idea. The spirits are silent on the matter."

Oh shit. Spirits again. First Cordy and her damn guides or whatever, and now Tommy and his spirits. What is with the other side mucking in my business all the time?

"I don't suppose you could, you know, give them a little jog?"

He chuckled. "Doesn't work like that."

Of course not. "So now what?"

"No idea." He turned from the stove, a silver pot in his hand. "Cappuccino?"

∽

"Tommy, have you ever heard of the djinn?" It was such a mad, crazy question, but I supposed if anyone would know about them, Tommy would.

Bright eyes twinkled at me out of an ancient face. "Now you are asking the right questions."

As he calmly sipped at his coffee drink, Tommy told me how the djinn had arrived on tribal lands centuries before the white man came. "They just appeared. Out of thin air." Tommy waved his cappuccino cup around, nearly sloshing his drink over the side. "Some people believed they were gods we should worship, but my ancestor was a shaman like me. He knew better."

"He knew what the djinn were?" I was completely enraptured by Tommy's tale.

"Oh, yes, he knew. He had seen them in his visions, and he knew they were powerful, but not without weakness. So"— Tommy shrugged—"he did what any good shaman would do."

"What was that?" Inigo asked.

"Why, exploited that weakness, of course. He used the power of the earth and the sun and nature all around him to trap one of the most powerful of the djinn—a marid. He forced it to admit that it had fled with its people to avoid being captured and enslaved by powerful magi in the East."

"What did your ancestor do then?"

"Let it go. After extracting an oath that he and his kind would never again trouble our people." Tommy drained the last of his cappuccino and began cleaning up. "They vanished into the high desert, never to be heard from again." He glanced over to me. "Until now."

A djinni had killed Agent Vega. A djinni enslaved by powerful magic. Magic that had also bound together a nest of vampires and demons and had immolated a vamp from a distance. Talk about bad juju.

"Can you trap a djinni, Tommy?"

"A minor djinni, maybe," he said, "but not a marid. I am not nearly as powerful as my ancestor was. There is no human left who can trap a marid. In fact, I know of only one creature alive today who can do it."

"Which creature?"

"The fairy queen."

I sighed. Who else? Eddie had been wrong, after all. "Of course it had to be the frigging fairy queen. I guess there's only one thing to do."

Tommy just smiled knowingly, but Inigo gave me a baffled look. "What is that?"

"We're going into the desert to look for the djinn."

"One thing I should tell you before you go…" Tommy spoke up.

I turned to look at the old man. "Yeah?"

"When you see your mother tonight, ask her about Alister Jones."

Chapter Fifteen

I winced as the Mustang hit yet another pothole. Poor thing just wasn't made for this kind of abuse.

"What the hell was that crack about my mother and Alister Jones?" It was a rhetorical question. Obviously, Inigo had no more of a clue than I did. But I couldn't get my mind off Tommy's last words. Why would my mother know Kabita's father, the former leader of MI8 and a genocidal maniac? And why would she have never mentioned the fact?

I pulled the car off to the side of the poor excuse for a road and killed the engine. The potholes were getting too thick to dodge, and I didn't want to break an axle.

"That's it. We walk."

Inigo raised an eyebrow. "It's freezing cold out there. We have no idea where we're going, and you want us to walk?"

"Yeah. Pretty much."

He shrugged and flashed a grin. "Let's get going, then."

I was glad I'd brought my puffy winter coat. It was possibly the ugliest coat I'd ever seen, but it was warm. Two steps from the car and I wished I had a second one. The wind hit me, cutting through my jeans and chilling me to the bone.

Inigo moved closer and wrapped an arm around me. Suddenly, it was as though the wind had died down and the air around us had warmed up. Except that the wind was definitely still blowing. The whipping branches of a stubby juniper tree proved that.

Have I mentioned how good it is to have a boyfriend with dragon magic?

The frozen ground crunched under our feet as we made our way toward…well, frankly, I had no idea. My plan didn't go any further than hitting the high desert and hoping for a miracle. According to Eddie, the djinn don't like humans intruding on their territory, so I figured if I wandered around long enough, they'd show themselves. I wasn't sure pissing off a supernatural was a good idea, but it was the only one I had.

"You sure this is the right place?"

Inigo's question grated on my nerves. "How would I know?" There was an edge of a snap to my voice. It wasn't fair, but I was feeling frayed and I couldn't help myself. "Sorry." I glanced up at him. "I know I'm being a bitch. I'm just…"

"Scared? Worried? Freaking out?"

I gave him a wry grin. "Something like that, yeah." Trust Inigo to understand.

"Well"—he tugged me a little closer—"why don't you try using your new superpower?"

"What?"

"Eddie said that the djinn were creatures of air. And you were able to see the one that killed Vega. Maybe you can sense them now."

He had a point. I was sort of embarrassed I hadn't thought of it. "OK. I'll give it a try."

I stepped out from the circle of his arm and was immediately overwhelmed with the icy cold of the wind. It whipped against me as though trying to throw me to the ground and bury me in cold. Suddenly, I was sure it wasn't a natural wind.

Instead of turning my back to it, which was probably the logical reaction, I faced it. Tears streamed down my face from the whip of the wind, and my lips turned numb from the cold. Still, I faced it. And from within the depths of my soul, something uncoiled.

My own wind rushed out of me, its silver strands sparkling in the winter sunlight like so much glitter. Instead of the usual wispiness, it was a giant wall, pushing against the other wind. Like two waves crashing together.

I had zero control over my air. It just poured out of me, raging against that cold wall of "other" air. Blue and white sparks flew where the winds met. I staggered under the pressure, beyond fear or panic. It was all I could do to hold on to sanity. I could feel it like it was my own body beating against the icy wall.

Morgan! Morgan!

Inigo's voice was faint. Distant. I wasn't even sure if he was speaking aloud or in my head, but it didn't much matter. I couldn't answer him. He was a fuzzy shape outside the wall of wind.

Within the wall of wind, other voices called to me. Faces, haunted faces, begging me to join them, hands reaching out to grab me. It was like that painting, *The Scream*, come to life.

Sorrow engulfed me. Deep sadness of souls lost in the wasteland.

I fell to my knees, the air still pouring out of me as I struggled to catch my breath. The edges of my vision were darkening as my lungs struggled for air, like an old photo when it first catches fire. I knew without a doubt if I didn't rein in the air, it would kill me. Unfortunately, I no longer had the strength.

So I did the only thing I had left to do. In desperation, I dived down into that place where my powers live, and I opened the cage and let out the fire.

Like opening the door to a blast furnace, the fire flashed out of me. It wrapped around my own air and then smashed into the icy-cold wall in front of me. For a second, the other wall shivered, then it flashed into so much mist, spattering the frozen ground with water droplets.

I stared numbly at the once-frozen ground, now covered in puddles of water. My mind was blank, my emotions exhausted. I hadn't the strength to pull the fire and air back, but oddly enough, they retreated anyway, winding their leisurely way into my body. Almost as though satisfied with a job well done.

It took me a moment to realize Inigo was kneeling beside me, cradling me against his chest. I must have been worse off than I'd realized, because he sounded truly panicked.

"Here, allow me." I didn't recognize the new voice. It was female and a little breathy. It reminded me a bit of Marilyn Monroe.

I opened one eye. *Dammit.* She *looked* like Marilyn Monroe. I must have hit my head on something. Maybe I was hallucinating.

"Inigo, is Marilyn Monroe here?"

A laugh rumbled through his chest. "No, sweetie. I'm pretty sure she's a djinni."

"Yes," the breathy voice said. "I am one of the djinn."

"Then why do you look like Marilyn Monroe?"

Her pretty face screwed up in a pout. "I studied most closely so I could replicate Ms. Monroe's exact form." The djinni glanced down at herself. "I was sure I got it right."

"You did," I said with a slight nod.

That brought a smile to the djinni's face. "Good. I wanted to choose a pleasing form. Humans respond so much better to those they find attractive." She appeared baffled by the notion. "Is Marilyn Monroe not the epitome of human female beauty?"

"I wish." I managed to get myself into a sitting position, but I still felt ridiculously weak. "But I'm afraid curves went out of fashion about forty years ago."

She gave me a baffled look. "You humans are so strange."

"Tell me about it." With the help of Inigo and pseudo Marilyn, I managed to stagger to my feet. "Now, who are you, and why did you try and blast me with that wind?"

"Oh, it wasn't me," fake Marilyn assured me. "That's just one of the barriers we put up ages ago to keep humans from wandering into our territory. Gets messy when humans wander where they're not supposed to. Though, it certainly has been happening a lot lately."

I just stared at the djinni. Not only did she look like Marilyn, right down to the glamorous curves and glossy blonde hair, but she was dressed like Marilyn, in a skimpy white frock and strappy heels. She appeared completely unaffected by the cold. Holy hell.

"Um, sorry, who are you?"

"Oh, right." She giggled and fluttered her hands around. "My name is Zipporah. But you can call me Zip. Everyone does." She beamed at me like a young child who'd just won first prize in a spelling bee.

A djinni named Zip. Right.

"OK, Zip." I stepped away from Inigo. I didn't want to appear weak in front of the djinni. "So, not to be rude, but what are you?"

"I told you. I'm a djinni." She crossed her arms over her chest and gave me a look that clearly said she thought I was a little slow.

"Uh-huh. And did you say others have tried to enter your territory recently?"

She bobbed her head, sending pale-blonde ringlets dancing around her face. "Oh, yes. A really handsome one."

"Dark hair? Olive skin? A black suit?" I was guessing about the suit, but he *was* a fed.

Her blue eyes widened with excitement. "You know him? Is he coming back?"

Inigo and I exchanged looks. Daniel Vega. Had to be. What was he doing on djinn lands? Did he know about them? Was he trying to contact them? Or was it just a coincidence? Not that I believe in coincidence, mind you.

"Probably not," I told her.

"Oh, that's too bad." She drew her little cupid's bow mouth into a pout. Cute, if you go for that sort of thing.

"Sorry, why are you here again?"

"I'm here to help you." More beaming.

I didn't trust that sunny smile for a split second.

I glanced over at Inigo. He shrugged, so I turned back to Zip. "So, you know why we're here?"

"Of course."

Her voice was so ridiculously perky it was starting to get on my nerves. I narrowed my eyes. "How do you know?"

She pointed at my chest. Right to where the amulet lay under layers of clothing. "I can feel it. It calls to me."

"Feel what?"

She gave me a coy look. "Don't play that game with me, Morgan Bailey. I know you wear the lost amulet of Atlantis around your neck."

"How do you know my name?"

She blinked. "I don't understand."

Was she stupid? "I never told you my name. How do you know who I am?"

Her laugh danced in the air like a living thing. "Because"— she shook her head, sending her blonde ringlets bouncing—"you are the key. We have been waiting for you for centuries."

∽

"What is it with everyone?" I snarked at Inigo under my breath as we followed Zip across the frozen ground studded with snow-dusted sagebrush. "Royal freaking princess. Stupid-ass Atlantean key. Are they all drinking the same Kool-Aid?"

This whole key business was starting to worry me. What was so damned important about me being the key? What did that even mean? And how the hell did Zip know about it?

Laughter danced in Inigo's eyes as he pulled me to his side and kissed me. It was a pretty thorough kiss and left me more than a little breathless. "Morgan, you are quite possibly the most stubborn person I know."

Somehow I didn't think he meant that entirely as a compliment.

"Fine." I sighed. "So I'm the key and a freaking Atlantean princess. But why does everyone have to get so bloody worked up about it? Every time I turn around, people go all cryptic on me. It's getting old."

My tirade was interrupted by a shriek from Zip, who was a little ways ahead of us. We both took off toward her at a run.

"What is it?" Inigo asked, his eyes scanning the flat country-side, nostrils flaring. I couldn't see a damn thing that would have made the djinni freak out, but it looked like he sensed something.

"Oh no," Zip whispered in her breathy Marilyn voice. "You have to run." She pointed to a low mound of volcanic rocks in the distance. "There. Fast as you can. It's coming."

"What's coming?" I demanded. I was damn tired of cryptic.

She turned to me, eyes wide with terror. "You have to run," she pleaded. "I can't stop it."

I was about to demand why when Inigo grabbed my arm. His voice was low and tense. "Run, Morgan. It's got our scent."

My feet took off, but my mouth was still running. "What is it?"

"Death worm."

"You have got to be kidding me."

Chapter Sixteen

The ground heaved and rolled under my feet, nearly knocking me on my ass. "Holy shit, what is that thing?"

Inigo yanked me up against him, practically carrying me as he hauled ass toward the low mound of rocks. Zip had disappeared into thin air. Something was definitely coming. Something really big.

We staggered over the increasingly unstable ground and scrambled up onto the rocks. "What is it?" I yelled.

"I told you, Mongolian death worm."

I must have looked as dumbfounded as I felt because Inigo laughed. Laughed! We were about to be attacked by a Mongolian death worm, whatever that was, and he was howling like a lunatic.

"Seriously. You are going to stand there and laugh?" I braced myself against one of the larger boulders as the ground gave a particularly vicious shake.

"Sorry, love." He made an effort to hold back the laughter, but his eyes still twinkled at me.

"Now, what the frakk is a Mongolian death worm, and why is it here instead of Mongolia?"

"It's a really big-ass worm that supposedly spits acid and can zap you like an electric eel. No idea why it's here instead of Mongolia."

I stared at him. "Are you nuts? There's a giant bug zapper out there, and you are *laughing*?"

"I'm a dragon, Morgan. This is *fun*."

"You are insane. That's what you are. You may be resistant to acid, but I am not." Another ground quake sent me tumbling on my ass. "You sure there's only one of those things? How big are they, anyway?"

The ground in front of us erupted in a shower of earth and a scream that nearly shattered my eardrums as the worm burst up from underground. The giant bulbous head of the worm was the size of a small cow and covered in sticky reddish-pink skin. Needlelike teeth jutted from a gaping maw. It was one of the most disgusting creatures I'd ever laid eyes on. And believe me, I've seen some disgusting stuff in my time.

"Um, it's big," Inigo said.

"No shit, Sherlock." The worm was bigger around than I am. No telling how long it was, but there was a good five feet of it sticking out of the ground, shrieking at us like something out of a really bad sci-fi movie. I figured it had to be at least twenty feet in length overall. Maybe more.

The giant head zeroed in on us and let out another scream. A second shriek answered it from the other side of the rock pile where we'd taken refuge. Then a third.

"Holy shit, Inigo. There are three of them."

"Yeah, I heard." His eyes had definitely lost their twinkle. Apparently, three Mongolian death worms weren't nearly as much fun as one.

"So what do we do?" I kept my voice low. I had no idea whether the giant worms could hear me or not, but I wasn't going to test the theory. "If they really do spit acid, we're in big trouble. Or, well, I am anyway." Inigo could transform. His dragon scales are impervious to acid.

"I'd say killing them would be a good start."

I rolled my eyes. "And how are we going to get close enough without getting either spat on or electrocuted?"

"Well…" He thought for a minute. "I don't actually know that they spit acid or electrocute people for a fact. It's just what I've heard."

I glared at him. "I am so not about to run out there in the hopes they don't."

"Well, I was thinking more along the lines of I fly over them and you chop their heads off."

I perked up at that idea. "They could still spit at us—you know, if they spit acid."

"And I can wheel and protect you. Since when has Morgan Bailey, vampire hunter, ever been afraid of a little old earthworm?"

I gave him a glare. "Since little old earthworms were the size of whales."

He pulled me tight against him. "I will protect you, Morgan." His voice was deadly serious. "I promise. I won't let anything happen to you."

I nodded against his chest. "I know."

"Good. Then I fly. You chop. Deal?"

"Deal."

∽

Cold wind slapped my face, causing my eyes to tear and my cheeks to sting. I was freezing my ass off, but I kept my mouth shut and my right hand firmly clasped around the handle of my machete. Thank the gods I'd thought to bring it with me.

Ready? Inigo's voice filled my mind.

I gave him an answering squeeze with my thighs.

With a smooth push of wings, Inigo wheeled in the sky, scales flashing blue and silver and gold in the afternoon sun. As beautiful as he is in human form, he is breathtaking as a dragon.

I lay low over his neck as we headed toward the first worm. The thing swiveled its head toward us as though sensing our approach. This was it. Either the creature was going to spew acid or…not. I was really hoping for not.

Inigo made a sudden jerk to the left, nearly tossing me off his back in the process. I was about to give him holy hell when I saw the spray glistening and sizzling against his scales just inches from my right foot.

Acid. Shit. So the rumors were true. I hoped the acid wasn't hurting him. Dragon scales are impervious to just about anything, but the worm spit looked nasty.

Don't worry. Can't feel it.

I gave him an acknowledging squeeze. I hoped he wasn't being all macho and lying to me.

Another pass. Ready?

I pressed myself against him as flat as I could. It was hard without a harness, but we'd practiced this enough times that I was fairly sure I wouldn't fall off and break my neck.

We wheeled again and came in for another pass, this time from behind the worm. It swiveled again, but not fast enough. With my muscles honed from years of dusting vampires, and boosted by hunter strength, a single hack was enough to separate the worm's head from its soft body.

The head splatted against the ground, spraying worm gunk everywhere. The body kept writhing as though still half-alive.

You ever hear about how you can chop an earthworm in half and it'll grow two heads? Inigo spoke directly to my mind.

Damn, damn, double damn. We couldn't let that happen. The last thing we needed was a whole herd of Mongolian death worms running around Central Oregon. Or crawling and burrowing around, anyway.

An idea struck me. Unfortunately, I couldn't mind-speak to Inigo like he could to me. I tried to yell my idea at him, but with the wind and the other two worms still screeching their heads off, it was obvious he couldn't hear me.

So I did the only thing I could think of. I closed my eyes against the wind and let my mind travel down to that place where the darkness lives. It blinked at me sleepily, like a napping cat, but I ignored it. I needed something else.

The fire came to me in a rush, but I gripped it tight. Tamed it. For once, I was in control. I wondered if it was Inigo's nearness, his natural affinity for fire, or if the fire inside me was just being cooperative for once. I'd like to think it was me gaining strength, but I wasn't that optimistic.

It curled out of me slowly and gently, blooming from the center of my palm and wrapping itself up along my arm. I would have had to be touching the worm's body for me to set the thing on fire, but that wasn't my purpose. Instead, I sent a tendril of fire dancing along Inigo's scales to tickle him under his chin.

Are you nuts, Morgan? This is no time to play.

I did it again, dancing the flame up and down the side of his neck. I knew the flame wouldn't hurt him while he was in dragon form, but he'd feel the warmth. And the tickle.

For gods' sake, Morgan... His voice trailed off. *Oh, fuck me, I'm an idiot.*

This time, when he wheeled, he opened his great dragon mouth and strafed the worm's still-twitching body with fire. The creature was immolated in seconds.

My fire stroked him approvingly before making its way back to my hand and slipping back inside me. It gave me a strange sensation, the fire. Normally, it burns with hunger, longing to feed, to destroy. This time it felt...different. Almost sensual. I wondered at the difference. Something I'd definitely have to explore. You know, sometime when we weren't trying to chop the heads off acid-spitting death worms.

One down. Two to go.

Inigo dived for worm number two. This time, with a bit of fancy flying, he managed to avoid the acid. One hack and its head dashed against the rocks below, spraying slimy chunks of worm. Nasty.

Unfortunately, Inigo's flame hadn't built back up, and I had to actually be touching something to set it on fire, so we'd have to wait to burn the thing. I really hoped they weren't quick regenerators. That would suck.

One more pass to get the last worm. It should have been easy, but just as Inigo wheeled in the sky, a ridiculously strong gust of wind hit me like the smack of a giant hand. I went tumbling off Inigo's back, barely managing to grab his neck.

Morgan!

I tried to climb back up, but my fingers were numb from too much time in the cold air. My arm muscles trembled at the strain of holding on midair while flying. I knew I had seconds, at best.

Oddly, I felt no fear, no panic. I was calm, focused. It wasn't that I wasn't afraid of falling, but that I had no room for fear. My entire being concentrated on that one task: holding on.

Morgan, hang on. I'm landing.

I tried. I really did, but there was no strength left in me. My fingers slipped, and I plunged toward the ground.

Chapter Seventeen

They say that right before you die, your life flashes before your eyes. It's bullshit. Mostly, I was just thinking, *Oh fuck, I'm going to die!*

Everything slowed, smoothed out. I could see the ground rushing toward me, hear the shriek of the last worm, and sense Inigo's panic. This was it. Strange. I'd always thought it would be a vampire that would get me. Again. I wondered what waited for me on the other side. The ground was mere inches away.

A pair of claws snatched me midfall, swooping down on me like a giant bird of prey. Only, the wings weren't those of an eagle, but the brilliant blue of a dragon. My dragon.

My heart tried to pound its way out of my chest. He'd saved me. I wasn't going to die. Not yet anyway.

Suspended in midair with giant talons wrapped around my middle, I couldn't see what was going on. I heard a worm shriek and then the answering scream of a really pissed-off dragon. Hot air brushed against me, and the worm stopped its shrieking. Heh. Mongolian barbecue.

Still, we had the other worm body to deal with, and Inigo was out of fire again. Strange how the mind works. Here, I'd almost died, I was dangling from his claws like a sack of potatoes, and I was worrying about frying a stupid worm.

Inigo set me down gently on the rocks, away from the splattered worm. The beating of his wings stirred up dust and debris as he hovered above me.

I reached out a hand and stroked his leg. "Come on, calm down. I need you."

Surprisingly enough, I meant it. Me, the badass hunter who needed nobody.

He landed beside me, his bulk shifting the rough black rocks slightly. In a shimmer of gold-and-blue sparkles, the dragon disappeared. I didn't even wait for him to regain his balance. I just wrapped my arms around him and buried my face against his neck.

"Thank you," I whispered against his throat.

Inigo hugged me to him, squeezing me almost too tight. "I would never let any harm come to you."

I pressed my lips against his throat. "I know."

I wanted to stay there in that moment, just the two of us, but we still had another worm to burn. And a djinni to find. Again.

"Do you think it's safe to go out there? Could it still be doing its electric thing?" I glanced over Inigo's shoulder at the still-twitching body of the giant worm.

"No idea. Why don't I transform and blast the worm the minute my fire builds up again?"

"Bad idea. Look." I nodded at the worm. Already, the slimy reddish-pink skin was bulging and stretching. The thing was growing a new freaking head.

"Crap."

"No kidding." I closed my eyes and inhaled. "I have to burn it."

"No way. You are not touching that thing." Inigo was adamant. But it was the only way.

"Listen"—I cupped his face in my palms—"I'll be fine, OK?"

"Morgan, I almost lost you." There was pain in his eyes, and it shattered my heart, then put it back together again because I knew how much he cared for me.

I kissed him then, full and deep. My tongue tangled with his as I poured every ounce of emotion I felt for him into that kiss.

I pulled away, both of us a little breathless. OK, more than a little. I gave him a smile and then hopped off the rocks.

"Morgan!"

"My soles are rubber, so stop worrying." I strode toward the twitching, growing worm. Its new head wasn't completely formed, so I was pretty sure it couldn't spit acid at me. I was not sure whether it could electrocute me. But what I couldn't do was let it get away to terrorize the countryside.

As I approached the worm, I called up the fire again. This time there was nothing lazy about it. It sensed what I wanted, and it rushed up out of me, hungry. My body glowed with flame, the warmth of it against my skin almost like a caress. I knew it burned, but I was unscathed.

Still, I hesitated at touching the worm's slimy skin. What if the skin were acidic? Or electrified?

The fire snarled at me. It wanted to be let loose. It wanted to feast.

That was when it happened. The air spiraled out of me in a whirlwind, snatching at the fire and turning it into a vortex of flames. It danced from my hands, independent of me. Within seconds, it had reduced the worm to cinders, along with the vegetation around it.

My hair whipped in the wind, my cheeks ruddy with heat. The fire and the air wanted to play. They wanted to dance across the high desert and eat everything in sight: sagebrush, juniper trees, everything. I'd seen the results of a wildfire in this desert. It wasn't pretty. And I wasn't about to let that happen.

With every ounce of strength I could muster, I used my mind to grab hold of the fire and the air and pull them back to me. They resisted. Of course they did, but I am nothing if not stubborn. I pulled back harder.

They turned back and snarled at me like wild animals. Or something scarier. Then they yanked so hard I felt my physical body stagger forward.

Part of me wanted to go with them. To run wild through the desert with the wind and the fire. But the other part of me instinctually knew that to do that meant losing myself forever.

I guess that thought gave me the boost I needed, because I dug my metaphorical heels in and hauled back on the reins. They jerked and bucked and danced like crazy, but eventually, I won out, either through sheer willpower or pure crazy luck.

Reluctantly, the whirlwind of wind and flame zigzagged across the ground back toward me. I think I heard Inigo call to me, but I was too focused on what I had to do. With one last pull, I yanked the fire and the air into my body. They hit me like a metaphorical freight train, sending me staggering backward. I slammed the lid down on them.

It had been easier this time. Controlling them. But for the first time, I saw why: I was becoming like them. One with them. They were no longer just random powers lurking inside me; they *were* me.

"Oh, gods," I whispered.

For a moment, I stood there, alone in the cold desert wind, my body drained of energy. Then I slowly slid to the ground. My eyes fluttered closed. Darkness swallowed me whole.

∽

I woke to Zip's face looming inches from mine.

"Holy hell." The shock sent my heart racing. Not every day you wake up to Marilyn Monroe six inches from your face.

"My goodness, she has a potty mouth, doesn't she?" Zip sat back primly, her pretty face twisted in a frown. She was still wearing that ridiculous white Marilyn dress. Completely unsuitable for the cold weather.

"I'm a hunter. Ladylike isn't my thing."

She pouted. "Obviously."

"Where's Inigo?"

She fluttered her hand around vaguely. "He's having a chat with the marid."

"The what?" I blinked. My brain felt slow, numb. Had she just said marid?

"He's the most powerful of all the djinn." She propped her chin against her fist. "He's like our king. He's way hot. Totally dreamy. Like Lou Diamond Phillips or something."

"Uh, right. And why has Inigo gone to see him?" I was getting a bad feeling.

"Well..." She seemed to think it over. "We don't really like people in our territory. You know, human people. We discourage it. That's why I had to make your hot friend go away."

She obviously meant Vega. "What do you do to human people who wander into your territory?"

"Well, usually, the winds take care of that. If that doesn't work, a few hallucinations. They get scared to death and leave."

"Is that what happened with Vega, the guy who came here before?"

She nodded. "Oh, he tried to fight through the wind, but the hallucinations got him eventually. He finally gave up, though I got the feeling he planned on coming back." She frowned. "I haven't seen him, though. Too bad."

"Yeah, too bad." I still couldn't figure out what Vega had been doing here, but I was pretty sure it had something to do with his death.

"You"—Zip gave me a pointed look—"are different."

No kidding. "So, what are you going to do to us?"

"Oh, it's not me," she assured me. "I like you. You're pretty. And fun. And you killed those yucky worm things."

"Speaking of those yucky worm things, where did they come from?"

She shivered. I wasn't sure if it was from cold or fear. I was going with fear. "Don't know. They showed up a couple months ago." She leaned in closer and whispered, "I think they were hunting."

"Hunting what?"

She shrugged. "Don't know. You, maybe. Maybe me."

I decided to take another tack. "So, if you don't decide what happens to us, who does?"

"I told you. The marid. That's why Inigo is talking to him."

"Right. Because what would happen if Inigo didn't talk to him?" I prodded.

"Oh, the marid would have killed you outright. But I convinced him to give you a hearing." She beamed at me like she'd just done something supersmart.

"So, the marid isn't going to kill us?"

"Oh, I don't know. Maybe yes. Maybe no. You never know with the marid. He's off coffee at the moment, so he's kind of cranky."

"Oh, for fuck's sake." I struggled to my feet, fighting the woozy feeling that came over me. Whatever had happened in the desert, it had really taken it out of me. "Take me to the marid." There was no way I was going let Inigo face the king of the djinn alone. I knew Inigo could take care of himself, but this was one of the most powerful beings on the planet we were talking about, and he could no doubt snap a half dragon in two.

Zip gaped at me like a fish out of water. "But I can't."

"Why can't you?"

"It's...it's not protocol."

I leaned into her face until our noses were inches away. "Listen to me, you"—I wanted to call her a twit, but that would have been mean—"you djinni. You will take me to Inigo and the marid. Now. Understand?"

"Yes." Her voice was barely a squeak.

I was surprised and somewhat baffled by her capitulation. I honestly hadn't expected my usual intimidation tactics to work on such a powerful being as a djinni. "Good." I smiled. "Let's go."

∽

Zip led me through a series of tunnels that wove their way through the volcanic rock that made up much of the high desert to what she called the Throne Room. I hadn't expected the djinn to live underground, and I had no idea how we'd gotten there. It was possible Inigo had just hauled me through some cave entrance no one knew about. More likely, Zip had led us through a portal of some type.

I don't exactly know what I'd expected from the home of the djinn, but not that. For one thing, there was the whole living on another plane of existence thing, which this definitely was not. For another, they were not creatures of earth, but of air. Not a lot of air underground.

The marid's "Throne Room" was surprisingly ordinary. The room was really a small cavern about the size of my living room back home. There was no throne, per se, just a large campaign desk with a leather swivel chair behind it and two visitor chairs in front. Much like Kabita's office. Or any office, really.

I scanned it quickly for Inigo. He was safe and sound, lounging in one of the comfy chairs with a glass of wine in his hand, looking for all the world like he was shooting the breeze with an old friend.

"Inigo..." I started forward, relief flooding me. And then I saw the marid.

My entire body froze. My feet wouldn't move, as if they were glued to the stone floor beneath me. I opened my mouth, but no sound came out.

The marid was anything but ordinary. He towered over me, close to seven feet tall, muscles rippling everywhere like a WWE wrestler. His skin was red. Pure, rich bloodred. His hair was a green so dark it was nearly black. His face had the breathtaking beauty of a fallen angel.

But that wasn't what had stopped me in my tracks. What had was one thing: the marid was the djinni I'd seen murder Agent Daniel Vega.

Chapter Eighteen

I'll admit—with only a minor amount of embarrassment—that, in that moment, I very nearly wet my pants. The man, the marid, was *huge*. And not only was he the freaking king of the djinn, he was a killer. I had seen him suck the life and soul out of a government agent. I had no idea what to do. Which was an unusual thing for me.

Inigo glanced up from his chair, a look of concern on his face. He must have read my expression, because I could feel that slight push of his mind against mine.

Morgan? Morgan, honey, what's wrong?

I marched across the room and grabbed Inigo's arm. I must have used my hunter strength, because he actually winced. It had been years since I let my extrahuman strength get away from me. Rattled was an understatement.

"We have to get out of here," I hissed.

"Morgan, the marid has asked us to stay—"

"No fucking way!" It came out a lot louder than I'd intended. And a lot ruder. Even Inigo seemed shocked, and he's used to my less-than-stellar manners.

"Morgan," Zip spoke up in her breathy little Marilyn voice, "it's an honor to be asked to dine by the marid."

"Yeah?" I snarled, whirling on her. "And what exactly is he going to dine on, huh? Is he going to eat our souls like he did Daniel Vega's?"

Zip's eyes went wide in horror as she looked from me to the marid and back. Not sure if she was more horrified at my behavior or at what I'd just said. Me and my big freaking mouth. Seriously, you'd think I'd have more control by now. Instead, everything was boiling inside me; the air and the fire and the darkness were raging, and I was this close to losing control.

"Marid, I apologize—" Inigo began, but before he could finish, anger boiled to the surface and my tenuous hold over the powers inside me snapped.

The amulet around my neck flared to life, turning the cavern sapphire blue. I could feel the heat even through layers of clothing, but that wasn't the worst of it.

The air rushed up and spilled out of my chest, hitting the room with gale force. It swirled around, ripping papers from the marid's desk and slamming furniture up against the wall. It whipped delicate knickknacks off the bookshelves, smashing them to dust on the stone floor.

Inigo opened his mouth to yell something, but I couldn't hear over the roaring of the wind. I couldn't even hear him inside my mind. All I could feel was the rage of the air as it fed off my own anger. An anger I couldn't seem to let go or control.

And for once, I wasn't scared of that loss of control. I reveled in it.

Zip cowered under the marid's desk as fire surged up out of me, spilling down my arms and over my body. As usual, it didn't hurt me, but I knew anyone or anything I touched would be immolated on the spot. I tried desperately to rein it in, but my control was gone. Completely shattered. The anger was gone, and along with it, the joy. Now I really was afraid.

My whole body shook with both terror and adrenaline. I wasn't afraid of the marid anymore. I was scared of myself.

Hot tears splashed down my cheeks as I tried desperately to regain control. But it was useless. There was nothing I could do.

The marid finally stepped out from behind his desk and strode toward me. I hadn't thought until that moment I could be any more afraid than I already was. I was wrong.

Blood surged through my veins, panic sending my heart into overdrive. It hammered against my breastbone as if trying to escape.

The air whipped and howled around the room, and the fire surged higher. I was a human flame in the middle of a tornado, and I couldn't stop.

As the marid approached, the darkness hurled its way out of my body and wrapped itself around the djinni's throat as though to strangle the very life out of him. The darkness was responding to my fear, but I had no control. I tried to grab onto its leash, but I couldn't. Sheer terror swamped me. I was going to kill them. All of them. Even my Inigo.

The marid ignored the darkness squeezing the breath out of him and pressed on through the whirlwind. He was inches from me. Close enough to kiss. It was a wonder I didn't just pass out from the fear. My heart pounded so hard I was afraid my ribs would shatter.

And then the king of the djinn placed his palm flat against the center of my chest. Instantly, the wind died down, the flames receded, and the darkness uncurled itself from around his throat. Then, slowly, each of my elements receded back to where they belonged, deep inside of me.

I collapsed. Fortunately, the marid caught me before I hit the floor.

"You need to learn more control, little one." His voice was deep and a little gravelly. Like if Barry White and Alec Baldwin got together and had a vocal baby.

"Normally, my control is just fine," I said, my voice still a little shaky. I clenched my fists against the trembling. It was part adrenaline and part unadulterated freak-out.

A greenish-black eyebrow went up. Why are people always raising their eyebrows at me? "Seriously," I insisted, "I usually have perfect control." Well, almost. Perhaps "perfect" was a slight exaggeration. Although my control was getting better, it was far from perfect. But there was no way I wanted him knowing that.

"I just don't meet a murdering lunatic every day." There was a lot less bravado in my tone than I would have liked.

"I can assure you that I am neither a murderer nor a lunatic. And obviously, your control is far from perfect, if you let the queen's magic overcome you so easily."

I glared at him. "What are you talking about?" Of course. My amulet. It had gone all glowy again. *Shit.*

"Ah, now that is a story to tell." He sat me down in one of the visitor chairs, which Inigo had pulled back to the desk after my little temper tantrum.

Inigo immediately knelt by my side. He ran his hands up and down my arms, my legs, his forehead creased with worry. "Are you all right, Morgan?"

"I'm kind of freaked out," I admitted. Not only had I lost control, but the king of the djinn had taken over my powers like taking candy from a baby. "And pissed. I can't believe he could control me like that. Are you OK?"

"I'm fine. I can hold my own, if I need to."

No kidding. "He's the one," I whispered. "The one I saw kill Vega."

"I know he is."

I blinked. I wasn't sure I'd just heard what I thought I'd heard. "Excuse me?"

"Please, little one, rest. I will tell you all." The marid sat behind his desk and leaned forward, forearms resting against the dark wood.

The incongruity of a giant djinni in his underground lair sitting behind an executive desk as though we were about to have a perfectly normal business meeting almost made me laugh. Almost.

Instead, I scowled at the marid. "Would you stop calling me 'little one'? Do I look little to you?"

Laughter spilled from his throat. "Everyone looks little to me."

Fair point. The man—djinni—was massive. As I leaned back in the rather comfy visitor chair, I noticed a small brass lamp on the side of his desk that had miraculously survived the air's temper tantrum. It looked like something out of the story of Aladdin. A djinni with a lamp. Seriously.

"Fine. I saw you murder Agent Vega." I didn't bother to clarify that it had been while channeling my new superpower. A superpower that had just gone completely haywire in his presence, and which he'd been able to control when I hadn't. That was what really worried me. Besides the fact that the trick card up my sleeve had been rendered useless. With the marid able to completely control my powers, I was as helpless as an ordinary human. Maybe more so. "What's your side of the story?"

"You saw me kill this Vega, yes," the marid said with a nod, leaning back in his seat, "but it was not I who did the killing."

"Sorry, could you run that through the wringer again?"

He smiled a little. "You know we can take different forms."

"Uh, yeah, thanks to Marilyn there." I nodded to Zip, who had moved out from under the desk and was now hovering around the edges of the room, blue eyes wide.

"Zip"—the marid's voice took on a very commanding tone—"please go find refreshment for our guests."

The female djinni did some bobbing and curtsying and made a few squeaking sounds before scrambling out of the room, her little kitten heels clacking against the stone floor. She was seriously adorable. I wondered what her true form looked like. Then again, maybe it was better I didn't know.

"OK, so you can look like Hollywood stars. What does that have to do with anything?"

"We can take on the form of many things," the marid said. "Animals, people, even one another." His eyes bored into mine.

"So, you're saying another djinni took on your form and murdered Vega?"

"Yes."

"Why? And why was Vega even out here to begin with?"

He shook his head. "I have no idea on either count. But as far as the murder is concerned, my guess is that someone forced the djinni to take on my form and murder your agent."

I frowned. "OK. Fine. That would make sense if someone was trying to frame you. But why should I believe you? How do I know that it wasn't you?"

"Because I have not set foot off this land in more than ten thousand years."

That got me. "Sorry, did you say you've lived here in this desert over ten thousand years? I thought the djinn were from the Middle East." Discounting, of course, my bizarre dreams of their planetary origins.

Again, a slight smile quirked his lips. "We are, in a way. But my people were sent here millennia ago."

I frowned. "All the djinn?"

He shook his head. "No. Just my clan."

"Why?"

The muscles in his jaw flexed. Anger. Whatever had happened all those ages ago, he was still really pissed about it. "It is not important."

Inigo reached over as though to warn me, but I squeezed his hand and ignored the warning. I knew I was being rude. I knew I was risking getting my ass handed to me on a silver platter. In that moment, I didn't see I had another choice.

"Oh, I think it is. You say that someone took on your form to murder a federal agent just miles from your land. Land you claim you haven't left since before the pharaohs. Land that that agent recently attempted to gain access to, and you don't think all of this might be somehow related to the reason the djinn are here?"

I didn't mention my dreams. The dreams always mean something even if I can't figure out what. If I was dreaming of the marid and the priest, then it had something to do with all this. I was convinced of it.

For a moment, I thought the marid really would jump across the table and rip me limb from limb. Fury was written on every inch of his face, and frankly, it scared me to death. But giving in to my fear wasn't an option. I had promised Trevor I'd find out who had murdered Vega, and the marid was my only real lead.

But then a calm came over him, as if he were reining in his own beast. "Our banishment was part of a binding. We were all banished to this land, but I alone am bound not to leave it."

"Binding?"

He scowled. "The djinn are very powerful. The marid the most powerful of all. Yet there are a few in this world with the ability to bind our magic to theirs and force us to do their will."

Something clicked inside my mind. Something so bizarre I could hardly credit it. "Why were you bound?"

"I cannot say."

"Excuse me?"

He shrugged, face impassive. "Part of the binding."

"Who bound you?"

"I cannot say."

Crap. I was getting a really bad feeling. I fingered the amulet around my neck. He'd known what it could do. "Atlantis."

I swear, if a being with skin the color of a fire truck can grow pale, the marid did. Yet he said nothing.

"You were bound by the last high priest of Atlantis."

His expression told me I was right. I just had no idea why a priest of Atlantis would bind a marid shortly before destroying the city. It was just…weird.

"OK." I was thinking it through even as I spoke. "So you were bound by the priest and forced to this land ten thousand years ago." I had to phrase this carefully. Pissing off the king would be a bad, bad move, so I kept my words nonconfrontational, my tone sympathetic. "I was told you only appeared here a few hundred years ago. That you came to escape an evil magi from the East."

The marid shrugged. "There was a time my people grew restless and began wandering outside our lands. I called them back, but not before they'd revealed themselves to a small tribe of humans who had taken up residence on this land. Got their shaman all worked up. So I had one of my people allow the shaman to capture him. The story we gave the shaman was simply what you might call damage control."

So Tommy's ancestor hadn't captured the marid, after all. And what Tommy knew of the djinn wasn't entirely accurate. I couldn't say I was terribly surprised.

"What does the fairy queen have to do with all this?"

"I don't know," the marid admitted. He nodded toward my amulet. "I know the amulet is from Atlantis and that it glows in the presence of certain types of magic. Particularly the magic of the queen of the sidhe. Her magic must be involved for it to react as it did earlier."

"You've seen my amulet before?" That was a new one.

This time his smile was genuine, full of fondness and memory. "Yes. I saw it shortly after it was made. Before the binding." His smile faded.

I sensed pain behind his words. Betrayal. Something that had happened back then still caused him pain now. Though I wondered at it, I knew better than to ask. He wouldn't talk, and it probably wasn't important. At least not at the moment.

"All right." I took a different tack. "This djinni that murdered Vega. Do you know who he is?" I was only assuming it was a he. For all I knew, there was no difference between he and she in the djinn world.

"I do."

"I need to speak with him. Please." And then I needed to kick his ass.

"That is not possible," the marid said with a slight shake of his head.

"What do you mean?"

"The djinn have ways of dealing with traitors," Inigo explained gently.

That brought a dark smile to my face. "Let me guess. Swift and final."

The marid nodded the affirmative. Great. Just great. How the hell was I supposed to find out why Vega had been murdered if the guy who did it was dead?

"OK, then, why would another djinni take on your form to kill someone?"

"I have no idea," the marid admitted. "My best guess is the queen is up to something and wants to frame me."

"Why on earth would she do that?" In my experience, the queen of the fairies isn't much interested in anyone but herself and her queendom. And, oh yeah, me, apparently.

"I suppose that would best be answered by knowing what she had to gain by the death of this Vega."

He had a point. But there was something else niggling at my brain. "That's true. But it might also be answered by knowing what she has to gain by *your* death."

A look of pure bafflement crossed his face. "I don't understand. The fairy queen has no sway here. I never leave my land, and no one can come unless I bid them. I would certainly not bid one of the sidhe. And my own people cannot hurt me. It's part of the binding."

The nasty little thought niggled harder. "I'm here."

Inigo and the marid both stared at me. Finally, the marid spoke. "I don't understand."

I leaned forward in my chair. "I am here. On your land. You couldn't stop me." I knew I was skirting a fine line between having some cojones and showing disrespect, but I needed him to know that, while he might be more powerful than I could imagine, I was still a force to be reckoned with.

"I admit, you have...interesting abilities. You seem partially immune to our defenses. Yet I am in no danger."

"That's where you're wrong."

"Excuse me?" The look of surprise on his face was absolutely priceless.

"You see," I said, "if I were to find out you're lying and you had something to do with Agent Vega's murder, there isn't a power on earth that would stop me from ripping your heart out of your chest."

I honestly had no idea if I could do that or not. Probably not.

I stood up and walked slowly to the desk. Then I leaned over right into the marid's face. "You know I can do it, don't you? Not me, but what's inside me." I was totally guessing that the darkness was one thing he couldn't control. His expression told me I was right. I smiled. "Lucky for you, I believe you're being framed." I waited a beat. "So maybe you should ask yourself, why does the fairy queen want you dead?"

Chapter Nineteen

Great way to win friends and influence people, love."

I rewarded him with a scowl. "Well, can I help it if he looked like the murderer? Besides, I want him to know I'm serious. Somebody obviously wants him dead, and I think it has something to do with this binding he keeps going on about. I keep dreaming about it, so it has to mean something." It was a stretch, but it was the only thing that made sense at the moment.

I'd double-checked with Zip before we left the djinn land, and she'd confirmed that the marid hadn't left their borders in over ten thousand years. Despite the fact that she was obviously smitten with her king, not to mention his subject, I was pretty sure she was telling the truth. There was just something so absolutely guileless about Zip.

Then again, millennia-old beings from another world would no doubt be able to lie through their teeth well enough to fool even a hunter. I slid my gaze toward Inigo. But maybe not a dragon. He can sense things I can't.

"What do you think about Zip? Was she telling the truth about the marid?"

He shrugged. "Near as I could tell. This is the first time I've run into the djinn, though, and they're very alien."

Of course, how the marid didn't go completely loony tune locked up on his land all the time, I don't know. But the point was that it was highly unlikely that the vendetta against him had been created in the last ten thousand years. It's not like he was going to dinner parties and pissing off the guests. It had to be about something that happened *before* the djinn arrived in America. Or pre-America, I guess. It was the only thing that made sense to me.

Though, how on earth I was going to find out about that something was beyond me. The marid wasn't talking, and my options for ten-thousand-year-old gossip were pretty limited. Jack is the oldest person I know, and he's only just over nine hundred.

I stopped midthought. There was one other person who might know something. Someone old enough to remember. Maybe.

"What is it?" Inigo glanced over at me.

"The queen might know about this vendetta thing."

"As in the fairy queen?"

"Yeah, that one."

"She might," he said. "Then again, she might be the one behind it."

I sighed. "Hell. Why can't things be easy?"

"If it makes you feel any better, she probably wouldn't talk anyway."

He was right, of course. But it didn't mean I wasn't going to try. But I'd wait until I was on my own to give it a shot. No sense putting anyone else in the line of fire. "I think we need to consult Eddie's book. Maybe have a talk with Jack."

Inigo frowned at the mention of Jack's name. "You sure?"

It wasn't like Inigo to be jealous. Protective, maybe, in his own way, but not jealous. "He's my guardian, remember? And he's connected to this whole Atlantis thing just like I am. I need to know what he knows." If he knew anything.

"It's just that you get so…upset when you talk to him."

I almost laughed at that. Inigo's oh-so-polite way of saying I get bitchy. He wasn't wrong. Jack always manages to get on my last nerve. I would rather not examine why that is.

Once we made it back to the car and onto the highway, I pulled out my cell and dialed Trevor's number. He answered on the second ring.

"Yeah."

"Hey, Trev. How are you feeling?"

A short bark of laughter. "Like I got the shit beat out of me."

"I don't doubt it. When are they letting you out? Do you need a ride?"

"Naw. I've got my rental."

Men. I swear to the gods they can be so thickheaded. "You just had the shit beat out of you, and you think you should be driving?"

"Stop worrying, Morgan. I'm fine. A little sore, but nothing that will affect my driving. Now, what did you find out?"

"Not much. I think we found more questions than answers." I told him about our visit with Tommy Waheneka, followed by our trip to djinn lands. I also had to tell him there would be no justice where Vega's direct killer was concerned. At least, no human justice.

"Damn."

"Yeah," I agreed. "But you'd better believe the marid made sure he paid for what he did." I didn't mention that, in the marid's eyes, the crime was turning traitor on his people, not the murder of Agent Vega. Trevor didn't need to know about that.

"So what does this vendetta against the marid have to do with Vega?" Trevor asked.

"No idea," I admitted. "But I mean to find out. Listen, we're headed back to Portland to do a little research. You staying here?"

"Yeah." His voice held a note of determination. "I'm not leaving until I know the truth."

"OK, I'll keep you posted. Let you know what I find."

If I found anything besides more questions.

"You going to have a talk with your mom?" Inigo glanced at me from the driver's seat.

"Not yet. But I will." Our visit with Tommy had brought up a lot of questions. I wondered more and more just what my mother knew about my father and the SRA.

She'd always insisted my dad had died when I was a baby. I'd believed her. Until I met Trevor. And now Tommy's mention of her having known Alister Jones. It was all just a little too crazy. She had to know something. How could she not?

Over the last few months, I'd come to discover that everything I'd ever believed about our family, about myself, was a lie. I honestly had no idea how I felt about that. Numb, I guess. But what really worried me was how much my mother knew. Had she known all along we were descended from the remnants of ancient Atlantis? Did she know what I am? Was everything, her blissful ignorance, all just an act? And if it was, how would I handle that?

If she'd been lying to me my whole life, I wasn't sure I could forgive her. And as hard as our relationship could be at times, I wasn't ready for that.

I just wasn't sure I could face her right now.

"First let's have a chat with Jack. Then we'll pay Eddie a visit."

I had no doubt things between Jack and Inigo would be awkward. I even thought about asking Inigo to wait in the car, but that would have been even worse. In the end, I kept my mouth shut and decided to grin and bear it. We are all adults, after all.

Jack was just wrapping up a piano lesson as we arrived. I still couldn't get over the fact he taught little kids to play piano. It was just so...normal.

He let us into the house with some reluctance and waved us to the couch. I tried really hard not to think about what had happened the last time I sat on that couch. Inigo didn't need to know about Jack and me and our clothing-optional evening. I managed to redirect us to the chairs opposite.

Jack lounged on the couch, his long fingers steepled together. He didn't speak, but irritation was written in every line of his body.

Inigo reached across the space between chairs to take my hand—a surprisingly possessive display that made me want to smack him. And not in a good way. What were they going to do? Pull out their penises and measure?

Looking at the two men side by side, or at least across the room from each other, I couldn't help but compare them just a little. Jack appears solid on the surface, but underneath, he is wild, untamable. Duty before love and all that bullshit. While Inigo, for all his flamboyance, is the true steady one. The one who always puts me, us, first. And yet both of them attract me in their own way.

A little stab of guilt wiggled its way into my consciousness at the thought. I cleared my throat. "Jack, what do you know about the djinn?"

He gave me a puzzled look. "The creatures from the Middle East? I haven't seen one of those since the Crusades."

For the hundredth time, I wondered about Jack and the lives he'd led over the last nearly millennium. But, unlike Inigo, Jack is a closed book. "No, I mean, do you know anything about their involvement with Atlantis?"

Jack crossed one leg casually over the other, but I could feel the tension simmering beneath the surface. My darkness could feel it too.

"As far as I know, they never had any involvement with Atlantis." His voice was cool, calm, emotionless. His gorgeous ocean-colored eyes flat. I couldn't tell whether he was hiding the truth of the djinn or if he was just hiding from me.

"We spoke to a marid." I nodded to Inigo. "Out in the high desert. He claims to have been bound by the last high priest, but he can't tell us why. You're telling me that when you were hooked up to this thing"—I flashed the amulet—"it never showed you the djinn?"

"No."

I wanted to growl in frustration. Why was he being such an ass? "OK. How about logic?"

Jack's eyebrow went up. "Excuse me?"

I could feel Inigo beside me trying desperately to suppress his laughter. I shot him a glare. "You know more about ancient Atlantis than I do." Hell, he'd lived with the dreams of the place for nine hundred years. "Surely there is some logical explanation as to why the high priest of Atlantis would not only have had a connection to the marid, but would have bound him and his people and sent them to live in the Oregon high desert."

Jack was silent for a moment, a thoughtful expression on his face. "The Atlanteans had dealings with many species for many different reasons. They had real, intimate relationships only with humans, but they sometimes traded goods or exchanged knowledge with other peoples."

I could have guessed that for myself. "But you don't know why they would be involved with the djinn specifically?"

"No."

His lack of detail was giving me the fits. "OK, fine. What about the binding? Why would the priest have bound the marid?"

"No idea." Jack shrugged. "I would have said the priest wanted something from him, but since the binding obviously survived the priest's death, it must be more than that. A task, perhaps, that he wanted carried out."

A thought flashed through my mind. I could think of two reasons why a person would use magic so strong it would bind someone to a single place centuries beyond your own death. Either the person was your enemy and you didn't want him to escape, which was not the case, according to my dreams. Or you needed that person to protect something and you wanted to make sure they didn't shirk their duty. That totally matched the conversation I'd dreamed about between the priest and the marid.

Holy shit, that was it. I had no idea what the marid was protecting or why, but it made perfect, beautiful sense.

The queen of the sidhe might know more, but first I'd check Eddie's book. Maybe it would reveal enough that I wouldn't have to contact her. I really didn't want to end up owing the queen another favor. If I could even get in touch with her in the first place.

"Right, thanks for your help." I stood up quickly, trying to keep the reek of sarcasm out of my voice with little success.

Jack's expression softened for a fraction of a moment before his face returned to its usual stoic expression. "Anytime."

I had a flash then of all the good times we'd had together. The heat between us and the gentleness. And more, the dreams of the future we could have had together. Longing and regret mixed with hurt and anger. My heart beat a little fast, and I could feel my cheeks flush.

I glanced over at Inigo. Had he picked up on my emotions? Oh, gods, I hoped not. But he with his superior hearing and his sort of psychic connection to me, how could he not?

I straightened my shoulders and pushed thoughts of Jack and our past firmly out of my mind. "We'd better get going. Thanks again."

Inigo politely shook Jack's hand. Points to him for not getting all jealous and insecure. Double points for his not giving me the third degree when we got in the car, because I wouldn't have blamed him if he had.

This time I drove. I needed the release that control gives me. I cracked the window and cranked the tunes. The freezing February air slapped me in the face, and the blast of eighties rock music assaulted my ears. I felt better already.

Inigo just leaned back in his seat without a word. I had no idea what he was thinking or feeling. I opened my mouth, but I didn't know what to say. So I didn't say anything at all.

∽

Eddie was still at his shop when we arrived. He glanced up at the jangle of the bell over the door, his cherubic face creasing in a huge smile. "Morgan! Inigo! Come in, come in. I was just getting ready to lock up. Flip the sign. We'll have tea." He glanced at me. "Or coffee."

I laughed and turned the Closed sign across the door before sliding the bolt home. Eddie knew me well.

While Inigo and I made ourselves at home around the big checkout counter, Eddie bustled around the little kitchenette in the back making drinks and piling cookies on a plate. He even had real cream for my coffee. Sometimes I could just kiss that man.

"Now"—he settled onto his stool at the counter and took a sip of his herbal tea—"to what do I owe the pleasure?"

"We need your help." I took a sip of my own drink, nearly scalding my tongue in the process. Strong and hot, creamy and sweet, just how I liked it.

Eddie's eyes twinkled. "Now, there's a surprise. Could you be a little more specific?"

"Yeah." I gazed at him over the top of my mug. "We've got a djinn problem."

Chapter Twenty

Eddie sputtered a little. Mostly with laughter. "You have such a way with words, Morgan."

I flashed a grin. "I do my best."

Inigo and I gave him a quick rundown while we munched on chocolate chip cookies. They were homemade. And had walnuts. Excellent.

Eddie gazed thoughtfully into his teacup. "Well now, that really is a doozy. A marid bound by an Atlantean priest."

"And not just any Atlantean priest," I pointed out. "The last high priest. The one who destroyed the city and hid the Heart of Atlantis." I fingered the amulet around my neck.

"Not just any binding either. The thing's lasted ten millennia," Inigo reminded us.

"What really gets me is that someone had to bind another djinni to kill Vega. Not only that, he must have forced the djinni to take on the marid's form. There aren't many creatures with enough magic to bind the djinn." In fact, as Tommy Waheneka had pointed out to us, there is only one: the fairy queen.

"Well"—Eddie pushed back from the counter—"I'd say it's time for the book."

I'd been expecting it. Eddie and his creepy sentient book. I could only hope it would cooperate. It sort of has a mind of its own.

There was the usual flurry of pages before the book stopped its flipping. The page it landed on was decorated along the edges in swirls of blue and silver. In the middle of the left page was a detailed painting of two men. I recognized both. One was the marid. The other the last high priest of Atlantis.

On the right was scrawled a flourish of words in black ink. I couldn't even begin to read it. "Is that English?" It sure didn't look like it.

"Norman French, actually," Inigo said, peering at the page.

"That's odd." Eddie adjusted his glasses and leaned closer to the page. "I wonder why Norman French? Why not Old English? Or maybe Sanskrit? Or better yet, ancient Atlantean?"

"Can you read it?" I supposed another bonus of having a four-hundred-year-old boyfriend is his ability to read really old languages.

"Yeah, though it's been a while. Let's see." He adjusted his glasses on the bridge of his nose while he and Eddie stared at the page. "It tells of the binding."

"Yeah?" I prompted.

"There's not much here. The marid and the high priest of Atlantis were friends for many years. Shortly before the destruction of the city, the high priest betrayed the marid and his people by binding them." Inigo glanced up from the book. "That's it."

"That's it?" My voice was practically a screech. So not attractive.

"That's it. Nothing to indicate what the binding was about or why it was done."

Shit. Fat lot of good that did us. "Well, what about whoever bound the djinni that murdered Vega? The book got anything to say on that?"

More flipping pages. This time they landed on a blank page. The book was giving us nothing.

"What next?" Inigo asked.

Good question. "Eddie, do you have anything at all on the sidhe? You know, more than the fairy-tale stuff you've got on the shelves."

Eddie pulled thoughtfully at his lower lip. "Maybe in the attic. There are boxes of things I haven't sorted through yet. A few of them were from the estate sale of a local sorcerer."

"Sounds like a good place to start. Lead on."

A "few boxes" turned out to be six stacks, floor to ceiling, filled to the brim with books, papers, drawings, and notes on random bits of paper. Most of them in languages I'd never even heard of. We all dived in, shuffling through the dusty pages.

A dozen boxes in and we were tired, sweaty, and covered in grime. And we still had a big fat nothing.

Frustrated, I sat back on my heels, my amulet swinging slightly against my breastbone. That gave me an idea.

I pulled the amulet out of my shirt and wrapped my hand around it. If the amulet glows when sidhe magic is near, maybe it could lead me to what I needed. I closed my eyes, took a deep breath, and focused my thoughts on the sidhe.

At first, nothing happened. Then the amulet began to slowly turn warm. I reached out toward one of the boxes, and it turned cold again. So I moved to another box. Still cold. A third and it warmed again. I continued until I found a box that turned my amulet white-hot.

This was it. "Guys, over here. I've found something."

Among the papers was an illustration—like one from the medieval illuminated Christian Bibles—of a man so beautiful and ethereal he looked like an angel, but his dark, soulless eyes were anything but angelic. I gaped at the image. "What is he?"

Eddie took off his glasses, polished them, and popped them back on. His expression was grim as he scanned the accompanying documents. "That is Alberich."

"Alberich?"

"Alberich was quite possibly one of the most evil creatures to ever have walked the earth. He was the twin brother of the queen of the fairies and the only one besides the queen powerful enough to bind a djinni. In fact, rumor has it he was actually much more powerful than the queen, thanks to his obsession with the demonic realms."

"What do you mean by *was* her brother?" I asked.

"Alberich is supposed to be dead. According to the legends, the queen executed him generations ago." Eddie frowned. "Unfortunately, according to the book, he's still very much alive."

Inigo and I both glanced at each other. I didn't need his telepathy to tell me what he was thinking. His expression mirrored mine. If Alberich was still alive, we were in deep, deep shit.

∽

"You still got that key?" Inigo's voice cut through my thoughts as we stood outside Eddie's shop.

"Key?"

He gave me a look. "The key from the queen of the fairies, Morgan."

Shit. Yeah, that key. "Yeah, I've got it." I'd been carrying the stupid thing around in my pocket with me. After all, she'd said it would save my life. Had she somehow known about Alberich? That he was targeting me? But why would she even care? I am just a lowly human, and the queen doesn't bother herself much with our kind. In any case, I really hoped I'd never have to find out.

"Good. I have a feeling we might need it." His voice was as grim as his expression.

I stared out into the darkness before slowly making my way to the car. "I don't like this, Inigo. This is not what I signed on for. I'm a hunter, not a…" I waved my hands in the air, searching for a word. Nothing came to me. There was no one in my world who had ever gone up against the sidhe. No one.

"Hey." He grabbed me and hauled me up against him. "Look at me, Morgan."

I gazed up into his eyes. The beautiful blue was swirling with gold, meaning his dragon was close to the surface. "You can do this. *We* can do this."

"You shouldn't have to," I told him. "This isn't your problem."

He shrugged. "I don't really care about what I should and shouldn't have to do. I care about you, and you are involved whether you like it or not. That means I'm involved too. You aren't in this alone."

I sighed and gave him a slightly wobbly smile. "That's probably the most romantic thing anyone has ever said to me."

He flashed me a grin, then pressed his lips to mine. I opened my mouth and welcomed him in, our tongues tangling with our breaths. I wrapped my arms around his neck, pulling myself tight against him as his hands found their way under my shirt, his fingers slipping beneath the edge of my bra.

"Inigo, we're in public." I admit my protest was more than a little weak.

His chuckle was low and sexy and turned my knees to jelly. "It's the middle of the night, and we're in Eddie's parking lot." His lips moved from my mouth to my ear and then down the side of my neck, each nibble sending a shimmer of desire coursing through my veins.

"People can see us." I'm not a prude, exactly. I just prefer to keep bedroom things...well, not in the middle of a parking lot.

He was nibbling along my collarbone. I wasn't exactly sure when he'd managed to open my coat and my shirt. He started walking backward, hauling me with him, his mouth never deviating from its southern trajectory. We ended up in an alley down the side of the building, deep in the shadows.

"Now they can't," he said right before he slid my bra strap off my shoulder and took my nipple in his mouth.

I forgot all about who might or might not have been watching as pleasure pooled low in my belly. I tangled my fingers through his silky hair, urging him to continue. I didn't even notice the cold.

His fingers popped the buttons on my jeans and then slid under the rough fabric until they found my sweet spot. I made a little whimpering sound. "Inigo."

"That's right, baby. I've got you." He pulled down my jeans and panties, baring me to the night. I should have been cold, but I wasn't. Dragon heat.

Next thing I knew, his mouth was on me, his clever tongue working its magic until I couldn't think, couldn't speak. Could do nothing but drown in the pleasure of his touch.

I was just about to slip over the edge when he stopped. "Inigo?"

"Shhh." I heard the rasp of his zipper. Then he lifted me as though I weighed no more than a feather. "Wrap your legs around me, Morgan."

I did as he'd asked, and then, oh, sweet mercy, he slid into me. I clung to him as the first climax hit. Then he moved. With each hard thrust, the pleasure wound tighter and tighter until this time I did slip over the edge, taking Inigo with me.

∽

I stood in the middle of a room. I assumed it was a room. Fog swirled around me so thick I could make out nothing of my surroundings.

"Hello?" My voice echoed weirdly in the fog.

No one answered.

Hands caressed my body as if they knew me. Intimately.

I realized I was naked and the hands were touching places they shouldn't have been touching. I tried to grab them, stop them, but I couldn't see anything. I could only feel.

Lips pressed against my throat, tiny kisses against delicate skin. I shuddered in pleasure and fear. I wanted more, and I felt guilty for wanting it.

"Who are you?"

Still no answer. Just the phantom caresses of my ghost lover.

I felt myself grow wet and languid with desire as lips and fingers stroked me to a fever pitch. Then I felt that long, intimate slide of thick, hard flesh inside me. The stroke of male inside female.

The dreaming me felt guilty, but the me in the dream was having none of it. The dream me wanted this. I rocked against my invisible lover, taking him deeper, begging for more. I could feel his skin, slick with sweat, against my palms, the muscles moving and shifting underneath. But still, I could not see him.

I lost myself to the pleasure of his touch, the thrust of him inside me. And as the first orgasm took me, he whispered in my ear.

"I will never leave you. I am always watching over you." The voice was low and gravelly and, oh, so familiar. As was the taste of his kiss.

"Jack?"

∽

I woke up in bed with Inigo sprawled out half on top of me.

Guilt suddenly stabbed through me. Granted, it had only been a dream, but it had felt so real. And worst of all, I'd enjoyed it. Thoroughly.

I stared blearily at the bedside clock. *Crap.* It was already ten in the morning, and I'd managed a whole four hours' sleep. The problem with having a dragon for a boyfriend is they've got way too much stamina.

OK, so it isn't a problem, exactly. Though it does make for some rather zoned-out mornings.

I glanced over at Inigo, who was snoring lightly, then slipped out of bed and staggered into the bathroom. My body was still slick with desire from the dream. I closed my eyes against the spray of the shower.

What the hell was wrong with me? How could I be having sex with my current boyfriend one minute, then dreaming about having sex with my old boyfriend the next? And not just any sort of dream, but a vision so real it felt like we'd actually been…doing it.

Obviously, I had issues. I needed to call Cordy.

And that was just for starters. Gods, there wasn't enough coffee in the world to wake me up for what I had to face: my mother.

And, oh yeah, the freaking fairy queen. But mostly my mother.

It wasn't that I had to so much as I needed to. With all this stuff coming up about my father and the revelations about his past, I had to find out what my mother knew, if she knew anything at all, in case it was all connected. It was time to open that closet and let the skeletons run free.

Don't get me wrong, I love my mother, but she is a challenge to deal with even on the best day. Ever since I'd discovered our Atlantean heritage, I'd assumed she didn't know. So I kept quiet about it. And about my powers. I know what it's like having your entire worldview turned on its head, and it isn't something I wanted my mother to have to deal with. No doubt she'd have thought I was crazy and insisted I call her therapist. But now, with the revelation that she had known Alister Jones, I didn't have a choice. If she'd been lying to me my whole life…

Well, I didn't know how I felt about that. I was still in a bit of shock over the whole thing. But whether she'd been hiding things from me or not, bringing up my father was going to result in just about the furthest day from the best you could possibly imagine. My mother doesn't talk about him, period. I am lucky I even have a picture.

But I needed answers about Alister Jones, and according to Tommy Waheneka, my mother had them. As I stood under the hot spray of the shower, my mind whirred through my approach. How could I confront her without causing World War III?

I finally gave up and got out of the shower. There is just no two ways about it. Drama happens.

Inigo was still snoring away facedown across the bed. He'd tossed off half the duvet, revealing a tantalizing length of thigh and a glimpse of shimmering scales across his hip.

Guilt reared its ugly head. One minute I'd been having hot mind sex with Jack and the next I was drooling over my boyfriend. But it wasn't my fault. It had only been a dream, after all. You can't control your dreams.

"You gonna stand there staring? Or are you gonna come have your way with me?"

I laughed, trying to shove aside the guilt. "I had my way with you, what, four times last night?"

One eye peered at me through tangled golden hair. "Wrong. I had my way with *you* four times last night."

I smirked at that. "Oh, no. That's where you've got it wrong, babe. I distinctly remember time two being all me."

"Oh, yes." He sighed with a self-satisfied smile and a lazy stretch. "That was a particularly good one." He gave me an innocent look. "Still, I could use a refresher course."

"I give you a refresher course and I won't be able to walk for a week. Now, come on." I tossed his jeans at his head. "Get your sweet ass out of bed, lazy boy. Time to brave the lioness's den."

"I like your mother," he said, ignoring the jeans. "She brings out the bossy in you."

I quirked a brow. Well, both brows, since I'm incapable of quirking only one. "I'm always bossy."

"Oh, I know. But you get extra bossy." He grinned.

I rolled my eyes. I needed to get out of there, away from the horrible feelings that I'd done something wrong, even if it hadn't been my fault. "You are a lunatic. And I need coffee."

His laughter followed me to the kitchen.

While Inigo was showering, I gave Cordelia a quick call. "Cordy, I need your help."

"Oh dear." Her voice was a little breathy. "That was some dream you had last night."

"What?" I very nearly shrieked. "You can see my dreams?"

I could hear laughter over the line. "Not exactly. More the emotions that come with the dreams."

Just fabulous. "OK, so tell me. Why am I dreaming about... doing *that* with Jack? I'm in love with Inigo, for crying out loud." And what if he'd picked up on those dream emotions? He is, after all, a mind reader. Sort of. Gods, I couldn't imagine what he'd be feeling if he knew about my dreams.

She sighed. "You know very well that you have many unresolved issues with Jack. You are still attracted to him, and there's nothing wrong with that." She muttered something along the lines of "damn puritanical morons" or something.

"Cordy?"

"Listen, Morgan, you are going to have to figure this one out on your own. I told you, your love life is hazy. Nothing is set in stone. Only you can decide what you want. What you need."

"I want Inigo."

"Of course you do. But that doesn't mean you don't want Jack too."

"Oh, gods, I'm fucked up."

"My darling girl." She sounded amused. "You know very well that I don't view life as most of our 'morally upright' citizens do." If her tone was anything to go by, she doesn't hold morally upright citizens in very high regard. "I believe that love is far too big a concept for most people's tiny little brains to handle."

"Um, what?"

"Stop worrying about things you can't control. When the time is right, you'll know what to do." And with that cryptic and entirely unhelpful bit of wisdom ringing in my ears, Cordelia hung up.

∽

"Morgan. Two times in one week. What a surprise." Her words were innocent enough, but my mother's tone was layered in snarky. I come by it honestly. She just has this way of making me feel guilty for pretty much everything: being single, not visiting enough, visiting too much. No matter how hard I try, I just can't do anything right in her eyes. So I pretty much gave up trying.

"Come in." She waved us through the door. "I was just making a cup of coffee. How about some? I've got croissants."

My mother knows I can't resist croissants. Inigo and I followed her into the kitchen. My mother also adores Inigo, and I was hoping his presence would keep her from ripping into me too much. Yeah, I'm a wuss. I'm not proud of it.

I know I make my mother sound like a monster. She isn't. She just has a very particular way that she needs things to be. When things aren't just so, she tends to get a little...snippy. And I've never been good at dealing with it. Especially since I'm usually the cause of her snippiness.

"What on earth are you wearing?"

I paused in the middle of hanging up my coat to glance down. It was my usual outfit of jeans, boots, and a simple long-sleeve T-shirt. Black with a Shakespeare quote in bloodred lettering. "What? It's my day off."

I couldn't very well tell her it was standard hunting gear. She gave the sigh of mothers everywhere who despair of their daughters' fashion choices and practically stomped into the kitchen.

"Listen, Mom, I need to ask you something," I said while she poured out cups of coffee and handed the croissants around.

"About?"

"Do you happen to know some guy called Tommy Waheneka?" I kept my tone casual, as if it were no big deal.

She frowned as she mulled it over. "No. It doesn't ring any bells. Why?"

"He's a shaman over at Warm Springs. He says he knew Dad."

If I didn't know her as well as I do, I might not have noticed the subtle shift in her expression, the tension that suddenly gripped her body. It was the reaction she always has when someone brings up my father and why I'd stopped asking about him years ago. "Oh?" Her voice was light, deliberately uninterested, but I could tell she was focused on every word.

"Mom, he seemed to think there was more to Dad's death than I thought. What really happened?"

She adjusted the pearls around her neck, a sure sign she was nervous, before taking a careful sip of coffee. There was a look of guilt on her face. "I don't know what you mean."

I knew then and there she was hiding something from me. Something about my father. I leaned forward, elbows on the kitchen table. She didn't even comment on my bad table manners. Another sign she was hiding something. "Mom, Tommy told me Dad didn't die when I was a baby."

She swallowed and toyed with her pearls some more. I tried to catch her eye, but she wouldn't look at me. There was no surprise in her voice. No reaction in her face.

"It's true, isn't it?"

"Morgan, we don't talk about your father."

I knew for sure then that she'd known the truth about my father's death all along. How much she knew of the rest of it was the question. I glanced up at Inigo, who gave me a brief nod before slipping out of the room. Mom would never talk about such intimate family things in front of someone else. Not even him.

"Mom." I kept my voice gentle. "It's time to stop the..." I started to say "lies," but I stopped myself. "It's time to tell me the truth. What really happened to Dad?"

She was silent for so long I thought she wouldn't answer. "He left me," she finally spoke, her voice so small and sad. Ashamed. Not like my mother at all. "He left us. I knew that story about him dying in a car accident was a lie." Her hands trembled as she picked up her coffee cup. "He just couldn't handle being a father. Or maybe..." Her voice trailed off.

Suddenly, I felt like shit. I knew exactly what my mother was thinking. That he hadn't loved her enough. That she hadn't been enough for him. She was the love of his life, and she didn't even know it.

"Mom." I reached out and grabbed her hands in mine. "Mom, that's not true."

"Yes, Morgan. Yes, it is. He didn't love us enough to stay."

This was going to be awful. "Did you know he had another family?"

She blinked at me, and I could see the tears she was struggling to hold back. After all this time, even believing what she did about him, she still loved my father. "What?" Her voice was a mere whisper.

"When he met you, he was already married. He had a son. He never told you?" Gods, I couldn't believe I was telling her this stuff. It must have been breaking her heart. As if it hadn't been battered enough already.

She shook her head, shock written clearly across her face. I hesitated, reminding myself to tread carefully.

"I met him, Mom, Dad's son. My half brother. His name is Trevor. He told me why Dad left."

My mother just stared at me. I had no idea what was going through her mind, so I pushed on. "Trevor told me that you were the love of Dad's life. That he was going to leave Trevor's mother for you." I still couldn't read the expression on my mother's face. "He didn't want to leave us, but...well, some bad people were after him, and he was afraid if they found you, they'd hurt you to get to him. That was why he faked his death. You didn't know any of this?"

My mother seemed to shrink into her chair. "No."

"That's the real reason he left. But Trevor said Dad never stopped loving you. Before he died, he made Trevor promise to look out for us." A small lie, but a necessary one. Our father had only made Trevor promise to look after me.

A tear rolled down my mother's cheek. I felt as though my heart would break, so I got up from the table and gathered her into my arms. I'd never realized before how tiny and fragile she is. I must have gotten my build from my father, because I am anything but delicate. "Mom, please don't cry." I stroked her back like one might stroke a child's. "You didn't know about any of this?" It was becoming increasingly clear my mother hadn't known much of anything. She certainly hadn't known about my father's true career or our genetic heritage.

She shook her head against my shoulder. "He was a traveling salesman. He never did anything wrong. Why would anyone want to hurt him?"

"I don't know, Mom. But I'm going to find out."

She leaned back, her face completely serious. "I swear, Morgan, I knew none of this. I thought he'd left us, and I couldn't bear for you to know that. So"—she shrugged—"I told you he died. Just like Alister told me."

So Tommy Waheneka had been telling the truth. "Alister, Mom?"

"Yes, dear. Alister Jones. Your father's best friend."

Chapter Twenty-One

I stared at her as shock coursed through my veins. Tommy had said my father had known Alister Jones. He hadn't mentioned they were best friends. My mind was whirling like crazy trying to make sense of it all. How on earth had my mother known the former head of MI8? My best friend's father? I knew my own father had met Alister. I had a picture of the two of them together. "What do you mean, Mom? How did Dad know Alister Jones?"

"They worked together, dear." She got up from the table and started clearing away the now empty coffee cups, for all the world as if we were at an ordinary tea party. "They were both salesmen for the same company selling machine parts." She paused, her expression tightening ever so slightly. "Or at least that's what they told me."

"And you actually met Alister?"

She gave me a funny look. "Yes. He came to dinner a few times. Why?"

"Did he…" I hesitated. "Did he know you were pregnant with me?"

"Of course," she said as she put the last mug in the dishwasher. "I told you, he's the one who told me your dad died in that accident. I didn't believe him, of course." She shrugged. "It was obvious he was lying about the accident. I figured your father ran out on us and he was just covering up for his friend by making up the accident story. Alister never liked me much."

I frowned. "What an ass."

"Morgan! Language."

I repressed a grin. Now, there was the mother I know and love. "Why didn't Alister like you?"

"I had no idea at the time, but maybe he was friends with the other wife." Her expression made it clear the very thought of my father's other family was unbearable. I couldn't say I blamed her. Everything he'd told her had been a lie. He'd done it to protect us, but she didn't know that. And I couldn't tell her if I wanted to keep her safe.

Knowing the truth had gotten me nothing but a heap of trouble. But I am a hunter. Trouble is practically my middle name. My mother, on the other hand, is the twenty-first century's answer to Donna Reed. "My guess is he wanted me out of Alex's life, and Alex freaking out over the baby was a good way to get it done. I wouldn't put it past Alister to have come up with the whole story and then convinced Alex to go along with it, just so he could get away from us."

"Except," I said softly, "he didn't freak out. He wanted me. He wanted *us*."

Mom shook her head, her expression stubborn. "If that were true, he would have stayed."

I bit my lip, debating how much to tell her. "Maybe he couldn't. Remember, there were people after him. He didn't want them hurting us."

"Morgan, I've made my peace with the past. Please let it lie." Her voice was firm. Final.

Though it was clear she'd never fallen for Alister's car accident story, it was also clear she wanted to believe that my father had left us high and dry. It was almost as if she found that more comforting than the truth: that Alexander Morgan hadn't had a choice.

I heaved a small sigh. "OK, Mom." I squeezed her hand.

There are some wounds that never heal.

∽

Outside, I drew in a lungful of ice-cold air, closing my eyes against the harsh winter sunlight. "That sucked."

"Yeah." Inigo wrapped an arm around me and pulled me up against him. "You handled it well." There was a note of pride in his voice.

I opened my eyes and stared up at him. "What do you mean?"

"You know your mother winds you up. You knew this day was always going to be tough. Yet you handled it, and her, with calm and sensitivity. Even when she wasn't being...rational."

I had to admit he had a point. I am never good with my mother. She has the most amazing way of getting under my skin. Much as I love her, she drives me nuts. But today I'd felt less like I was someone she was fighting or trying to control and more like...her daughter.

"I just don't understand why my dad would be friends with Alister Jones. The man is a psychopath."

"Maybe he wasn't always. I mean, your mom said he and your dad worked together," Inigo pointed out. "Maybe Alister was one of the good guys back then. Or maybe your dad just didn't realize what kind of person he was."

I frowned. "Trevor didn't know Alister Jones other than as an MI8 agent. Surely, if he and my dad had worked together at the SRA, Trevor would have known about it."

"Not necessarily. The SRA was in its infancy back then," Inigo said. "It's possible that MI8 was helping out by sending their agents here to train Americans. A lot of things that went on back then weren't exactly documented."

Before I could say anything else, a familiar heat burned my chest. I yanked the amulet out from under my clothes. "It's doing it again. The damn thing is burning hot."

The sapphire was glowing like a beacon. If it had been night, I'd have looked like a Blue Light Special. Fortunately, it was broad daylight on a residential side street, so no one noticed.

"There's sidhe magic nearby." Inigo kept his voice low.

I scanned the street, but I couldn't see anything that looked like one of the fae. "Where is that thing? Why doesn't it show itself?"

Inigo tugged me to the car, a look of strain crossing his face. "Come on, Morgan, we need to go."

"Inigo—"

"Now, Morgan. We need to go now."

I nodded, letting him drag me to the car as I tucked the amulet carefully under my clothes. "You sense something?"

"Nothing good. We need to get in the car."

Before he could reach for the door handle, a blast of bluish light hit him, and he crumpled to the ground. He lay there next to the car, eyes closed, unmoving. His skin was deathly pale. I wasn't even sure he was breathing.

"Shit! Inigo..." I knelt beside him, trying to feel for a pulse. Relief flooded my system. Inigo's pulse was strong, which was a good sign. Whatever had hit him had knocked him out, nothing more.

My eyes searched the street for any sign of his attacker as I hovered over Inigo, trying to protect him from any further attack. I couldn't see anything. There was no one around. I couldn't sense anything either, which wasn't a total surprise. My Spidey senses only work on vamps, and vamps wouldn't be out in broad daylight unless they had a death wish.

There was no one visible on the street, and I didn't know what else to do, so I pulled out my cell to call Kabita for backup. But before I could hit the call button, something grabbed me by the hair and yanked me away from the car.

Pure instinct took over, and I snapped my head back, my skull connecting with what felt like a nose, then followed that up with a swift backward kick to the shin. I couldn't see him, but my attacker let out a string of cuss words. He was male, and he was pissed as hell.

Unfortunately, he didn't let go. Instead, he shook me hard by where he had hold of my hair. The sting across my scalp sent tears welling in my eyes as I tried to pry his fingers out of my hair.

I was pissed as hell also. I didn't know who the hell he was, but how dare he knock out my boyfriend and try to choke me to death?

I was a little scared as well. Because, whoever he was, he was strong. Really strong.

Without warning, he picked me up off the ground and flung me. I flew across the sidewalk and crashed into the cyclone fence around my mother's front yard, hitting the ground with a very audible thud. I glanced around, but I still couldn't see my attacker anywhere.

"What the fuck?" I whispered to no one in particular.

I winced as I staggered to my feet. My ribs were definitely bruised, if not broken. Shit. The amulet was glowing like crazy. I could feel the heat clear through my heavy winter coat.

What if my mother heard and came out to investigate? Shit, that was all I needed. I checked the house, but everything remained quiet. I could only hope she was distracted by something else.

I started back to Inigo—I had to protect him, and without a visible foe, there was no one I could fight. But before I could take more than a couple of steps, something grabbed me again, a large hand wrapping around my throat. This time I grabbed back. My hand closed around what felt like a forearm. Human. Or human-like. Good. I wrapped my legs around the invisible thing's waist so it couldn't throw me and threw a solid punch right into its jaw. The thing let out a grunt and gave me a good shake.

There was only one creature it could be, though I'd never heard of the sidhe going invisible. Then again, there was a lot we didn't know about the sidhe. "Listen, you freaking fairy," I snarled at my unseen foe. "You do not know who you are messing with." It was total bravado. I was seriously starting to doubt my ability to kick his ass, but sometimes bluffing is a really good defense. I learned that watching Perry Mason.

"Oh, I know exactly who I'm dealing with, Hunter." The voice was surprisingly musical. Lilting and bright. The sound wrapped its way around my senses, threatening to pull me under its spell and send me off to la-la land as my attacker tightened his grip around my throat.

"Ain't...going to work, fairy boy," I snapped, my voice coming out a little strangled as I struggled against his hold. "As you say, I'm...a hunter. Your tricks don't work with me," I lied through my teeth. I have no immunity to sidhe magic. Hopefully he didn't know that. I decided it was time to play my trump card. "If you hurt me, you'll answer to the fairy queen."

My words certainly had an effect, though I wasn't sure it was the effect I was looking for. Without warning, the sidhe snapped into visibility. His face shifted incarnations so fast it made me dizzy.

"I do not give one fuck what the so-called queen has to say," he snarled. His fingers around my throated tightened even more until dark spots danced in front of my eyes. He leaned his face close to mine, breath hot against my cheek. Like all the sidhe I'd encountered recently, he smelled of cloves and peppermint. "If she loves you so much," he taunted, "maybe she should save you."

I could feel my consciousness slipping from me. Struggling against the sidhe's powerful grip was useless. Even my extra hunter strength was no match for him. And with my energy slipping away, so too was my ability to control my other, stranger powers. They should have been raging out of control. I reached for them, but instead of them waiting, it was almost as if there were a door up between me and them. A door that wouldn't let me through.

"It's no use, Hunter." Alberich laughed. "Don't even bother."

In panic, I bucked under him, trying desperately to shake him loose. But without access to my powers, I was completely at his mercy, and looking into the eyes of a madman, I didn't see a whole lot of mercy.

As I struggled for breath, something clicked inside my mind. I didn't know how he'd cut me off from my powers, but it left me only one option.

This will save your life.

The key. The queen of the sidhe had given me a key. A key she'd said would save my life.

And what else was a key for but opening doors?

I had no idea what was going to happen if I used the queen's gift, but I couldn't see another way. Dark spots danced in front of my eyes. I was out of time. I slipped my free hand into my pocket, reaching for the little key.

"But she isn't going to save you, is she?" Alberich taunted. "Because she doesn't give a damn. She only cares for herself and her throne." He pressed his face close to mine. "So first I'm going to kill you, and then I'm going to finish what I started with your boyfriend."

His facial incarnations stilled long enough for me to make out a leer. "And I'm going to take my time." He nodded to where Inigo still lay crumpled on the ground. "Oh, yes, I'm going to take it nice and slow with that one. Until he begs for me to kill him."

Shit, Inigo. The only chance either of us had was for me to get free and kick Alberich's ass.

My fingers finally touched the small gold key. I had no idea how it worked. So I did the only thing my fading brain could think to do. I whispered a name inside my mind—a name no mortal should know. A name that suddenly appeared in my mind as though someone had placed it there. *Morgana.*

∽

"Now, that is a name I have not heard in a while."

The surface under my palms wasn't concrete like I'd expected. It was highly polished black marble, smooth and cold to the touch. Tiny silver veins flickered through the black, almost like it was alive.

I glanced up at the speaker, and for a moment, I could hardly breathe. She was quite possibly the most beautiful woman I'd ever seen in my life.

Of course, that was to be expected from the fairy queen. Her alabaster skin gave off an otherworldly glow, the only color a soft pink flush to her cheeks. Hair the color of red gold shimmered as though under a spotlight as the delicate curls shifted in an unseen breeze. She looked all of eighteen, but her eyes—those painfully blue eyes—were older than those of any creature I'd ever seen. Maybe older than time itself.

The scent of peppermint and cloves swirled about her so strong it made my nose tickle. I wondered if the scent getting stronger was somehow connected to the power of the sidhe. Something to ponder later. When I wasn't in the presence of the most powerful and deadly creature I'd ever met.

I had no idea how a person was supposed to address the queen of the fae, so I went with whatever spilled out of my mouth. "Uh, hey, Your Majesty." Not my most brilliant move, but it was all I had at the moment. "I guess your key worked."

Boy, had it. One minute I was being strangled to death by a psycho sidhe. The next I was facedown in fairyland.

I glanced around me. "Where's Inigo? Is he OK?" Panic coursed through me. "Alberich said he was going to kill him."

And I'd no doubt that crazy sidhe meant every word. "You can't let him kill Inigo." Probably not wise to make demands of the queen, but I wasn't exactly in the right frame of mind to care. All I could think about was Inigo.

₁ The queen gave me a cold look. "Dragons are not allowed in the other world. They are of fire. We are of earth. As for Alberich"—she shrugged—"what he does is of no concern to me. Nor is the status of your lover."

"Send me back, Morgana. Now. Please." I had to get back and save the man I loved.

"Careful, Hunter, you tread a thin line," the queen snapped.

The consequences of angering the queen of the fairies could be disastrous, but my fear for Inigo overrode my common sense, making me reckless. And stupid. Because I knew Morgana could squash me like a bug. And still I couldn't keep my stupid mouth shut. "I beg you, Your Majesty. Please, send me back," I whispered it between lips stiff with terror.

She glided closer until her face was right up next to mine. The look on her face was downright chilling as anger came rolling off her in waves. I swallowed hard as she hissed, "If you want to save the boy's life, you had better start cooperating."

Hearing a four-hundred-year-old dragon referred to as a "boy" was kind of funny, but I couldn't dredge up any laughter. Inigo was in danger from a psycho, and there was nothing I could do but cater to the whims of the queen of the sidhe, who could kill me easily as look at me. I didn't really have a choice but to obey. "O-OK, Your Majesty. I'll cooperate."

The queen leaned back, a smile on her face. It wasn't a happy smile. "Of course you will."

"May I ask you a question?" I kept my voice as humble as I possibly could.

An arched eyebrow was all the response I got. I took that as a yes. "I have fire. Why am I allowed in the other world?"

"Because I bade it to be so. And I am queen."

Right. OK. Talk about double standards. But it made about as much sense as everything else did.

"So, the guy who just tried to kill me, that's your twin?" I'd already figured it out, but I wanted confirmation.

"My, you do get around." She moved toward me, her delicate feet scarcely brushing the marble floor. Her sheer green gown spilled out behind her slender frame, wafting slightly in a wind I couldn't feel. Unlike most sidhe, her face did not change. It remained still in a single permutation of breathtaking beauty. She reminded me a little of Michelle Pfeiffer as Titania, complete with ringlets spilling down her back, except the queen made poor Michelle look positively ancient. The only flaw, if it could be said to be a flaw, was the tiny gap between her front teeth. It was oddly charming.

She held out her hand to me. "Come."

I hesitated. One thought and she could burn me alive. But refusing would be an insult she would not ignore. I sucked in a deep breath, trying to get my racing pulse under control.

I took her hand, so dainty compared to mine. Like I could crush her bones with my hunter strength. Of course, her appearance was totally deceptive. She was, without doubt, one of the most powerful beings in existence.

"Walk with me," she said in that beautifully lyrical voice that sounded so much like her brother's. Minus the hate and the nasty, of course.

Despite my worry for Inigo, I couldn't help but notice the bizarre beauty of the place. I gazed around the room, trying to take it all in. Every surface, from the fluted columns to the intricately carved ceiling, was made of the same black marble shot with silver. We were the only spot of color. In fact, the only light in the room came from the fairy queen herself.

As we walked, bright flowers sprang from her footsteps. Spots of color against the darkness. Within seconds, they withered and disappeared as if they had never been. That's fairy for you. A facade of beauty wrapped around an empty husk.

"I brought you here to save your life," the queen said finally. I had no idea why she deigned to tell me anything, but I was grateful. "I knew that when Alberich's initial plan failed, as it was bound to, he would come after you next. He would not be able to help himself. His thirst for revenge would be too strong."

"So you decided to help me?" Out of the goodness of her heart, no doubt. As if.

She laughed at that. "Oh, no. You see, Morgan Bailey, I have saved your life. And now you owe me a favor. A favor that I will one day collect."

Now, that I believed. "Why me in particular?"

Her expression didn't change. "It was not about you in particular. I simply saw an opportunity, and I took it."

It was a lie. I could almost smell it. Technically, the fae cannot lie. They can skirt the truth or omit important details, but lying is impossible for them. Somehow the queen was getting around the rules. Or maybe there was some grain of truth wrapped in the lie, but in those seconds when Alberich was squeezing the life out of me, she'd given me her name. Not something the sidhe take lightly. But accusing the fairy queen of lying would be so not good for my health, so I held my tongue, hoping she'd tell me something about Alberich and his plans. Anything to help me stop him.

Her face serene, she turned to me. "Alberich wants to start a war."

Chapter Twenty-Two

B ut why? Other than the fact that he's batshit crazy," I blurted. *Shit. Me and my big mouth.*

She threw me look that said she was clearly not amused and folded her hands neatly in front of her. We were still walking through the hall of black marble. I was starting to wonder if it went on forever. Was the entire other world made up of the same dark stone?

"He wants to rule the other world, of course. We are twins, you know. Born mere minutes apart."

"I picked that up..." I said, then cringed at the sarcasm in my voice and added a quick and humble, "Your Majesty." I even gave a little wobbly curtsy for good measure. I was seriously surprised she hadn't smitten me yet.

She ignored my gaffe. "He was born first, and so he should have been king." She shrugged. "But as you say, he is batshit crazy. Our parents deemed him unfit to rule. As did our people. And so when the time came, I took the throne. I should have killed him then, but I was weak." The ice bitch peeked through again. "I banished him instead, with the understanding that the rest of our people would believe him dead and he would never return to the other world."

It made sense. If the others thought she'd killed Alberich, it would protect her position. Make her seem badass. People don't generally mess with women willing to kill their own brothers.

"I thought I had seen the last of him," the queen continued.

"It would appear not."

"Indeed." Her voice was dry as dust.

We walked on a bit, silently. I wondered where we were going or if we were even going anywhere at all. The scenery never changed, just column after column of black marble. Darkness everywhere save the light of the queen herself. I'd always thought of the other world as being light and bright and filled with beautiful things. Though I suppose the stone had a strange beauty of its own.

"So, there is no vendetta against the marid?" I had to ask the question.

Her expression was inscrutable, and I wondered what was going on behind that icy facade. "Not that I am aware of, no. Killing the marid is merely a means to an end for Alberich." Her voice was so cool and detached it made me shiver at the inhumanity.

"How does starting a war with the djinn get Alberich closer to the throne?" I asked.

She ignored my question, continuing her smooth glide through the endless black. I hurried to catch up with her, my feet echoing in the vast space. I had to rethink my approach.

"Are the sidhe powerful enough to control a djinni, my lady?" I kept my voice and posture as subservient as I possibly could.

For the longest time, I thought she would not answer.

"The sidhe are, perhaps, the only beings left who have such power." Her tone was careless, as if the answer and the question were of no importance.

"So a sidhe could control the marid."

"I alone have the power to control a marid," she snapped.

Something about the way she said it struck me. "You and your brother?" I goaded her ever so gently. I was probably lucky she didn't chop my head off or something. The look that crossed her face told me she'd have liked to do just that. Obviously, whatever favor she expected of me was a doozy.

"My brother can no longer draw from the power of fairy."

It didn't exactly answer my question, but I knew I was edging over the line, and her patience was wearing thin. I had to be extremely careful, so I mulled it over in my mind. Alberich had been born a king, after all. Plus, he had started playing around with some serious demonic stuff. If a sidhe could draw power from the others of his kind, why not demon kind as well? Still, I decided to keep that little speculation to myself and not piss off the queen any more than I already had.

OK. So that explained why Alberich had snagged one of the djinn and forced him into taking on the marid's appearance. He hadn't been able to get to the marid himself because of the protection of the binding and Alberich's own lack of power, but he knew I'd go after the marid if I believed him a murderer. I frowned. "Why on earth would Alberich think that my killing the marid would start a war? Why would he even think that I was capable of killing the marid?" I was so not about to mention the darkness, just in case she didn't know.

The queen's face remained expressionless, her silver eyes focused straight ahead. Her silence spoke louder than words.

"Shit. You lied to me. He wants to start a war between the djinn and the humans." My insides turned to ice, and I felt the blood drain from my face. For a moment, I'd completely forgotten about the stupidity of calling the queen a liar.

Before I could blink, Morgana flicked a finger and a cut opened across my cheek from eyebrow to jawbone. For a moment, I felt nothing but shock, then the pain hit, so fiery and intense I thought for a second I might pass out. I reached up to touch my face, and my hand came away slick with blood.

She flicked her finger again, and suddenly, the wound, the blood, the pain were all gone. I knew I'd just been given a warning. I swallowed down bile as my stomach threatened to give in to the fear flooding my system.

"I did not lie. As you well know, the sidhe cannot lie. Not even the queen." Her expression had an icy imperiousness that was absolutely terrifying. "You assumed I meant a war between the sidhe and the djinn. I did not specify."

My mind raced. I bowed my head slightly to indicate obeisance. "Since Your Majesty is the only one with enough power to control the djinn, the SRA would ask you for help once the war started."

"Yes."

"I still don't see how that would gain Alberich the throne. Surely the sidhe can defeat the djinn."

Her smile was grim. "Not without hurting themselves. I could stop the djinn, but I would destroy myself in the process, leaving my people ripe for the plucking."

"I don't understand." I felt a little like I'd just fallen down yet another rabbit hole. Nothing was making sense.

"You do not have to," she snapped. Her face changed from one of ethereal beauty to something altogether more frightening. Her features looked almost skeletal, her eyes pools of black. I had a feeling I was seeing her true face at last. "I am queen here. All you need know is that should my brother succeed in his machinations, a great deal of power will be his for the taking. And take it he will."

With the djinn gone and the sidhe under his control, I had no doubt she was right. There would be nothing and no one to stop him. Maybe the dragons. Maybe. But their numbers have been small since the genocide wrought by Alister Jones's ancestors centuries ago.

"Shit," I said with a great deal of feeling.

"I could not have said it better myself." Her face returned to its ethereal beauty, and although she radiated the same icy coolness, it felt almost as though she were amused.

"I still don't understand how Alberich's killing me would further his plans."

She shrugged delicate shoulders. "It would not. I told you, Alberich has a very short temper and a very strong desire for revenge. He wanted payback for losing his throne, nothing more. His…passions got the better of him. For the moment."

"My lady, may I ask you another question?"

She quirked an eyebrow. "You may ask." Her tone clearly told me she might not bother to answer.

"Do you know why Alberich murdered Vega?" I had no proof, of course, but I also had no doubt it was the truth.

She studied her long nails. "I do not care about such things." Her tone was one of boredom, and I knew she would not answer even if she did know. And if she didn't know, she'd never admit it in a million years.

I pondered that a moment as we walked on in silence. Perhaps it was the tomb-like calm of the other world, but my brain seemed to be working more clearly than usual. A few possibilities came to mind. Perhaps Vega had gotten in Alberich's way. Or perhaps Alberich had simply needed to draw me to where I needed to be. All the supernaturals know that hunters are the ones who investigate supernatural deaths. And I am the only true hunter within hundreds of miles of djinn land.

"And Trevor? Why beat him up?"

She continued in silence.

"Please, my lady. He's my brother."

I don't know if it was the "please" again or the fact that I'd brought up family, but once again, the queen deigned to answer.

"My brother may not be entirely sane, but he does have a twisted sort of logic. I imagine," she said dryly, "that the plan was to kill Trevor. No doubt Alberich thought it would make you angry enough to storm onto djinn lands and kill the marid yourself."

"But we all know I can't kill the marid."

Silence again. And somehow that silence was telling. Was it true? Could the darkness inside me really kill the most powerful djinn in the world?

"How do I stop Alberich?"

She smiled coldly, once again the perfect image of the serene fairy queen. "You have already put a—how do you humans say it?—monkey wrench in his plans. The marid is not only alive, but you now know he is innocent of murder. The control my brother seeks is now far from his grasp."

I actually hadn't known for sure that the marid was innocent. I'd suspected it was so, but she'd just confirmed it for me.

"But he'll try again." Of that I had no doubt. Alberich wouldn't stop until he got what he wanted.

"Oh, yes. He will try. But you will stop him."

I wasn't sure she should put quite so much faith in me. What I was sure of was that she was still hiding something from me. Something big. There was more to Alberich's bid for power than the queen was letting on. Her comment about stopping the djinn resulting in her own destruction was ringing all kinds of alarm bells with me.

As we walked, I noticed a slight glow of light from up ahead. The light was tinted with green as though filtering through tree leaves. So there was more than black marble in this place. It grew brighter as we drew near.

"You still haven't told me how I'm going to stop Alberich." I so wasn't looking forward to hunting down the sidhe version of a serial killer.

"You are a hunter," the queen said with a smile. "Plus, you bear the name of a queen. You shall figure it out." With that, she dropped my hand, and I found myself sucked down into deepest darkness.

∽

"Morgan? Morgan. Morgan, you wake up right this minute, or I'm going to wave a can of tuna under your nose."

I opened one eye to find Kabita standing over me with a distinct glare. "You know how I feel about fish. Why are you glaring at me?"

"You used that damned key."

Kabita never swears. Well, almost never. Which meant I was in deep doggy doo. I sat up, wincing a little at the soreness in my ribs. Remembering my lovely conversation with the queen, I touched my cheek where she'd sliced it open. My fingers met smooth flesh, and I mentally breathed a sigh of relief. "Listen, I didn't exactly have a choice..."

"Oh, please. Don't give me that," she snapped.

I froze, suddenly remembering. "Where's Inigo? Is he OK? He was hurt..."

"He's fine. I just talked to him."

My panic subsided slightly, along with my blood pressure. "How on earth did I get to your office?" The faux-leather couch squeaked as I shifted on the cushions.

"Actually," Kabita admitted, "I don't know. You just sort of... poofed."

"Poofed?"

"Yeah. One minute I was alone. The next minute you were sprawled out on the couch—drooling."

I gave her a glare of my own. "I was not drooling."

One black brow hit her hairline. "You were so drooling."

I rolled my eyes and changed the subject. "Inigo? You're sure he's OK?"

"Like I said, he's fine. Has a bit of a headache from that fireball or whatever it was, but that's all." She sank down into one of the chairs in the outer office. "Said some crazy guy attacked the two of you and that you'd disappeared into thin air."

I breathed a sigh of relief. "Crazy guy. Heh. Yeah, sounds about right." I tried to get up again, but my ribs practically shrieked in protest. I pressed my hand against my side and breathed shallowly until I could get the pain under control. "I thought...I wasn't sure he was OK."

"He's a dragon. Why wouldn't he be OK? And sit down before you fall down." Ever the bossy one, Kabita.

"We were at my mother's."

"Your mother likes Inigo. I doubt she'd bash him over the head with a skillet."

I shot her another glare. "When we left her place, we were attacked by a sidhe. And not just any sidhe, but the king."

That got her attention. "Excuse me? King?"

I told her all about Alberich, his threats against me and Inigo, me popping over to the fairy realm, and how I was supposed to stop a bloody war between the sidhe and the djinn before humans got caught in the middle. "I have no idea what the hell I'm supposed to do next. I mean, obviously the marid is fine. Alberich is hardly going to be able to start a war with the marid alive and the fairy queen fully aware of his actions."

"But what he can do," Kabita said, "is avenge himself on you."

"Avenge himself? That's a little melodramatic, don't you think?"

She shrugged. "You messed up his plans, and it doesn't sound like he's exactly stable."

"True."

"Still, the whole vengeance thing sounds a bit over the top. I mean, I know that's what Morgana said, but that's just...insane."

"That's your first problem. You're trying to ascribe logic to a crazy person. Why do you think he was waiting for you outside your mother's house, Morgan? To take you to prom?"

"I never went to prom."

Kabita looked like she wanted to strangle me.

"OK, fine." I sighed. "Probably, he's not real happy that I spoiled his super-evil genius plan. It just means he might be a little harder to catch, that's all."

"You want to catch Alberich, the second-most-powerful sidhe in existence? Did you hit your head?" Her voice was overflowing with incredulity. I wasn't sure whether to laugh or be offended by her lack of faith in me.

"You got a better idea?"

She sighed and pinched the bridge of her nose between her thumb and forefinger. "Why me?"

I snorted back a laugh. "Yeah, it's all about you." This time I managed to get myself off the couch despite the pain. "I just got beat up by a sidhe, so I'm going home for a nap." And to call Inigo to make sure he was OK. Or better yet, I'd go to Inigo's house and take a nap with him. It wasn't that I didn't trust Kabita; I just needed to know for myself.

"Your car is back at your mother's house," Kabita reminded me.

Oh yeah.

She shook her head. "I'll give you a ride."

"You are too kind."

"Yeah, and if you get yourself killed hunting this guy, I am not going to be happy. You don't want to make a witch unhappy."

I grinned. "Don't worry. I'll just haunt your ass for the rest of eternity. And I'll keep all the boy ghosts out of your shower."

That made her laugh.

∽

I slipped into Inigo's apartment building behind his elderly neighbor and, impatient to see him, took the stairs instead of waiting for the world's slowest elevator. The door swung open before I'd hardly had time to knock.

"Morgan." There was relief in his voice. Obviously, he'd been as worried about me as I had been about him. He hugged me so hard I was half-afraid he'd snap a rib.

"Alberich said he was going to kill you," I blurted out, unable to keep the fear out of my voice.

"Hey, it's all right," he soothed, running his fingers through my hair. "I'm fine. I'm tougher than I look."

That caught my attention. "What did he do to you?"

He sighed as he pulled me into his tiny living room. "The minute you disappeared, he threw another one of those fireball things at me." His tone was definitely disgruntled, which brought a slight smile to my face.

"And?" I prodded as we sank down on the sofa together.

"And the first shot had worn off a bit, so I managed to roll out of the way. He tried again and I…uh…changed."

"Changed."

"Yeah."

"In broad daylight in the middle of the street?" I could just imagine what my mother's neighbors thought about a ginormous blue dragon wandering the neighborhood.

He laughed. "No one saw. But psycho boy took off really quick. I was worried about you, though. Where did you go?" His tone told me he'd been more than just worried. Freaked out more like.

"To the other world."

There was a beat of silence, and I felt his whole body tense up. "Excuse me? Did you say the other world? As in the land of the freaking fairies?"

"Yep, that's exactly what I mean." I tucked my feet up under me and snuggled in against him. "Remember that gold key the queen gave me for my birthday?"

"Of course."

"Well, apparently it's a round-trip ticket to fairyland."

Another beat of silence. "Holy shit."

"No kidding," I said. "Imagine my surprise when I touched the thing and landed on the floor of the queen's court." I left out the part where I called the queen's name. That was between her and me, and I was pretty sure giving away her secrets would piss the queen off. I did not want to piss of the queen of the sidhe. It would no doubt be very bad for my health.

"So what did she want?" Inigo asked.

"She wants me to stop a war."

After a pause, he said, "Piece of cake."

∽

"I thought we were friends, Priest," the marid snarled, drawing himself up to his full seven feet. Fury pulsed from him like a living thing.

"I am sorry." I attempted to soothe him, but there was no calming the enraged djinni. "I truly am sorry, my friend, but this is necessary. It is the only way."

We stood on a balcony overlooking the sea. The wind whipped up, snatching at our robes.

"And how many others have been ensnared in such a fashion?"

Sadness gripped my heart. I hated what I was doing to him. To the others. But I had no other option. Not if I wanted Atlantis to survive. "Four. There are four of you. I wish I could explain, but I can't. In time, you will understand."

The marid turned his back on me. "I will never understand the betrayal of a friend and a brother."

"No"—infinite sorrow—"you would not. But I swear to you, I had no other choice. This is the only way to save the Key of Atlantis."

"There are always choices. Always." The marid whirled on me, fists clenched. But he did not strike.

"This time there was but one choice. And when the key returns and the binding ends, you will know I made the right one."

Muscles flexed under red skin. "So you say."

"If I'm wrong, there is no hope—for any of us."

∽

I woke with my heart in my throat. I was really starting to hate these dreams. Dreams that were actually memories given to me by the amulet. I could feel the rage of the marid, the true regret of the priest, almost as if it were my own rage and regret.

The marid had told the truth about the binding. And about the betrayal. Ten thousand years of betrayal. Talk about sucking big-time.

I lay there for a moment, thinking things over. I still had no idea why Vega had been on djinn lands. In fact, I might never know. But I did know his death was tied into Alberich's bid for power. There was no vendetta. Just pure, unadulterated greed. I wasn't sure that made things any better.

I threw back the duvet and managed to haul myself out of bed without too much pain. The tenderness in my ribs had already decreased, which meant my hunter healing ability was doing its thing. Three cheers for hunter superpowers.

I padded barefoot to the kitchen, where Inigo was tapping away at the keys of his laptop. His glasses had slid down his nose. He looked totally geeky and totally adorable. "Hey, sexy."

He glanced up, a slow smile spreading across his face. "Apparently, I'm not the only sexy one around here."

I hadn't bothered with the robe he keeps for me. I figured he'd seen me naked, so what was the big deal about a T-shirt and panties?

"Perv." I laughed, walking over to wrap my arms around him. "Did I mention I'm glad you're OK?"

"Once or twice." We just held each other for a while. I think my absolute favorite thing about Inigo is how much he loves to cuddle. I never thought of myself as the cuddly type, but apparently I am. Who knew?

My cell phone rang, jarring us out of the moment. I leaned over to grab the phone out of my bag, my ribs protesting a little. "Hello?"

"Morgan, it's Trevor. What the hell is going on?"

"Uh, what do you mean?"

"There's a woman in my hotel room. She says she's a djinni, and she keeps babbling about you being in trouble and the marid going missing. And why on earth does she look like Marilyn Monroe?"

Shit. "That's Zip. She's a...friend." Friend was, perhaps, stretching reality a bit, but it was the easiest explanation.

"Why is she in my room?"

"I have no idea. Maybe she doesn't have a cell. Wait"—I frowned—"did you just say the marid is missing?"

"Hang on." I could hear him having a muffled conversation with what was obviously Zip. I'd know her breathy Marilyn voice anywhere. Finally, he came back on. "Yeah. Apparently, right after your visit, he vanished off djinn lands."

"That's impossible. The binding won't allow him to leave," I insisted.

"True. Not willingly."

"You're saying someone kidnapped the marid?"

"It's looking that way," he admitted.

"How is that even possible? No one can get onto djinn lands— oh shit." It hit me then.

No one could get onto djinn lands without the permission of one of the djinn. Zip had given me permission because she knew who and what I was. There was no way a djinni would give any- one else permission. Unless they were coerced.

And other than the fairy queen, there was only one person alive who could coerce a djinni: Alberich.

Chapter Twenty-Three

Sounds like your buddy Alberich has been a busy boy."

I shot Kabita a look. "No kidding. I seriously think the guy has a screw loose." I ran my blade over a whetstone until the steel sang. Is it wrong that I love the sound of a really sharp blade?

"Don't underestimate him, Morgan. He may be nuts, but he's a very dangerous nuts." She was filling up some kind of aerosol can at my kitchen sink. After the phone call with Trevor, I'd called in the troops, then headed home. I'd need my arsenal if I was going up against Alberich.

"What are you doing?"

She grinned. "Salt water."

"Salt is for demons and ghosts, not the sidhe." Though I had to admit the whole idea of salt in a spray bottle was kind of awesome in its simplicity.

"True," she admitted, "but this sidhe is different. He's been corrupted by demon magic and hate. I doubt the salt will hurt him much, but it might slow him down. Besides, he could have more demons under his control."

She made a good point. I checked over the rest of my weaponry. Machete or dao? Machete or dao?

The machete is more multipurpose, but since I wasn't headed into a jungle, I settled on the dao. It's sharper. Unfortunately, I knew very well that none of our weapons would stop Alberich for long. Even chopping the head of a sidhe wouldn't kill it. As far as I knew, there was no way for a human—or a hunter, for that matter—to kill a sidhe. That wasn't my plan, anyway. My plan was to trap the bastard and get him to the other side for his sister to deal with.

There was a knock at my back door. Kabita and I exchanged glances before she shrugged and went to open it.

"Kabita, how lovely to see you." It was Eddie, a smile beaming from ear to ear. His curly gray hair was even wilder than usual, as though he'd been running his hands through it.

"Eddie, we're about to go on a hunt," Kabita began.

"I know, I know." He waved her away and plopped into the kitchen chair across from me. He withdrew a hand from his coat pocket and laid a thin, silvery strip of metal on the table.

I picked it up and turned it over in my hands. It looked just like the plastic zip cuffs a lot of the cops use now, except it was made of some kind of metal etched with what looked like Norse runes.

I glanced up at Eddie. "What is this?"

"You're going up against a sidhe, Morgan. And not just any sidhe, but a fairy king."

"He was banished."

Eddie shook his head. "Doesn't matter. He was born king, and king he remains. At least when it comes to power. You will not be able to kill him, but you may be able to capture him." Eddie tapped the metal strip with his finger. "With this."

"How?"

"This little zip cuff not only contains iron, which is anathema to sidhe magic; it's also imbued with the most powerful magics I know"—he glanced at me through his thick spectacles, an odd expression on his face—"and a few I don't. After we discovered Alberich was involved in all this, I had Tesselah get to work on these babies. They're the only pair in existence. Get this thing around his wrists, and he'll be powerless long enough to get him to the other world."

So all I had to do was track down a crazy sidhe, subdue him, slap on a pair of cuffs, and haul his ass over to the fairy realm. No problem.

∽

I let Inigo drive. There was one person I needed to talk to before we faced Alberich.

Before I could dial the number, my phone rang. I frowned at the caller ID. "Tommy? I was just about to call you. What's up?"

"Trevor is in serious danger. I can feel it. But he isn't answering."

"Yeah, I know. He's dealing with a djinni at the moment. Don't worry, I'm on my way to help him."

Tommy Waheneka breathed a sigh of relief. "Good. He'll be fine, then." He said it with such finality I wondered if he knew something I didn't. I didn't have time to get into it, though. I needed answers.

"Tommy, I talked to my mom about my dad and about Alister Jones. She didn't know anything. Except for the fact that my father didn't die when I was born. And that Dad and Alister were best friends."

"Never said she knew any more than that."

I gritted my teeth in frustration. "Tommy, this is important. What else do you know?"

"It is important, yes," he admitted. "But not now. Now there are other things more important."

"Alberich."

I could almost see him smiling through the phone. "Yes."

"What do you know about Alberich?"

"Only that I believe he is behind the disturbance in the force."

What? He was quoting *Star Wars* now? "Seriously, Tommy?"

"Why do you think I brought Vega here in the first place? I knew something was wrong out here, but I needed someone with the right kind of training to help me figure it out."

Tommy was the reason Vega was in Madras? But why would an SRA agent help a tribal shaman in the middle of nowhere? There was only one reason I could think of. "Wait…was Vega a sentinel?"

No answer, but I knew Tommy was still there.

"He was, wasn't he? That's why he came when you asked him. You two knew each other." And Vega had been Trevor's close friend. "Was he helping you guard Trevor?"

Again, no answer. But I knew beyond a shadow of a doubt I was right. Vega had died in the line of duty. Just not his duty with the SRA.

"I regret Vega's death more than you know." Tommy's voice was quiet. "He will be honored as every soldier should be. It's up to you now, Morgan." And with that, he hung up, leaving me staring at the phone.

∞

Trevor was waiting on the edge of the djinn lands when we pulled up. Zip was with him, still dressed in her ridiculous white Marilyn dress and practically dancing with excitement. I hadn't realized a djinni could be so…perky.

Another vehicle pulled up behind us. I immediately recognized Jack's truck. "What are you doing here, Jack?" I demanded the moment he got out of it.

He moved around to the bed and started strapping on various weapons. I recognized one as the sword he usually kept over his fireplace. He'd gotten it off a soldier he'd killed during the Crusades.

"I'm here to help, Morgan. It's my duty. There is no way I am letting you go into battle against a sidhe alone."

"I'm not alone."

He gave me a look. Obviously, there wasn't any arguing with him. I didn't even ask how he'd found out what we were doing. I just shrugged and said, "Suit yourself." Then I headed over to the rest of the group.

"How do we know the marid is still on djinn lands?" I asked after everyone had done the greeting thing. "Alberich could have taken him anywhere." If he could break the binding. Normally, I'd say that was impossible. The high priest had possessed abilities far beyond anything most of us could imagine, but Alberich had been playing with demons.

"We don't," Trevor admitted. "But Zip says she can track the marid, so this seemed a good place to start."

I glanced over at the djinni, who gave me a little wave and flashed Inigo a far-too-flirtatious smile before practically purring at Jack. I managed not to roll my eyes. "That true, Zip?"

She grinned merrily, as though we were all about to go on a picnic instead of hunt down the evil sidhe who had her marid. "Oh, yes. All djinn can sense their marid. It's part of the…" She trailed off, eyes going wide. Very Marilyn. "Oh! We're not supposed to talk about that."

"Because of the binding. Yes, I know. What I want to know is, how did Alberich get to the marid in the first place?"

She pouted a little. "I don't know. The binding is supposed to protect the marid. Keep him on our lands."

"Unless Alberich used the magic of the binding to control one of the lesser djinn. He did it once; he could have done it again," Kabita pointed out. "The djinni would have allowed Alberich to enter djinn lands, where he could have snatched the marid. If anyone could do it, that crazy sidhe would be the one."

Frankly, it was the only option that made sense. Somehow Alberich had tapped into the magic the last high priest of Atlantis had used to bind the djinn. The very magic that was supposed to protect them had now become their Achilles' heel.

But that brought up another question: Why hadn't he done it before? With the first djinni he'd bound? He wouldn't have needed to kill Vega or Trevor. He wouldn't have needed me.

"Shit." I turned back to Trevor. "What about the SRA? Surely they can't care about keeping a low profile at this point. Can't they send—I don't know—backup or something?" After all, they'd helped out with my last baddie: a dragon hunter gone rogue. The woman had been serious bad news, and while Kabita, Trevor, and I did the actual takedown, the SRA had backed us up and hauled the crazy lady off to jail.

Trevor shook his head. "They're refusing to get involved."

We all stared at him in absolute shock. Except for Zip, who was still smiling perkily.

"What do you mean?" Inigo spoke up first.

"I had a little chat with a friend of mine who works in Operations. She told me on the down low that the SRA is well aware of the possibilities of a war between the supernatural races, and they want to…wait and see."

"What about a war between the djinn and the humans? Or the sidhe and the humans? Have they thought about that?" I practically shouted.

"Apparently, there were some questions after the last operation," Trevor said.

The last operation being the one where we captured Dara Boyd, aka Jade Vincent, psycho hunter extraordinaire—and unfortunately did not capture Alister Jones, former head of the MI8 and the brains behind the murder of an MI8 agent and the attempted genocide of the dragon race. "And?"

"The agency is trying to keep a low profile. So they decided to let the chips fall where they may."

That didn't take much mulling over. "They're going to deny everything, aren't they? Hope it all blows over."

Trevor nodded. "Plausible deniability. They can claim no involvement and say I did this on my own. If a war breaks out, they'll join whatever side looks like it'll win."

"They hung us out to dry." My voice was practically a snarl.

"That would be correct."

"Bastards." The irony that I used to paint my brother with the same brush was not lost on me. "Fine, they want to keep their lily-white hands clean, let them. We've got a job to do."

We followed Zip onto djinn lands. This time there was no wind. No Mongolian death worms, either, thank the gods.

"Zip, did you ever figure out where the worms came from?"

She shook her head, sending blonde ringlets dancing. "Nope. And we haven't seen any more, either."

I frowned at that. Something niggled at the back of my mind. Something about Alberich, the binding, and the worms, but I couldn't quite grasp it.

"OK, Zip," Trevor prodded. "Can you sense the marid?"

She closed her eyes and screwed up her rosebud mouth. "Yes!" She gave him a triumphant grin.

"OK, where?"

"Oh, there." She pointed toward the distant mound that made up the djinn underground home.

The rest of us tried not to roll our eyes. Of course she'd sense the marid in the place where he'd spent the last ten thousand years. Trevor held back a smile. "Anywhere else?"

"Yes." She etched her fingers along the horizon toward the west and the mountains. "There. It's faint, but he's definitely that way."

"Without a car, that trek is going to take hours," Kabita pointed out. "Surely we can get our hands on some dirt bikes or something."

Kabita and her motorcycles. Frankly, I'd rather give myself a paper cut and pour lemon juice on it.

"Oh, no, we don't need anything like that." Zip giggled. "Hold hands."

We all stared at her like she'd grown a second head.

"Hold hands." This time it was an order worthy of a drill sergeant. No giggling. No breathy Marilyn voice. For the first time, I felt the true power of the djinni. Frankly, it was a little scary.

We grabbed one another's hands, Jack very reluctantly standing between Kabita and Inigo. It was beyond strange to see my ex-whatever holding hands with my current.

Jack leaned his head down slightly and said something to Inigo. His voice was so low I could only hear a faint rumble. Inigo nodded, face serious. I was dying to know what Jack had said.

With the snap of Zip's finger, we flashed out of sight. And reappeared in a small sagebrush-filled valley at the base of the nearest mountain.

Ingo squeezed my hand and whispered, "We could have just flown."

"Now, where would be the fun in that?" I grinned back.

"OK, Zip, now where?" Trevor looked ridiculously official with his flak vest, badge, and assault rifle. I hoped he had something more than ordinary rounds in that thing, or it was going to be pretty much useless.

Zip screwed her eyes closed again as though she thought it might help focus her concentration. "Over there." She pointed toward a copse of stunted junipers across the valley.

I couldn't see anything other than a bunch of trees and rocks, but then again, I hadn't been able to see Alberich when he'd attacked me in broad daylight in the middle of an open street either. Apparently, invisibility is his thing. Which meant that, without Zip, we wouldn't have had a snowball's chance in hell of finding the sidhe or his victim.

Zip bopped ahead over the rugged terrain in her kitten heels and floaty white dress. How on earth she didn't break an ankle on a rock or snag the chiffon on some brush was beyond me. What was even more beyond me was that I actually knew what chiffon was.

And then our resident djinni let out a bloodcurdling shriek.

Trevor was by her side in a flash, Jack close on his heels, but it was too late. The demon had come out of nowhere and slashed Zip across the front of her chest with its long talons. She collapsed in a heap, bright-red blood pouring from the gaping wound. I could see white bone shining underneath the severed muscles. So not good.

For a moment, I thought maybe she'd be fine. The djinn are incredibly powerful beings, after all, but her expression told me another tale. I'd seen that look before on hundreds of other faces as I'd stabbed them through the heart. It was that resigned look of those who are at the end.

Dammit.

The demon turned on my brother. Trevor managed to get off a shot, but it barely fazed the thing. Its fist smashed into Trevor's chest and sent my brother flying a good ten feet. Fortunately, he didn't get caught by the demon's claws.

The demon was huge. About the same height as the marid, but built like a tank, complete with armor plating and talons like razor blades.

Jack grabbed what looked like a katana and charged the thing. The blade, sharp enough to chop a grown man in two, glanced off the demon's hide like a butter knife.

"What the fuck is that thing?" I hollered at Kabita.

"It's a behemoth."

"No shit."

"No, I mean that's the kind of demon it is. There's no way we're going to get through that armor plating. Not even with salt."

She was right. If Jack's blades couldn't penetrate the demon's hide, mine sure wouldn't. "What the hell is he doing?"

Inigo had slipped into his dragon form and was fighting the thing tooth and nail. In between attacks, Jack would jump in and keep the thing distracted with hits from his blades. They worked in perfect tandem, as if they'd been fighting together their whole lives. It was at once beautifully deadly and totally surreal.

Jack danced back, and Inigo hit the demon with a blast of dragon fire. It didn't even blink. *Shit*. This was so not good.

"Morgan"—Kabita grabbed my shoulder—"you're the only one who can stop it."

"Are you kidding me? Have you seen the size of that thing? You're the demon expert. My hunter strength is no match for it. And without weapons—"

She gave me a little shake. "That's not what I'm talking about. I can't kill it; it's too strong. I'm talking about your powers. You have to use them to send this thing back to the demon realm where it came from." Her expression was fierce. I knew she was right, but I was more than reluctant.

I swallowed as I stared at my brother and my boyfriend, not to mention Jack, getting the shit beat out of them. At Zip lying on the ground, blood spilling from her chest and the corner of her lips. "Last time I let them out, I couldn't control them. Not without the marid." It wasn't so much I was worried I'd lose control, but that when I did, those powers inside me would go after my friends.

But if I were honest, it was more than that. I wanted them out. I wanted them to kill. I enjoyed it.

And that scared me half to death.

Kabita gave me a little shake. "It's either that or we're all dead."

I screamed in frustration. "I don't know how."

She looked straight into my eyes. "The darkness does."

A chill ran down my spine.

I nodded. "Stand back."

She moved back a few steps. Far enough to be out of my way, but not so far she couldn't get to me if she needed to. I hoped she wouldn't need to.

I closed my eyes against the battle in front of me and reached down to that place where my powers live.

The air came first, its silvery tendrils spilling up and out of me. The wind kicked up, spinning into a whirlwind that tore at the surrounding brush and sent dust whipping into my eyes.

The whirlwind danced across the space between me and the demon. Inigo and Jack managed to move out of its way before the air wrapped itself around the behemoth. The giant demon screeched in anger, tearing against the wind, but the air held fast.

Slowly, almost in a daze, I walked across the space that separated us and right into the whirlwind. The demon tried to swipe at me, but the air held its claws back. I placed my palm in the center of the thing's chest, like the marid had done to me. Then I let loose the fire.

The flames poured from me, encasing both me and the demon in a spinning tornado of fire and air. "Shall I banish you?" My voice held a strange hollow quality. The darkness. I could hear it in my voice, see it dancing along the corners of my vision. A thrill ran through my body at the power, the freedom. That was followed hard by fear of the thing inside of me that I could barely control.

The behemoth opened its mouth as if to speak, but all that came out was a scream of rage. The amulet flared to life, burning the tender skin of my chest. That was when I knew. I don't know how I knew, but there wasn't a shadow of a doubt this demon wasn't at all what it appeared. I had to expel the magic from the creature.

The darkness boiled out of me, a living thing, echoing the demon's scream. I placed my other palm against the chest of the giant, and with a voice that was my own—yet not my own—I said, "Magic of Alberich, I banish you."

I had no idea what I was saying or doing or why. The darkness knew and the darkness was in total control, and it was as though it knew the words coming from my mouth had power somewhere out there in the universe.

There was a slight thump, like one of those percussion bombs used on TV shows. It was as though all the air was sucked from our lungs. Then a whoosh of wind that flattened everyone and everything except me and the creature standing in front of me: the marid.

∽

The marid's big hands curled around my upper arms. "Zipporah."

I swallowed. "I'm sorry."

The king of the djinn practically tossed me aside like a rag doll in his hurry to get to the fallen djinni girl. Surprisingly, she was still alive. Barely.

"Zipporah." The marid knelt next to the girl, ignoring the blood that quickly stained his clothes. He cradled the fragile djinni to his massive chest. "Oh, Zipporah, I am so sorry."

Blood bubbled from her lips. "Marid, it is not your fault." Her delicate white fingers stroked his cheek, leaving a smear of blood behind, slightly brighter than his own skin.

"I should have stopped him," the marid choked. "I should have been stronger."

"Were it not for the binding, you would have been," she whispered. "'Tis I who was supposed to protect you. I love you, my marid. Always. I should have told you sooner, but—" Her hand dropped to her side and lay still.

"No. Zip, no." Tears spilled down the marid's face, anguish etched in every line of his body.

But Zip wasn't there to answer. I felt the air stir inside me, and I watched as a tiny spiral of silver twirled out of Zip's body and danced away on the wind.

Chapter Twenty-Four

Marid"—I placed my hand gently on his shoulder—"if we have any hope of stopping Alberich, we need to know what happened. Tell me, please."

The marid still sat on the frozen ground, his body hunched over Zip's crumpled form, while everyone else stood around looking helpless. I understood the guilt and grief that must have been ripping him to shreds, but it wasn't his fault. Yes, he had killed her, but it had been Alberich who'd been behind it, controlling those slashing talons. Of that I had no doubt.

"Alberich forced the change, didn't he?" I prompted. If the queen had told the truth, it was a power Alberich shouldn't have had. *Change.* Such a polite word for the horror Alberich had forced on the djinni.

Muscles moved in the marid's massive jaw. That he was furious was an understatement. "No sidhe has ever before forced a djinni to take on its demonic form."

I glanced over at Kabita, who gave a little shrug. I'd known the djinn could take on a variety of physical shapes, but I hadn't known they had a natural form other than pure energy. Apparently, the demon-looking thing is one of their natural forms. The sidhe had only brought out what was already there. I tucked that little nugget away for future reference.

"Alberich isn't like other sidhe," I told him.

"This I know—now."

"I'm guessing he subjugated one of your people to get himself onto djinn lands."

The marid nodded. "Yes. He used the binding magic in a way I've never even heard of before. Once he was here, he was able to—" He choked. "He should not have been able to do this thing." He stroked Zip's golden hair, an expression of such sorrow on his face it made my heart hurt.

"But he did. And the worms weren't there this time to stop him?" I guessed.

But I didn't need the marid's answer. I was betting that Zip had been wrong about the worms. They'd always been there, protecting the djinn. It was only Alberich's magic that had awakened them and sent them on the hunt. He probably hadn't even realized it was his own magic working against him, aggravating the worms.

Once I killed the worms, Alberich had been able to get onto djinn lands and take the marid captive. When we got too close, Alberich had forced the marid into taking on its demonic form. And apparently, demon form doesn't allow for clear thinking. In fact, I'd bet anything Alberich had been able to control the demon form without even breaking a sweat.

"Do you know where he went?"

The smile that crossed the marid's face was a little scary. "Oh, yes. Yes, I do." He nodded to the copse of juniper trees I'd noticed before. "He's still there. Watching."

I stared at the little clump of trees. I couldn't see anything. "Why?"

"He gets off on pain and suffering. And"—the marid glanced over at me—"he'd like to finish what he started with you."

"He must be pissed as hell I escaped into the other world." The very thought made me smile. Then I sobered as a thought struck me. "He can go invisible. What if he's listening in right now?"

The marid shook his head. "I'd be able to sense him. He's still there in the junipers."

"What about super-hearing?"

He raised one greenish-black eyebrow at me.

"What?"

"It's a thing."

"Perhaps. But that psycho doesn't have it."

"OK, I've got some special cuffs that should hold him long enough to turn him over to the fairy queen."

A look of pure outrage crossed the marid's face. "You are turning him over to the queen?" He glanced around as though making sure the queen of the sidhe couldn't overhear him. Then, in a low voice, he hissed, "That bitch is the one who let him go in the first place."

"I know." She'd admitted as much during our little meeting. Her unwillingness to kill her own brother despite how evil he was had, in a way, led to all of this. Not that I could entirely blame her. "But no mortal can kill him. She's the only one with enough power." Frankly, I wasn't sure that was true, but it was the best I had.

A calm seemed to settle over the marid. "Very well. I shall help you capture him."

"Good." I nodded to the others. "We need to surround the trees, hem him in."

"Won't he just flash out?" Trevor asked.

"And how do we even know he's there? Don't forget he can turn invisible," Inigo pointed out.

"Oh, he's there." The marid's voice was a low growl. "I can smell the bastard."

I fingered the gold key that was still in my pocket. "I think I can prevent that. If only we could just surround him without him knowing—"

"I've got that covered," the marid interrupted. Apparently, Zip hadn't been the only one with tricks up her sleeve.

"OK, then," I said. "Let's go."

224

I don't know how the marid did it, but one second we were standing around hashing out our plan and the next we were spread out in a circle around the copse of junipers. It made Zip's teleportation trick look like child's play. With Zip, it had been bumpy, for lack of a better word. And it had taken a few seconds. With the marid, the teleport was smooth as butter. And almost instantaneous.

Now it was up to me.

I spread my hands out from my body and closed my eyes. Fire and air weren't going to help here. Alberich was immune to them. But there was one thing at my disposal that might: darkness.

Yes, he'd cut me off before, but that was because I wasn't prepared. Now I was ready for his tricks. I'd tried to force my way to the darkness. This time, as I faced the door Alberich had put up in my mind to bar me from my powers, I smiled as I summoned the darkness to me.

I felt it beyond that door. I sensed its eagerness, like a hound scenting blood. With a howl, it shot through the metaphysical door, out of my body, and into the trees, pulling me along with it.

My feet flew over the ground, my vision tunneling down to a pinprick. There was me, and the darkness, and the wild around me. And in front of me, the beating heart of Alberich.

Unfortunately, he was waiting for me. I managed to dodge the fireball of sidhe power he'd thrown at me, but I couldn't dodge him. Breath whooshed from my lungs and stars danced in my vision as he landed on top of me, his hands at my throat.

What was with people and strangling me lately?

Panic threatened to swamp me as I struggled to breathe. The stars were turning dark as my lungs heaved for oxygen. I would not go out like this.

I placed my palm against his chest and willed the fire to burn him, but nothing happened. Of course. He was immune. The panic surged higher, threatening to turn my reason to chaos. I kicked and twisted, but I couldn't dislodge him.

Alberich laughed. "What's the matter, Hunter? Fire won't burn?" He leaned down, hissing his words in my face. Beneath the scent of cloves and peppermint, his breath was foul. The stink of death and decay. Alberich's association with the hell dimension was taking its toll. "You are not a true creature of fire. You cannot burn me. Nor are you a true creature of air, so that won't work, either."

Once again, I could feel myself fading as I clawed at his hands. Even the darkness wouldn't come. I gasped for air and thought I heard the shriek of Inigo's dragon and maybe Jack yelling. Where were they?

"They can't come for you, Hunter. Did you honestly think I didn't know your plan? I allowed you in." The smile that creased his face was downright creepy. The beauty I'd seen in Eddie's book twisted by evil and hate. "I wanted to play. Before I rip out your heart and send it to my sister."

Why his sister would care if he'd ripped out my heart was beyond me. She'd insisted I was a means to an end, nothing more. Still, I kind of liked that particular organ right where it was.

Oh, this was not good. Some instinct had my fingers fumbling for the amulet around my neck. The Heart of Atlantis had once again grown incredibly hot against my skin. I yanked it out from under my coat and slapped it against Alberich's throat.

He shrieked in pain as a blast of sapphire light sent him tumbling across the small clearing. I stumbled to my feet and charged across the clearing toward Alberich, the amulet blazing against my chest. Before I had half covered the distance, he was back up. It was my turn to run.

I didn't get far. Alberich grabbed me from behind, spinning me around to face him. He wrapped his hand in my hair and yanked my head back so hard my eyes stung with tears.

What really scared me were his eyes—swirling twin vortexes of infinite darkness. The kind of darkness that made my own darkness look warm and fuzzy. There was madness there. And evil. So much evil.

So I did the only thing I could think to do. I kneed him in the junk. What can I say? It's my go-to move.

Alberich dropped to his knees, and for a moment, I thought I had him. Then he glanced up at me, and his face was a mask of pure, unadulterated hate. Laughter spilled from his throat and chilled me to the bone. "Do you actually think I'm human?" The way he said *human* made it clear he thought we were lower than cockroaches.

Alberich let loose another blast of sidhe power. The fireball hit me square in the chest, lifting me clean off my feet and sending me crashing into the magical barrier around the juniper copse.

Dark spots danced in front of my eyes as I slid to the ground in a heap. *Shit, that hurt.* I'd probably have been dead if not for my extra hunter abilities.

Or the fact that you're a sunwalker. The thought whispered through my mind, but I just as quickly banished it. It was not something I wanted to think about.

I lay there, unable to move, as Alberich stalked toward me. I knew if he got to me, I was dead. Nothing in my arsenal of "superpowers" could stop him. Not even the amulet, though it sure could give him a good kick in the backside. But maybe, just maybe, I could buy myself a little time.

Without Alberich restraining me and with the amulet glowing like a beacon of power, the door in my mind weakened. I reached down where the things inside me live. Air stirred in eager anticipation, so I summoned it. With a rush, it too broke through the door and out to play with my darkness.

The two rushed out of me, a dark wind. They slammed against Alberich, tossing him into his own barrier like a rag doll. The force field shattered.

Inigo and Jack were on him in seconds, but the would-be king of the fairies wasn't that easy to restrain. A single blast of power sent both men tumbling off through the sagebrush.

"Inigo! Jack!" I turned toward them, forgetting Alberich in my fear for the two men.

Too late, I saw movement out of the corner of my eye. "Kabita, no!"

There was nothing I could do. One minute she was charging toward Alberich guns literally blazing; the next she was dangling in midair, the sidhe's hand around her throat.

So much for the fae hating iron. Her bullets hadn't even fazed him.

"Let her go, Al."

His laughter taunted me. "Or what? You pathetic humans. You are nothing. Nothing! Not even my sister can save her pet human."

"Let her go, or I swear I will hunt your ass to the ends of the earth." Melodramatic, but what are you gonna do?

And then I saw something. In her hand, Kabita had my aspirator weapon. The one I sometimes use against vampires. The one filled with salt water.

"One more chance, Al," I yelled at him. "One more. Do you surrender?"

"Never!"

And with that, Kabita plunged the needle of the aspirator into Al's arm. One squeeze of the blub sent salt water flooding through his veins. With a howl of pain, he fell to his knees, dropping Kabita in the process.

The salt wouldn't kill him—he was far too powerful—but it had obviously hurt like a son of a bitch. Plus, salt is a purifier and is anathema to demonkind. It would negate his connection to demonic magic for just a moment.

And a moment was all I needed.

I raced toward the fallen sidhe, yanking the cuffs out of my pocket as I went. Kabita already had him facedown, hands wrenched behind his back.

"Hurry up. The salt is wearing off."

The urgency in her voice lent my feet wings. The air and the darkness swirled around me, boosting my speed beyond what was humanly possible, blurring the countryside around me.

I dropped to my knees beside Alberich's prone body and slipped on the cuffs, tightening them a bit more than strictly necessary. The runes flashed and shimmered, binding the sidhe's power.

Kabita stared down at Alberich struggling against the cuffs. "We'd better get him to the other world fast. I don't think those are going to hold him for long."

Inigo and Trevor hauled the struggling sidhe to his feet while Jack covered them with his sword. Though none of our other weapons had worked on Alberich, I supposed separating his head from his body would do the trick if we really had to. At least temporarily.

As the guys dragged the sidhe from the clearing, I got a good look at his face. Unlike the first time I'd seen him, Alberich's features didn't permute, but kept a single incarnation—something that I had thought only the queen could do. That incarnation was breathtakingly beautiful. He had the same shimmering red-gold hair and blue eyes rimmed in silver as his sister. He even had that tiny little gap in his front teeth. But unlike the queen, there was more than darkness in Alberich. There was, dare I say, pure evil.

"You wanted back in the fairy realm, Alberich...consider your wish granted." I started to reach into my pocket for the key, but the marid stopped me.

"I want to speak to him for a moment."

The marid's hand on my arm was warm. Too warm. I felt a little dizzy, and then my air swirled out of me to wrap around the marid's fist.

"What the hell?" I could barely get the words out. I watched in shock, and no little awe, as my own power abandoned me for the king of the djinn.

Before any of us could so much as blink, the marid punched Alberich in the chest. His fist crashed through skin and muscle and bone like it was nothing. And when he pulled his fist out of the gaping hole in Alberich's chest, he held the still-beating heart of the sidhe in his hand.

"For Zipporah," the marid declared, and then swallowed the heart whole.

I stared, stunned, as Alberich's lifeless body crashed to the ground, his words playing in my head. *You are not a true creature of fire. You cannot burn me. Nor are you a true creature of air, so that won't work, either.* The marid was a creature of both and an immortal. He'd used my air to bolster his own magic.

And with the magical cuffs on, Alberich was forced into corporeal form. Vulnerable to the marid's magic.

As we all stared down at the dead brother of the most powerful queen in existence, I had a bad, bad feeling.

"The queen is not going to like this."

"You are so right," a familiar voice whispered in my ear.

Between one heartbeat and the next, I found myself standing once again in the black marble hall of the other world. This time, instead of silver veins flowing and twisting through the stone, the veins were bloodred, as though the other world itself were bleeding.

Before me stood the queen herself, dressed in equally bloodred robes, her eyes dark as the tomb. Even the whites of her eyes had turned pitch-black. Frankly, it was freaky as hell.

"What have you done, Morgan Bailey?" The fury in her voice was barely restrained as it echoed through the dark hall.

She may have hated her brother. She may have wanted to stop his plan, but he was still her brother. And he'd been murdered at the hands of the king of the djinn, thanks to me. Not that I could have stopped him, but I doubted that would factor in. So not good.

You know that saying people have that fear turns their bowels to liquid? Yeah, I got that now.

"I did what had to be done, Morgana." I walked a thin line, using her name, but it was the one thing that might save me. There was power in using the name of a fairy queen. I hoped.

A cold smile spread across the queen's lips. "Yes. You did what had to be done. Thank you."

I licked my lips, my mouth bone dry. I wasn't sure where this was going, and I didn't like it. Why was she thanking me? "Sure, no problem."

"Follow me. It is time your actions were rewarded."

As I followed her, relief flooded me. She had thanked me. She was going to give me some kind of award. But as she led me across the floor toward a pool of ink-black water, I started to feel really uncomfortable and just a little nervous. I was pretty sure the pool hadn't been there on my last visit.

The queen waved her hand over the water, her face expressionless, her eyes cold as the grave. The water rippled and shimmered, and then an image appeared. An image of my friends standing around a copse of junipers calling my name. Searching for me.

"These are the ones you love."

I swallowed. I didn't want to answer her, but there wasn't much of a choice. "Yes."

"Good." She flicked her finger toward the water, and I watched in horror as a huge hole opened up in Inigo's chest. Blood spilled down the front of his shirt, soaking his clothing in seconds. He crumpled to the ground.

"No!" I sank to my knees on the cold marble floor, reaching out toward the water, but with another wave of the queen's hand, the image went dark. "No, no, no!" I screamed until my throat was raw, pawing at the water as though I could slip through it, back to my own world.

"Why?" was all I could get out past the raw tightness of my throat. I could barely see the queen for the tears that welled in my eyes and spilled down my cheeks. All I could do was lie there on the icy floor as agony burned its way through my chest.

The smile she gave me was so far from human I could hardly comprehend it. "For the death of a sidhe, there is always a price, Morgan Bailey."

She held out her hand, palm up. The little gold key she'd give me suddenly appeared in her hand. "Your services will no longer be required, Hunter." She closed her fist around the little key and squeezed until gold dust trickled in a shower to the floor.

I stared at the sparkles of gold, my mind completely numb. Inigo was gone. How could he be dead?

"I thought I owed you a favor?" I could have kicked myself for reminding her, but my brain wasn't functioning at full capacity. All I could see was Inigo's face as his life drained away. "Does this mean I've given you what you wanted?"

Her smile grew brighter, but didn't reach her eyes. "Oh, you have, Hunter. Most assuredly you have." She turned and strode away.

Terror struck as I knelt there on that hard, unforgiving marble. There was nothing I could do. My superpowers were useless. No tricks left up my sleeve. Inigo was gone. My heart was broken. The marid had struck the first blow, and I had no doubt the queen was about to answer in kind.

I was pretty sure we'd just witnessed the start of a war.

Acknowledgments

There's nothing quite like knowing you've found a place where you belong. Where your own personal crazy is nothing compared to the collective crazy and everyone loves you just the way you are.

To my tribe:

PJ, Heather, Ed, Julia, Lizzy, Alan, Robyn, and Stephanie,
Live long and write hard.

Thanks as always to my critique partners, Lois and PJ, and to my beta reader, Bonnie. Your questions, comments, and screams of moral outrage are invaluable.

Thanks also to my uncle Jim, a retired police chief, for the insight into Madras funeral homes, suspicious deaths, and tribal shamans. Any screwups are entirely my fault.

Don't miss more kick-ass adventures with Morgan Bailey!

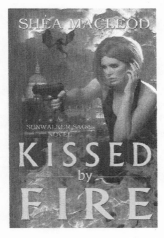

Available now on Amazon.com

About the Author

Photo by Razzaq Digital, 2012

Shéa MacLeod spent most of her life in Portland, Oregon, before moving to an Edwardian townhouse in London located just a stone's throw from a local cemetery. Such a unique locale probably explains a lot about her penchant for urban fantasy post-apocalyptic sci-fi paranormal romances, but at least the neighbors are quiet. Alas, the dearth of good doughnuts in London drove her back across the pond to the land of her birth. She is the author of the Sunwalker Saga and Dragon Wars series.

Made in the USA
Charleston, SC
05 December 2012